The
Three Camels

D C Bourne

Trevennick Books

Published by Trevennick Books 2008
Reprinted 2009

Copyright © D C Bourne 2008

ISBN 978-0-9559577-0-3

Printed by
TBC Print Services Ltd, Blandford, Dorset DT11 8ST
Typeset by the author
Cover and artwork by the author
Cover photograph, near Pentire Point

**To all who have loved
Cornwall**

**The landscape is a palimpsest
Each step we take treads on the past**

Part 1

Chapter 1   **Phyllite**

Even by Cornish standards, the weather had turned suddenly foul. What had started as occasional heavy rain had degenerated into a series of violent squall lines rushing in with all the vigour of three thousand miles of unopposed travel across the North Atlantic to hurl their violence against the cliffs that stood as bastions to their assault. The weather was behaving more like November than July.

Nathan packed up his things, turning over the pinkish rocks in both hands before lowering them into his rucksack. He was particularly pleased with the last piece – it was rounded and slightly more orange than pink. It had taken him a long while to chip it gently from its surroundings and prise it loose but it had been satisfying work sheltered in the lee of one of two small, granite outcrops. Sometimes he had paused, watching the cormorants and guillemots fishing and the gulls wheeling against the wind, seemingly stationary in it before turning and flying by at speed, casting him a casual interest; oyster-catchers had joined them in their distinctive black and white, hugging the water near the cliff where it was less blustery; and a bobbing, black blob might have been the seal that often appeared between the rocky, uninhabited islet of 'The Mouls' and where he was working. The gathering swell rushed forward and sucked out again, forcing the occasional rapid retreat from his task, as it sought to exploit each tiny weakness and claim back the land for its own.

Strange, he mused, that with all his care for detail De la

Beche had not marked the feature he was working on when he completed the first geological survey of the area in the 19th Century. But then, he argued, there was no reason for him to have scrambled down to where he was. After all, Nathan had only found it by chance himself.

Tying the rucksack, he stood for a moment, reflecting, before taking a final photograph. It would make a good opening slide for the lecture he was preparing and would test the students – there wasn't much pink rock in North Cornwall; in fact, he chuckled, he could probably confound a particular colleague with it as well.

He picked up the rucksack. It was heavy now. Moving up over the irregular rocks he began to run over the lecture in his mind: the pink rock had been molten once, extruded from the ground below in some great upheaval. Breaching the surface it would have cooled rapidly, hence the crystals composing it were not visible to the naked eye … the students should get that. The cleft it now formed pointed to it being less resistant than the adjacent granite, thus worn down more easily by eons of water and weather … he would have to describe working between two higher outcrops of granite to give them a clue there. Good, that would make sure they had to listen to find the answer … and it was also younger than the granite – they would only grasp that if they did the background reading. Excellent, he thought, that little puzzle would provide a nice exercise. Stepping over the cliff top and onto the lighter coloured granite, he turned to look at its two outcrops – 'The Rumps' they were called, and it amused him to think that he had been carefully gathering what nature had excreted from between them.

A blast of wind and wall of rain caught him unawares and he staggered for a moment before regaining his balance and picking his way onto the path. Crossing it was a low ridge that curved away to tumble over the cliff tops to either side together with a ditch that paralleled this course; he knew the feature well and didn't need to look to recall its shape. The books described it as the remains of an Iron Age fortification and, staggering again under the next horizontal deluge, he wondered both about the amount of work that had gone into its construction and the sanity of trying to eke out an existence in such an exposed spot; it was not even as if it had a good water source, and he could picture animals and children huddled uncomfortably against the onslaught of the elements. Flimsy wooden huts would not stand against this and there was nothing by way of anchorage for foundations – only bare, uneven rock. Perhaps it was a last attempt to gather against some group of invaders, he thought, or maybe it was a look out point from which to scan the coastline.

Another squall hit, knocking Nathan off balance and peppering him with its armament of raindrops. This was worsening rapidly.

Veering slightly to the right, the path pursued its route straight up. Already, it was becoming a water course as torrents flowed over the granite boulders causing the crystals of mica and quartz to glisten in the wetness. Each boulder was just the tiniest fragment of something vast and ancient – a mass of once molten rock larger than the whole of Greater London that stretched from beyond the Scilly Isles to the far side of Dartmoor and which had cooled ever so slowly in the darkness of the Earth's bowels, buried thousands of metres below a mountain chain that had rivalled the Himalayas for splendour. Over millions of years that had all gone – denuded away – and now he was stepping on stuff 280 million years old.

Wind shrieked up the cliff. Unable to go round, it was being driven upwards, almost unwillingly it seemed, and gusting angrily in response. Glancing out to sea, Nathan saw what looked like lightning. There was little chance of hearing the thunder in this wind, he considered, as he found his senses becoming numbed, dulled and deafened by its continuous buffeting and pounding.

Nathan glanced back to the cliff path. Not long before the black rock took over now. Forbidding and dropping away in cascades of steep smoothness and verticality to the hungry water below, it was much younger than the granite and rich in basalt. Black it was now; but at its genesis it had poured out red and liquid in the dark beneath an ancient ocean as fold upon fold of pillow lavas – molten rock boiling the water that it contacted and moving forward in voluptuous curves, building up layer upon layer. A few more steps and he would be onto it. Fifty more steps and he could gain the shelter of the old dry-stone wall.

The squall hit without warning and with a huge crash of thunder, gusting and sucking viciously. Nathan was knocked sideways, losing his balance. He fell and hit the ground. The rucksack crushed against him and he could feel warm blood pulsing down his face. He was sliding now, scrabbling for a grip. A clump of thrift gave way ... and another; another slide ... and his right hand wedged painfully in a crevice, like a flimsy anchor that might or might not hold. His legs were dangling over the edge of the cliff. Updraughts laden with spray from the waves crashing 200 feet below swirled around them. His knees were moving uselessly over the drop, buffeted by the wind and scrabbling desperately for a grip that the slippery thrift and coarse grass would not give. All that held him was the throbbing hand. Rain and wind were sapping strength. Now it was turning to hail – not gentle and soft but sharp and stinging, driving horizontally into the face he could not protect.

His body was screaming at him to release his jammed right hand, and his mind started chipping in. Perhaps the fall wouldn't be so bad really ... then his hand would stop hurting ... he could be free of the bullets that kept drumming into his face ... it might not hurt as he fell ... he might fall clear of the rocks ... his body might not be shattered by them ... if he let go he could be out of the wind and rain ... he could be warm ... it would be so easy. Of course, the body wouldn't be found – the heavy rucksack would weigh it down beneath the waters. He would sink into a dark oblivion. Perhaps he would be able to lie there in another existence and see the sun and clouds above but not be able to reach out to them. No one would know that he had gone. No one would notice until term began again. After all, he had lived alone for years with the dog in the old bungalow at Trevennick. Not that it was really a bungalow – that word came from the days of the British Raj in India, long after it had been built; it was more a single storey cottage to which he had added a verandah on two sides; but he thought of it as a bungalow. Memories came flooding back: sitting there shelling peas with the dog by his side waiting for one to drop then putting a soft paw on it and snuffling at it with her black nose to see if it was worth eating … a bundle of yellow being stroked … a tail flying across the sand, barking at the seagulls, nearly reaching them before they lifted off at the last moment … walking the cliffs with the faithful retriever until she had become so laboured that it had seemed unfair to take her. And that last morning, coming into the kitchen to make her meal. She had lain there looking at him with her big doleful eyes and golden face, giving him a half wag with her tail. He had bent down with the meal and she had struggled, raising herself onto her front paws before sinking back, her eyes open but unseeing, as if to say, "Thanks, but I'm tired; it's time for me to go."

He had buried her in the garden.

Something snapped in Nathan's mind. He wanted to see her grave again. He wanted to be buried on land; not slip into some unmarked oblivion below.

A small fragment of his mind was still working and seemed to be insisting to him, "hammer … the hammer." Slowly it came to him. The geological hammer was attached to the back of his rucksack by its usual velcro fastenings. If he could reach it with his free hand maybe he could use it like an ice axe and obtain a purchase to pull himself forward. Again the wind buffeted and he felt himself move sideways as the next volley of hail struck. But his mind was working now: he had used an ice axe countless times, the flatter end to cut steps on ice-crusted snow much more steep and slippery than this, and the old rhythm came back – cut left, remove axe, step right; thrust the climbing boot with its steel crampons into the previous cut and test for grip; cut right, step left, test again; repeat left; repeat right; keep repeating; keep going – and he had used the sharp, serrated pick to arrest a fall, practising throwing himself with and without a heavy rucksack down a steep snow slope and stopping his momentum by swivelling and using his body weight to drive the pick into the snow. Three times he had

had to do it for real.

Briefly he felt a surge of confidence, until the wind hit him again and his hand shrieked in agony. He'd been properly equipped then … and he had been balanced before he started … and he hadn't been hanging half over the edge of a vertical drop with the sea pummelling the rocks expectantly below him. Moreover, the geological hammer had only one chisel-shaped end – no serrations – and the other end flat, rectangular, unlike even an ordinary claw hammer … but it was that or nothing. Moving his free left hand infinitely slowly, it seemed, and stretching behind him, his numbed fingers found the shaft and moved down towards the fastening. Nathan's sense of hearing had long been deadened and he couldn't tell if the velcro was unfastening. Suddenly it gave and the shaft was sliding through his two smallest fingers until its head rested uncertainly between their knuckles. Another gust now and it would be gone, his thoughts screamed at him. Eternity stared unblinkingly at him as he brought the hammer up and over his shoulder, and down in front of his face, grabbing the leather loop in its base with his teeth before slipping his left hand through it and twisting the hammer so that the leather thong tightened round his wrist.

"Chock," said the bit of mind that was trying to fight its way through exhaustion and panic; "use it as a climbing chock in a crevice."

"Yes," came the dull response. "Use it like a climbing chock. Get it in the crevice where my right hand is. Then pull. Get purchase with my knees."

Now his arm was working without his mind willing it; the skill had been practised long enough for it to become automatic, able to be performed even when the body and mind had reached beyond the extremes of endurance. Now the hammer was turning and resting in the crevice. Now it was crushing the fingers in his right hand; it was in deeper than them and felt secure, still crushing the fingers that had lost any sensation of pain. The left arm was pulling and the knees coming forward thrusting him up and over the edge of the cliff. Again and again the left arm dug in, twisting the hammer to its chisel end. Another scrabble forward ... feet purchasing now ... another thrust – and he lay on the inner edge of the path, his body spread-eagled low against the wind, gasping for breath.

Muddied water cascaded into his mouth and he coughed and choked. He couldn't stay here. As he crawled upwards, his right hand was throbbing badly and would barely take any weight, whilst his left wrist trailed the hammer. Once it had looked like thirty steps; now it seemed like a marathon. A clump of thrift flew by him, finally loosened from its shallow grip on life. The stone wall loomed ahead. A few more lurches forward and there was a low entrance. Pushing himself sideways through it, he collapsed into the sheep pen and lay shaking against the leeward side of its wall.

How long he lay there he didn't know. Congealed blood on the right side of his face had hardened with the sheep droppings that he had been lying on; but his hand had stopped throbbing. Slowly he unwound the hammer from his wrist and restored it to its place on the rucksack. The mechanical action seemed to prompt him further and groping clumsily to untie the buckles he delved inside, seeking the chocolate he had bought in Padstow early that morning. With an effort of will he forced himself to eat each piece until it was all gone. Some strength was returning and he shifted, testing his ability to stand and walk. The wind was screaming less now and even the squalls had lost some of their violent intent as they hammered into the old, protecting wall.

The sheep pen gave entry to a large field. Following its boundary along two sides and disturbing the sheep that were sheltering in the lee of the wall, Nathan climbed over it and regained the coastal path a mile or so from Polzeath before stopping at a small stream. He endeavoured to wash away the worst of the embedded sheep droppings from his face and sat on the nearby memorial seat, looking at the scene. The wind was abating and the wrack of angry cloud had thinned so that there was a shaft of light far out to sea beyond Gulland. Clearly, the weather had been so extreme that even the most hardened of surfers had abandoned the bay below and the sands were entirely empty; the wind had flattened the swell, blowing the tops off its incipient waves, but he could picture the scene tomorrow if calmer weather followed. That vast energy expended over the water would yield train after train of curling waves, holding their crest line until the very last moment and breaking in a slight diagonal across the bay, allowing the boards to pursue them. It would not be surprising to see a two metre surf in the bay and, as if reading his thoughts, the first few black-suited figures were appearing to test the weather's legacy.

Food and tiredness were beginning to fight for pre-eminence in Nathan's mind – and somewhere was the reminder that he needed to go back across the estuary. He came down the steps from the cliff path onto the sand. Polzeath was a possibility … there were places to get something to eat, but it would be packed with tourists who were staying in tents or caravans and for whom little alternative venue lay within walking distance. Already it looked very busy from a distance, and he did not fancy queuing for food and having people stare at his face. That ruled out the cliff top restaurant opposite as well, and he found his feet carrying him towards 'The Choughs'. It was larger, he argued, and uphill so it would deter the casual walker; besides, it had some dark recesses.

As he drew near, he realised that he had been mistaken in his assumptions. A dozen smokers thronged its entrance, some of them of doubtful age and talking in public school speak, others inured by the years to their habit. Taking a step past them, he was hit by the smell and noise of a massed humanity that had been confined inside for several hours. He hesitated before the second wave hit his senses – chips, fried oil, sausages, tomato ketchup – and his stomach moved his legs forward.

The bar was full and he elbowed his way to a position where he was only three deep from it and near the till. That sounded like a New Zealand accent from one of the girls who was serving. Unsurprising really, since there were so few year round jobs in the area: the local young people had left for the cities and now the seasonal work was filled from abroad. He watched her in the bar mirror as she rang up the most recent round, pushing the plastic covered buttons. As she turned, her eye paused on his face and he mouthed 'doom' at her. Whether it was the face or the eye contact he wasn't sure but she pulled the drink on her way back to the crowded section and it was passed back to him. Mutterings of, "Why's he being served before me?" and "Blimey, look at his face," caught him as he passed three coins back along the chain and waved that he didn't want the change. Forcing his way back for food could come later, he thought, as he slurped the top inch of his pint of 'Doom Bar' to stop it spilling and used a combination of elbows and rucksack to retreat to a distant corner. There was a complete mixture in the place: large numbers of teenagers, mostly eight or more to a table that would seat four, talking excitedly and presumably awaiting exam results and GAP years; desperate parents, not talking except to assure their accompanying children that their food would not be long coming; equally desperate parents, talking to each other and pretending that the loud children nearby were nothing to do with them; a few walkers, who actually were four to a table; and a pair who looked like newspaper reporters fabricating a story – he would steer well clear of them – and somewhere he spotted a dog's tail.

The far corner was out of sight of most people and contained a table with only two occupants but three chairs. He negotiated his way towards it, narrowly missing another tail that swept instinctively away from the point where his foot landed, and pointed to the chair. Two girls who looked in their twenties nodded to him, indicating that it was vacant, and continued an animated conversation between themselves.

Somewhere around the point where the glass of Doom was beginning to look more empty than more full, Nathan began to be aware of the girls' conversation penetrating into his mind. The one, Zadie, by the sound of it, was showing the other a piece of green and purple rock, rounded at the edges and shaped rather like an artist's hand-held palette with holes in it where the thumb and paints would have gone. He found his eyes drawn to it and his ears picked up on the conversation, "...yes, found it on Greenaway at low tide. I think it's slate."

"Phyllite," said Nathan, without thinking.

Both girls stopped talking and the half of Nathan's face that could do so, blushed. It was a bad habit of years of teaching to make uninvited corrections.

"Sorry? What did you say?" said Zadie.

"Phyllite," he repeated. "It's a weakly formed slate common in the Camel estuary, particularly over this side."

The one girl got up.

"I'm sorry," Nathan apologised to the remaining girl. "That was rude of me…"

"It's OK," said the owner of the rock, "she's just gone to chat to that Australian barman. She's been looking for an opportunity for the last half hour and now the weather is clearing the crowd around the bar is thinning out."

Nathan looked across and rather agreed. He thought about making a bid for a food order but stayed seated.

Zadie's voice continued, "If you know about rocks, tell me about this then," offering him the green and purple stone.

He took it in his hands. It was common but rather nice. The palette-shaped rock had been worn smooth by the waves and had rays of green and purple radiating out from the point where an artist would have held it. There was a larger hole at that point, ringed by a slightly raised ridge of white quartz veining; towards the upper edge of the palette were five other smaller holes, similarly ringed, and connected to the larger one by thin white veins. He could see why she had picked it up. It would have looked even better when she had seen it wet and he dipped his fingers into the forgotten beer several times, wiping them over it. An appreciative murmur came from his left. Strange how nature could throw such beauty into such a small object … and it had taken 350 million years to fall into its owner's hands – not that you could really claim ownership to beauty, nor would this last much longer before it fragmented and became different again. He could feel the professionalism beginning to kick in, and also her eyes watching him. He was glad that she was on his left and couldn't see the damaged side of his face.

"How much do you want to know?" he said.

"Everything," came back the unexpected reply, with a smile.

Now it was his turn to smile. That was a mistake and he winced in pain. "The full story would take a day," he continued. "Do you know what this began life as?" he asked. She shook her head. "I'll give you a brief outline. It was a silty, muddy mess in the bottom of a shallow sea near a great land mass ..." and he was off, talking about ancient upheavals in the Earth's crust and molten rock, heat and unimaginable pressure, explosions of super-heated water rich in minerals that only made good answers to obscure crossword clues – and he'd barely scratched the surface. After twenty minutes, he handed the rock back to her and absent-mindedly downed the rest of the pint.

"There was also this," said Zadie, giving him an irregularly-shaped, greenish lump that sat easily in his palm. It was heavier than he had expected and much more interesting to him, although it had no intrinsic beauty. He rubbed his fingers across it and dislodged some particles.

"Where did you find it?" he asked.

"Same place as the other."

"Odd," he said, as much to himself as to her. "I wouldn't have expected it to be there. It's rich in copper – hence the green. Might be worthwhile brushing away some of the encrusting and seeing what's underneath," and he passed it back to her. "The other one, you could use some clear lacquer on to keep the colours looking vibrant."

"Been having a good chat about rocks?" said a face arriving back at the table and smirking in a slightly self-satisfied way.

The return of Zadie's friend jarred Nathan into realising the time and accelerated his departure. "Look, I've got to go," he said rather abruptly. "I have to catch the ferry." He hesitated a moment.

"I'd like to know more about the landscape," Zadie observed.

On impulse he blurted, "OK, I'll be walking the cliffs

tomorrow, I ..." he trailed off.

"I'll find you," Zadie ended for him.

Nathan felt confused as he set his way to the Rock ferry, walking on auto-pilot. Already the light was fading, although the evening had relented of the day's storm. As he reached the highest ground and paused, the westering sun sent a shaft of gold to illumine the distant windows of St. Breward, high on the edge of Bodmin Moor, so that they shone like golden mirrors. For the first time they struck him as eyes keeping watch over the ancient landscape below.

They shut; and he walked on.

Chapter 2   A Few Steps

A combination of sunlight streaming in through the open window and chickens scratching noisily woke Nathan early. For a moment he struggled to place his thoughts in order, until his hands encountered the right side of his face. The resultant expletive shocked the chickens into silence and they flew on top of the run down shed with its sagging roof of thick, uneven slates, looking down in disapproval before deciding that it was safe to return to their foraging. The bruise was rivalling the purple and green of the Trebetherick slates across the estuary, although it had some copperish tinges as well. "Pretty good geological specimen," said Nathan to himself as he looked at his face in the bathroom mirror and bathed gingerly.

Blast! He was going to have to go across the estuary again, he thought, slowly recollecting the day before and his parting conversation with Zadie. The day looked like it was going to be Cornish perfection and the cliffs would be full of walkers, the beaches packed, and the ferry queue a nightmare later. What's more, he would be meeting an unknown girl, at an unknown location, at an unknown time. He distinctly didn't like the place when it was jammed with people and now that the dog had gone he preferred his own company and the solitude of the cliff top.

Staring through the kitchen window, he went out onto the verandah and into the rambling cottage garden. The translucent blues of the morning glory flowers were nodding in the light breeze, mimicking the early morning sky with its few puffs of fair-weather cumulus drifting lazily across in promise of a beautiful day; Californian poppies had self-seeded along the top of the wall and were tight-curled in their orange and yellow cones, some still crowned with their little green hats and waiting to wave their welcome; mesembryanthemums were tumbling down the south facing side of the old, dry-stone wall that separated his garden from the gentle munching of dairy cattle in the neighbouring field. It was one of a few farms that hadn't given in to the attraction of oil seed rape and arable subsidies. He sighed. When the old farmer died he doubted that it would continue in the way that was half love, half labour. Soon the flowers would be a blaze of varied, vivid colours as the sun reached them and they opened to greet it. Even the belching of cattle sounded vaguely pleasant on a day like this and he contemplated staying put in Trevennick … after all, the girl probably wouldn't turn up, or he wouldn't find her. It would be a waste of time.

He decided to decide by the end of breakfast, and set to searching through the garden to find where the hens had laid their eggs. He knew their favourite places but sometimes they could be quite inventive. Half an hour later, the frying pan was on and the fusion of aromas from eggs, bacon and toast was beginning to permeate the kitchen; the coffee percolator exuded its own contribution as he brewed the last of the strong black coffee that he had obtained a few weeks ago in exchange for garden produce. So long as the hens kept laying and the garden producing he didn't have much need for money in the summer time and he guessed that was how it had been for a long time in this part of the world: what didn't need paying for in cash, couldn't be taxed.

The last piece of fried egg was proving particularly troublesome. It was very small and tinged that bright yellow that the yolk of really fresh eggs can give. It was sitting on a very slightly larger piece of toast … and Nathan was pushing them both around his plate with a fork that had one prong missing. He had decided to decide by the end of breakfast. Of course, he could cook another egg … or he could do the washing up – in a sense that was part of the meal.

Nathan went into the garden and started gathering runner beans and carrots. He stuffed them into a couple of plastic bags and put them in a half-filled rucksack before carefully placing a box of half a dozen eggs on top. Scattering a handful of grain as a peace offering to the chickens that he had so offended earlier – not that they really needed the grain at this time of year – he pulled the door to. If he took the inland path he would come out in the lane behind Prideaux Place and could be down at the harbour by eight-thirty. There had been a Spanish fishing boat docked last night when he had passed and he wanted to see one of the crew anyway.

Early mist had burnt from the estuary and it was still only ten o'clock when he stepped off the ferry and strode along the beach from Rock, seeking out the firmer sand near the strand-line of the night's spring tide. Footprints from early walkers combined with paw-prints sinking into the soft sand towards the estuary as they had deviated to investigate anything of interest. Soon the dunes were beginning to open up on his right and he struck through them, following the path that led to Brea Hill until he stepped onto the solid rock and paused. The estuary was staggeringly beautiful. No matter how many times he came here, it hit him like a pain. It really was so beautiful. Beauty so intense, so immanent, it hurt.

His eyes strayed to the south as he sat for a while. There was Padstow nestling in its little valley, sheltered from the strong south-westerly winds. It had been called other names before that – Petrockstowe after its founding saint, and Lanwhenock in the Doomsday Book, although that was almost certainly a phonetic rendering of something different; what was certain was that it was a good site for a settlement with its little harbour and fresh water supply. The names of some of the streets still betrayed the origin – Mill Square, for instance; and some were strange – Lanadwell, Fentonluna and The Drang. Each had a history.

His eyes moved slowly to the right. There was the Metropole; there was the top of the tower of St. Petroc's church; there was St. George's Well with its golden sand still illumined by the morning light, like a vanquished strip of gilded dragon-hide wrapped around the little indentations of the cliffs. Further on were the patchwork of fields and low abandoned cliffs before the vast expanse of Tregirls or, as the Ordnance Survey insisted on calling it, Harbour Cove, came into view. Its beach was shimmering silvery-gold and widening by the minute as the ebbing tide yielded it to those who would later make the effort to park and walk down to it; even at the height of the season there was always space there.

Nearer was the Doom Bar, the shallowing water over it reflecting differently the sky above and the retreating water. Again the scene changed as his eyes met Stepper Point, surmounted by its Daymark built to guide and warn vessels before all the modern navigational aids. He looked again at Stepper Point: its cliffs paralleled those across the estuary in colour, although different in type; and between them both the water was racing and rippling as it sought to return to the ocean. Drifting patches of cumulus cloud produced a kaleidoscopic pattern of moving colours. All eternity in a moment, it seemed to breathe to him.

Tearing his eyes away, he followed the path around the hill and Daymer Bay opened up before him. The car park was several rows full already and he smiled as he saw the early arrivals seeking to claim a patch of this beauty for their day. Soon the car park would be very full and, later, the traffic would be arguing over whose right of way it was up or down the narrow lane that led to it as late hopefuls met early departees and walkers, and push-chairs and dogs complicated the whole affair. On he went, down the cliff and across the little stream engrossed in its twice daily chore of carving braided channels in the sand as it sought its final escape to the retreating sea, each island in its course a work of art. He looked at the first wind-surfers struggling to match its unspoken eloquence as they laboured after it with their boards and sails and sought their pleasure for the day. Briefly, there was contact with humanity as he stepped on concrete and passed the metal and glass that had brought others to this place. The wide sward of short grass, trampled by a thousand feet, led him round Trebetherick Point until the black cliffs of Pentire swung into view.

Nathan had been lost in the landscape and had almost forgotten why he had come across the estuary. He walked more slowly now, partly because the path was becoming busier and partly due to the conflicting thoughts stabbing through his mind. The distant cliffs did not appear fore-boding today and the distance fore-shortened their height, yet he found himself checking his pack and touching his face in memory. For a long while he stood looking. How could such beauty and danger co-exist so closely in time and space? Why had he come this way again? It had been a lovely walk. Perhaps he should just turn and go back. And his feet began to move.

She was a solitary figure. Behind her was the backdrop of Pentire, its dark cliffs softened by the gorse above and white-crested waves below. At her feet lay the little beach with its coarse sand and proliferation of rock pools, their surfaces rippling gently in the breeze. Her golden-blond hair was pulled up under a flat, white cap and she wore a light blue top. As Nathan approached, he was struck by the thought that she should be a cloud floating in the sky. Turning to face him, sunlight flashed a greeting from the gold chain plunging below her neck and the copper bracelet on her wrist.

"I wondered if you would come," she said.

So did I, thought Nathan.

"Wow! Nice face – even better than in the pub last night!"

"I didn't think you saw that," Nathan said in surprise.

Zadie smiled and described how her friend had seen it and quite a group in the pub had been talking about it, speculating on how it had occurred and starting a competition for the best answer. "That's how I knew I would recognise you," she ended. "Anyway, I've sat here long enough. You were going to tell me about the rocks and landscape, in case you've forgotten. Let's go."

"Which way?" asked Nathan.

"Your choice," Zadie replied.

Nathan was filled with a sudden urge to show her the areas that meant the most to him. "Would you like to go across the estuary – it's quite a long walk?" he suggested tentatively. Zadie smiled again and reached under the bench, standing and slipping on a small back-pack before saying, "That's fine. I've got all day."

Nearby, uneven steps led down to Greenaway beach and, having descended, they struck off to the left, dodging through a vigorous game of frisbee that sent the coarse sand flying. Towards the sea young families were exploring the rock pools, catching seaweed in their little nets. In the middle there was a taller rock with a deeper pool beside it and a pair of black labradors were swimming in it trying to fetch the stones lobbed in by the children and emerging unsuccessfully only to shake themselves vigorously from nose to tail, spraying the children in the process and causing further shrieks of delight. It was a pleasant scene as they clambered onto the platform of rocks three or four metres above the level of the pools. Its surface was riven with deep clefts where the sea had etched out each line of weakness, and they stepped from part to part, sometimes straddling a cleft and looking down into deep sand-lined pools below or admiring the smoothed flanks of rock plunging down to them. Each was a miniature chasm; each pool a microcosm, yet each unique. On the landward side rose a sandy cliff, largely covered in grass with clumps of thrift and ladies slipper and a few pebbles at its base where it joined the rock they stood on. For a while they halted, drinking in the view as if, by some osmotic process, it was becoming part of them.

Nathan turned and sighed. "Well, we may as well begin here," he announced, reaching forward to touch the sandy cliff. "What do you make of this?"

Zadie sat and reached forward to grasp a handful of the sand, expressing surprise as her fingernails grated across it and she came away empty-handed. She tried again but it appeared that the sand could not be picked up lightly.

"Try this," offered Nathan, giving her his hammer. She was slim but looked stronger and more determined than he had imagined at first glance and, chipping twice, a chunk fell neatly into her hand. Nathan took it and put it on a rock. "Now hit it with the flat end." Zadie did so and the sand separated into its constituent grains. Picking up a small amount he ran it through his fingers from hand to hand, before pouring a little into her palm and drawing a small set of magnifiers from his pocket, flicking one of them open.

"Have a look. How many different types of grains can you see?"

A considered reply came back, "Three, no possibly four."

"Good," said Nathan. "There should be two lighter and two darker." Zadie nodded. "Look at the dark ones first. One should be slightly brighter but both should be flat." Again she nodded. "The dull one is a fragment of broken slate from around here, the other is mica from the granite of the moors. Now, can you see a lighter one that looks rounded under the magnifier?"

"Yes," she replied.

"That's quartz, again from the granite of the moors. It's the most resistant, hence it becomes rounded, although under a true microscope it looks very different."

"What about the other one?" said Zadie, developing an interest for this.

"Ah, that's the key," he replied, and that's why you couldn't pick up the sand without using the hammer. It's a tiny fragment of sea shell."

Zadie looked blank and waited for him to explain. Instead he turned and pointed to the vast expanse of sand on the opposite side of the estuary at Tregirls and the dunes behind it and, as they sat looking at it and out to sea, he began, "There's no difference in composition between these grains and the sand on the beaches today – or the dunes at Tregirls, or Daymer, or near Rock – this sand is a little bit coarser, but that's it. Once these grains were like those are today – the back of a large sandy beach." He was in his element now and as she listened an older landscape unfolded before her: dunes abandoned by the sea, becoming inactive; rainwater dissolving some of the tiny fragments of sea shell and then cementing the grains of sand together until they were in the first stage of becoming a rock – lithification, he called it.

"But could the wind have blown the sand so far up here?" queried Zadie.

"A good question," came the answer. "Possibly, but the real answer lies where we are sitting," and he reached behind him tapping the pebbles at the base of the sandy cliff with his hammer. They failed to move. "Cemented in the same way," he continued; "an old shingle beach but now stranded higher than the highest high tide." Looking back towards the sea again he said, "See what is in front of us? This higher platform we've been walking on was once like those rock pools the children are playing in down below – a platform cut by the waves. Now, it's been abandoned by the sea."

Zadie could visualise the level now and stood looking across to the cliff where she had been sitting on the bench. "I can see a similar level over there," she said, "and it matches up with the top of that large rock near those dogs." This time he nodded. She paused. "So, once the sea level was here and this would have been a beach and rock pools like those down there." It was a half-question, half-statement and he nodded again. "When?" she fired at him.

"Oh, recently," Nathan answered casually.

"What does that mean?" Zadie interrogated.

"Within the last 100,000 years, certainly; perhaps within the last 5,000 years," he responded. It was a rather different definition of 'recently' than she had expected. "It's actually a complex landscape and there have been quite a few changes in sea level," he added.

They were walking as they talked now, shifting from place to place among the rocks, picking or peering at items of interest but making their way generally up the estuary. Nathan was tapping idly at a bit of rusted metal – the last skeletal remains of a vessel driven onto the rocks near Trebetherick Point.

"People are strange," he said, pointing at the crowded expanse of Daymer Bay as it came into view. "Some of them come year after year, seeking out the same spot on the beach and expecting it to be the same. They think of it as their landscape, their spot – unchanging – able to be possessed, managed, maintained. It's not. It's dynamic, living; change is building all the time." Turning and pointing in the opposite direction, he continued, "You see that island out to sea? Barely 14,000 years ago we could have walked to it … and perhaps 30 miles beyond it was the edge of a great ice sheet. Sea levels were over 100 metres lower than today. That's how much and how rapidly they have risen naturally without any of the impact of our 19th Century Industrial Revolution, or China's industrialisation today. Those triggers have yet to take full effect. Mankind has always advanced onto land that has been yielded as sea levels have fallen and retreated as they have risen. It was easy when buildings were made from wood and subsistence agriculture dominated, and the global population was less than half a billion. Now it's over six billion and half of that lives within 25 metres of sea level. Even in 1900, perhaps 10% of the world's population was urbanised; now it's 50%. Cities are complex, immobile. Many of them sit as jewels in the crown of King Canute awaiting the rising tide."

They argued as they walked across the beach – not in emotional terms but in a detached, intellectual sort of way. Northern accents mingled with southern from nearby families; games of beach cricket and children flying kites mixed with the trudge of wind-surfers back from the increasingly distant water; and a steady stream of dogs and walkers passed in the opposite direction. Undulations between the hard ripples of sand gave an irregular sploshing as they walked.

"The trouble with triggers," Nathan was saying, "is that you don't see them until you've passed them and they already start taking effect. We know about Carbon Dioxide and the effect of thermal combustion in power stations and vehicles in creating Greenhouse gases but we are powerless to change the past and can't do much about the future. Even if we reduce our emissions, it is a pretence – we just buy our microwaves and consumer durables from abroad; China is opening a new coal-fired power station every three weeks … and it's a global atmosphere not a parochial European one. What's more there are some natural triggers that we know little about and they can act as a self-reinforcing spiral – take thermal expansion of the sea, for instance."

"What's that?" interjected Zadie.

"As the atmosphere warms, so the sea loses less heat to it, and it warms. As it warms, it expands and floods onto the land nearby. The shallow waters warm more, and so it goes on."

"But it can't expand by that much," she objected.

Nathan ducked beneath a kite string that threatened to

garotte him and Zadie threw a tennis ball back to a child who was in rapid pursuit of it.

"If two thirds of the planet is water, not expanding by much actually means quite a lot. And then there are the Clathrates."

"What are they?" she said.

"Deposits of methane gas locked beneath the permafrost in Arctic regions. Warmer temperatures allow the permafrost to melt and, quite suddenly …" (which Zadie took to mean over a few decades, given her experience with the word 'recently') "… the methane erupts into the atmosphere adding yet more to the Greenhouse Effect. More permafrost melts, and more methane enters the atmosphere, etc."

"OK, but all that is unproven," she countered.

"Yes," he acknowledged, " and that's the problem because by the time we can measure it happening, it will be too late."

They walked in silence for a while, crunching over some dead mussels stripped from their environment by the previous day's storm.

After a while, Zadie said, "New Orleans was flooded by a one-off event, 'Katrina'; and Banda Aceh was destroyed by a tsunami; but London and lots of towns and cities on the coast have protection against flooding from the sea, and there are planning restrictions about where you can build. I suppose you're going to say the politicians don't know what they are doing."

Nathan was very tempted to say exactly what he thought about politicians but a stray frisbee reminded him that it was a family beach and he concentrated on the plight of London.

"Some cities will be safe and some won't," he began, "and it's not just coastal ones. Arguably the largest in the world – Mexico City, 25 million people – sits in a hollow between two active volcanoes; most of the cities in the west of the USA lie within reach of a dormant super-volcano under Yellowstone National Park. However, leaving that aside, let's take the case of London." They hopped across the braided islets the stream had made in the sand and headed for the left edge of Brea Hill. "You can build an ever higher Thames Barrier for London but you can't protect the whole low-lying coast of Essex, Suffolk, Norfolk, The Fens," he continued. "As sea levels rise, the water will flood onto the land and start seeping into the permeable strata of chalk that underlie most of SE England, moving along them. The land water won't be able to drain so far into the chalk; water tables will rise by the same amount that sea levels do, since water finds its own level. Eventually, London will be flooded from below, not from above. The first to go will be the deep Tube lines, then the deeper cellars and basements ... it will be an insidious rise, almost undetectable in the usual measurements of fluctuations in the deep bore-holes and, when it is, it will be too late – another trigger taking its effect."

"What's the time scale?" asked Zadie.

"Just about the worst – 25 years, 50 years maybe."

"That's a long time. Why is that bad?" she exclaimed.

Looking at her, he answered, "If it was shorter, it would be a matter of urgency – not just for London – and there would be the motivation to do something about it. If it was longer, there would be time to plan; 'time for amendment of life', as my grandfather used to quote from the old Prayer Book. As it is, this generation can see all of this as a confusing problem to pass on to the next generation, blind in their belief that they will rest easy in their own graves by then and that technology will have developed some magical answer for the next generation."

They had only scratched the surface of a conversation that pitted property developer against purchaser, generation against generation, and scientist against scientist. Perhaps wisely, they allowed their thoughts to wrap around them as their feet drew them to the foot of Brea Hill and, spiralling away from the busy cliff path, they sat on an empty bench by an old quarry, overlooking the small church of St. Enodoc.

"If you had a choice," Zadie said slowly, "where would you live?"

"Other than Cornwall, you mean?"

"Yes," she answered.

"Probably Alice Springs," he laughed, and for once it didn't hurt.

"And if all the ice melted, would we be safe here?" she persisted.

"We would, but our children wouldn't be," he answered, blushing slightly.

"…And their children?" she continued.

"Maybe on top of the hill."

And they fell silent, looking at the view below.

Chapter 3   From Enodoc to Polgodoc

The bench was a pleasant spot to sit and few walkers chose to come round this side of the hill. The slightly crooked spire of the old church sat in the middle of its rectangular graveyard, bounded by a dry-stone wall overgrown with tamarisk. Beyond it the land sloped irregularly upwards, a profusion of different shades of green. In front of it was another green and a fairway leading to it. It was a pretty hole, and a difficult one.

A cry of, "Fore!" alerted Nathan to the presence of golfers and he saw the file of walkers following the nearer edge of the fairway duck and cover their heads as the ball hooked left into the marshy area by the little stream at the bottom of the steep slope below them. Yellow irises bloomed there earlier in the year and now there would be purple orchids in the drier patches; no chance of finding the ball and anyway it was out of bounds, he thought, reaching for his binoculars to follow the game. Four more distant clunks of driver on ball carried at intervals. The first golfer had presumably decided the same as Nathan and taken the penalty, playing 3 off the tee. Probably he was the last to play as that ball had hooked as well and was resting improbably on a short, shiny downslope near where the walkers had been; at least it was in bounds this time. Two had driven well and were near the middle of the fairway – they had a good chance of making the green in two; the fourth had sliced into the steep slope of longer grass on the far side of the fairway and was endeavouring to find his ball at least twenty feet away from where Nathan could see it resting in a thick patch of wiry grass. It would be an interesting stance, even if he found it. There were two blue caps and two red caps and Nathan had the impression that it was a father and son competition – in which case, age was doing rather better then youth at present.

'Blue Son' had given up on his ball and taken a drop. Both youngsters had taken two more shots to reach the green while 'Red Father' had chipped neatly to within four feet of the pin; 'Blue

Father' had gone through it but had a stroke of good fortune in ricocheting back off a white painted stone marking the edge of the walkers' path round the green. 'Blue Son' and 'Red Son' both two-putted to give them scores of 6 and 7, respectively, on the little par 4. So, it would be up to the 'Fathers'. 'Blue Father' had a very long and undulating putt, slightly uphill, and with a nasty little borrow at the end. Not much chance there, thought Nathan, as the ball was set off slightly to the left and rather speedily; but it seemed to take a borrow that Nathan had missed from his eyrie seat and was looking good now, slowing, seeming to resist each rotation as it trickled to the very edge of the hole … and toppled in. Animated comment, mixed with laughter, floated up to him. So, 'Red Father' had a four-footer to halve the hole. Not so easy as it looks, thought Nathan, after yesterday's rain and wind and today's sun it would be a bit crusty … and it was downhill. A group of walkers were watching in silence near the edge of the green, probably in the periphery of 'Red Father's' vision as well. There was the ball on its way, looking true and not too fast, slowing now and borrowing left. It caught the edge of the cup, running round it and speeding 7 feet beyond the hole. Nathan had never really worked out why a golf ball seemed to have the capacity to do this and accelerate away from the hole at a greater speed than it approached it. At least the next putt went in.

It had been fun to watch and, as the golfers walked towards the next tee, he switched his attention to the churchyard. There was the grave where Betjeman was buried, with a group gathered round looking at its slate headstone. They probably didn't know that his mother's grave was also in the cemetery. A friend had talked of meeting the old man once – old, so old – walking unsteadily with sticks across the fairway over which the pall-bearers had finally carried him before resting the coffin on the plinth in the lych gate. Petronella's seat at the top of the graveyard was occupied by a family as their children wandered around the graves looking for the oldest date or most interesting inscription. He thought fondly of that seat. On a day like today it probably gave the most fabulous view in Cornwall with the spire of the old church and Stepper Point framing the vista out to sea whilst the low tamarisk hedge and stone wall enclosing the graveyard seemed like a gentle glove holding the dead safe against misadventure. His mind strayed towards the tombstone in the lowest corner to 'A Seaman of The Great War … Known unto God' and he began tracking back through history.

"That church," said Zadie, "it's a funny place for it."

"Yes," he said. "It's old, probably Saxon or before. The east end is hewn into the solid rock and may have been built over a cave and spring. Once there was a village between it and the sea but it was overwhelmed by the sand blown up in storms. By the middle of the 19th Century only the spire and roof remained above sand level and, before it was dug out and restored in 1863, the priest was rumoured to let himself into the building by a hole in the roof once a year to perform communion and keep the building consecrated."

"The old village," began Zadie, "how rapidly would it have been overwhelmed?"

"Very rapidly," Nathan replied, "or else they would have had time to dig themselves out and regroup. Possibly a year; maybe just one stormy season. I expect they just put their things in their boats and paddled off elsewhere, or moved inland towards St. Minver. It must have been rapid if the rumours are true."

"What rumours?"

"That there are still the shells of old wooden houses under the dunes and some of them were left with furniture in them."

"When do you think it would have happened?" she continued.

"Probably the 14th or 15th Century. That would coincide with when another village was buried, at Rhossili in Wales – both faced in a similar direction and both had large expanses of sand drying in front of them at low tide. Also, this parish has a record of vicars stretching back as far as 1255 AD and there are gaps in the 14th and 15th Centuries that suggest something pretty disastrous might have occurred."

She thought of a little community struggling against monstrous conditions, shut inside day after day, huddled with their animals. Unable to fish and with their boats destroyed or buried, food supplies would dwindle rapidly; malnutrition and illness would follow swiftly. She wondered what the priest would be saying to allay the old superstitions or fears of divine wrath: maybe he didn't; maybe he was one of those who blamed the people and called for repentance and sacrifice; or maybe he had left for the safety of the monastery at Bodmin before conditions became too bad? And she pictured the survivors leaving before they were finally buried alive – a straggle of weary people with a few emaciated animals, abandoning the life that they had known and seeking shelter in the unknown.

He thought of the cliffs at Pentire and the strength of the wind. It had been bad enough for just a few hours. If it were to go on for day after day, that would be unimaginable; it would drive to insanity. Yet, there had been a great storm in 1857 that had stripped a depth of twelve feet from across the whole of the beach, burying the church with the wind-blown sand and exposing on the beach the remains of a part-fossilised forest of oak, hazel, yew, and holly, and the antlers of deer and teeth of other creatures, before it had covered them again with sand from the estuary.

Zadie shook her head slowly whilst scanning the fairway below with the binoculars. "The original village wouldn't have been by the sea – too exposed," she stated. "They would have moved there when the boats became larger and needed hauling up beyond the tide. The original village is much more likely to have been beneath that fairway. It would have been out of sight and sheltered from the south-westerly winds. There's a good fresh water source that flows round the foot of the hill and they could have prised boulders to build with from this slope and let them roll down the hill. The surrounding land would have provided wood for building and fuel and those irregular slopes beyond the fairway look like strip lynchets."

Nathan raised an eyebrow in enquiry and she explained, "Small fields only a few feet wide and maybe thirty yards long, hugging the contours of the hillslope and typically on south-facing slopes. Initially, they would have been worked by hand and foot-tools; later, by draught animals with elementary wooden ploughs. They were the first kind of sedentary arable farming in this country and you can still see good examples on the chalk land of south Dorset where it has never been ploughed over. That slope would have been ideal as the soil is thin and the land could have been cleared easily. It's not a big area and they could have used the surrounding woodland to provide protective fencing from wild boar and wolves." Nathan listened with respect as she went on to describe the complex organisation and the hazards faced by a typical Iron Age village. "Besides which," she ended, "Brea Hill is recorded as a Roman signal station and the Romans usually only constructed anything of a formal nature where there was some existing settlement to dominate or something worthwhile to them – this is a long way west of their last big base at Exeter."

She spoke confidently of the Romano-British period and the Celtic fringe with its fragmenting Iron Age settlements. Soon, they strayed into legend and King Arthur at Tintagel. There were other legends, too. The source of the stream below them stemmed from near Jesus Well, an unusual name amongst the proliferation of Celtic nomenclature. Some had told of Joseph of Arimathea being a trader in tin and bringing the young Christ-child to Cornwall, subsequently returning with a fragment of the Crown of Thorns and planting it at Glastonbury, where it yielded its white flowers, tinged pink, whenever Good Friday fell. Certainly, the Phoenicians from Tyre and Sidon traded in tin and the main ore of tin was Cassiterite, called after the name those traders gave to Britain – 'Cassiterides' – 'The Tin Islands'. It was difficult to know in Cornwall where history ended and legend began.

*   *   *

The vista from the top of Brea Hill rewarded the steep climb up. Away to the far north-east, the rugged silhouette of Rough Tor cut the skyline. "Standing on the rocking stones on top of that," Zadie was saying, "and looking down its southern flank, there's a whole Iron Age village with the remains of its huts still visible as small circles of stone amongst the scatter of debris fallen from further up the slope." Nearer, were the fairways of the golf course and to their right the dunes that led to Rock, hidden beyond; in the distance, across the estuary, were the old, iconic viaduct and Padstow itself. At the end of their rotation they looked towards Stepper Point with its angular indent at the base of the cliff as if a giant had taken a knife to it and then forgotten what he was about – the result of 19th Century endeavours by Padstow Harbour Commissioners to prevent ships being driven onto the Doom Bar by the eddying winds, and of Canadian servicement quarrying during the Second World War to provide hard-core for the airfield at St. Mawgan. That had been a time when invasion fears had closed and fortified the beaches, according to his grandfather; and those locals who were too old or too young for service had helped man an RNVR motorboat; an armoured train operated by escaped Polish forces had proceeded defiantly up and down the estuary.

Zadie looked across the estuary again and observed, "The old iron bridge looks attractive in this light. It must have been difficult to build."

"It was," said Nathan. "That creek was a major obstacle. The line reached Wadebridge in 1834 but it took another 65 years to find a way to Padstow. There's a story behind it – my grandfather told me it once, and his father told him; there's supposed to be a photograph of the old man – my great-grandfather – amongst the dignitaries welcoming the first train in1899, but I've never identified him. It caused a great rift in the village when the railway came."

"What village?"

"Trevennick, where I live."

"What's the story?"

"Well, I'm not sure quite how true it is – grandfather was a bit selective in his stories sometimes – but he said there was disagreement between those involved in building ships at the yards in Padstow, or sailing to Sea Mills in Little Petherick Creek, and those who wanted the railway. Some of the villagers supported the shipping men and others bought into the railway, thinking they would make a fortune. It had the delusion of turning Padstow into a wealthy port. There was a lot of debate and families were polarised. For years the route was blocked. Then the railway brought the steels – great cylinders cast in iron – and drove them fifty feet through the mud of the creek into the solid rock so that the track could vault it and the viaduct was high enough for the wooden ships to pass under. The yards had closed but the delay cost the railway. By the time it reached Padstow, the whole estuary was silting up and the new ships had too large a draught; it never made any great profit."

"So, what happened to the villagers?"

"A few made money; most lost everything. They emigrated: those who knew about sheep to Australia; dairymen to New Zealand; arable to Canada; and miners all over the colonies, wherever there were holes in the ground and minerals to be found. It's always been the way; you'll find the Cornish names wherever the map was painted red. 'There are two things you can never stop, son,' my grandfather use to say, 'progress and greed.' That generation never questioned what was meant by progress. It was a new age, a Steel Age, I suppose – steel, guns, ships, missionaries. They thought they could change the world; and they did."

Zadie thought a while and asked, "What happened to the railway?"

"It took fish to Billingsgate in London, and brought the first tourists here. The hotel was built for them by a local lad who made a fortune in South Wales. Sometimes, my grandfather used to come over near this spot to watch the 'big train' cross the viaduct and spill out its passengers for their stay." Nathan thought of what the railway had meant to Padstow.

Even as late as 1959 the journey began at Waterloo as the big, old clock ticked onto 11am; the guard's whistle blew and the Merchant Navy class engine coughed and barked to move the eleven or thirteen fully laden coaches that formed the Atlantic Coast Express, smuts, cinders and smoke enveloping a generation that would forever associate their smells with holidays. Only the front two carriages went to Padstow – others were detached for Bude, for

Newquay, for St. Ives, and the other forgotten termini of the SW. At Okehampton, the big Merchant Navy with its Bulleid shielding and perforated, flanged wheels was replaced with the lighter West Country locomotives for the last part of the journey. As the engine and its two coaches pulled through Wadebridge the level crossing closed, blocking the main road and causing tail-backs two miles long, before it continued down the estuary, smoke drifting like the early mist evaporating and its whistle echoing plaintively over the water, inviting reply from the steam ships that were no more. Finally, it would steam over that viaduct with a kind of deliberate, slow majesty before sighing to a halt in Padstow station at exactly 5pm. Outside a pub on the waterfront was still one of the last line-side markers of the journey – 259/1 – two hundred and fifty nine miles and one chain from London, Waterloo.

Of course, the line was long gone now, severed by Dr. Beeching's axe in the mid 1960s, along with countless other branch lines up and down the country. The last steam train, a shabby mixed goods, had chuffed into obscurity – a mobile anachronism of a former era – in 1965. In a strange way the line had survived more successfully than ever because now it was a cycle track, carrying daily more people than the railway had ever done at its height and opening to each the vistas of the Camel Trail; the station was a car park and the quays a venue for restaurants and tourism – ever and always, the mutation of the past could be seen in the present.

"My grandmother used to tell me stories but they were rather different," said Zadie as they walked down onto the dunes, "about her grandmother and the woods and the wild boar, and tales of Tintagel." Soon she was speaking of The Saints' Way – the ancient route of Christianity that Celtic priests had travelled from Normandy to southern Cornwall, thence overland to Padstow before embarking in their coracles to christianise Ireland. Their names were partly lost in time but others – Petroc, Menefra, Merryn, Enodoc – were remembered in names that had no dates. Once, she had listened to a university lecturer attempting to explain the difference between faith and insanity but she had been left unmoved by the semantics. Thinking of how rough the water at the mouth of The Camel could be even on a calm day, Nathan was inclined to think that any attempt to paddle west in a coracle was definitely insanity.

"How old are these dunes?" asked Zadie.

"They might have formed at the time Enodoc was obliterated," answered Nathan, "as there's a good variety of vegetation and some depth of soil on them in places. Back there is the abandoned cliff that they have almost buried; there are places where bits of it can still be seen and even something like a cave." Passing an apple tree, grown from some long discarded core, he continued, "But probably they're older as the name of 'Rock' suggests a solid landing point amongst the shifting sands and its name is recorded in the charter granting rights to a ferry in 1337, although then it was called the Black Rock ferry."

By this time they had reached the ferry queue. It was remarkably short and the tide was at its lowest ebb. The full moon had brought the spring tides and it almost seemed as if they could walk the few strides across the estuary. Nathan was glad that they would berth at the lower steps and could walk up the Stile Field. Although he liked the place, Padstow would be hot and busy on a day like this. Seagulls were crying in the distance as the little ferry zigzagged its course through the shallows and he imagined them diving and squawking at the tourists sitting by the pretty harbour in an attempt to force them to drop their chips or pasties, and the birds fighting over the remnants of the food.

At the top of the field, Zadie leant on the slate stile, worn smooth and curved by countless hands and feet, looking alternately at the view to south and north. Each was superb in its own way. "Accident of history," said Nathan, reading her thoughts. "This is the Memorial donated after the 1st World War in memory of those men from Padstow who lost their lives. Their names are on that Celtic Cross – a whole generation that went but never came back – the field was bought later by the town as open space in perpetuity," and he felt a depth of gratitude that through some distant sacrifice those men had unknowingly assisted in giving succeeding generations the opportunity of such a view. "Prime building land," he went on, "worth millions – and so is the land to the north but that was blocked from development by the family who have owned it since Tudor times, and before that it was church land. There was a monastery here – quite wealthy one – but it was sacked by the Vikings in 981 AD."

They walked on, dropping down into the dunes at the back of Tregirls. "I can see the abandoned cliff at the back of these," Zadie observed. "It even has miniature headlands and little inlets still there."

"Yes. These dunes are much younger," he replied. "They don't even show up on the first geological survey map of the area – it's shown as open water right up to those cliffs." They paused, trying to locate a skylark that was trilling above, watching it land away from its nest to protect its young from any airborne predator before scuttling towards it out of sight. Five minutes of fruitless search for the nest showed the skill of the bird in camouflaging its fragile home. "In medieval times skylark tongues were a delicacy," he added absently, thinking of the difficulty of trying to catch them and the number of birds sacrificed for a meal in a society that could have so great inequalities of wealth and power that some could require such a trifle and the majority struggle to meet their basic needs for food.

Crossing through the marshy area where a little stream slithered slowly to the sand, they regained the cliff path and walked past the old life-boat station, its boat long since removed from the silting cove to Trevose, and arrowed up the slope towards the Daymark. Again gorse blazed its welcome in the early afternoon sun; valerian vied with campion – intense in its pinkness – for the butterflies' attention and, to their right, wind-surfers vied with each other to complete some improvised course. Pepper Hole and Butter Hole came and went but they were content largely to walk and look, rather than talk, until they came to a point where the path veered away from the cliff top for a while and Nathan stepped off it down a lesser-worn track.

"Polgodoc," he said. "Not many people come here; it's a hidden spot."

There was a seal playing in the waters below and cormorants standing like sentinels on the rocks, waiting for it to go away so that they could resume their fishing. Nathan lowered his rucksack with a dull clink. For the first time today he did not feel the pain as he smiled. He looked at her eyes and saw them smiling back. Emotions stirred and he remembered how other eyes had looked like this; it was distant, disconcerting.

"Look, would you like some lunch?" he asked, to turn his thoughts aside.

The simple, "Yes," disarmed him.

The grassy slope faced south and was warm. A flat rock provided a convenient table and Nathan produced a bottle of red wine from his rucksack, followed by a cheese in the shape of a small grapefruit, and a fresh white loaf. Seeking his large penknife with its varied attachments, he rummaged further but succeeded in producing only a large runner bean. Zadie broke into gales of laughter and the sun flashed its mockery at him off her jewellery as she writhed in mirth.

"… often open a bottle with one of those, do you?" she sobbed between bouts of further laughter.

It wasn't helped by Nathan holding the slightly mis-shapen bean between his thumb and finger about six inches from his nose, and staring at it. He flung the offending item at a passing gull and finally succeeded in locating the penknife, setting to work on cutting the bread and cheese. A satisfying pop as the corkscrew attachment did its work was coupled with an unsatisfying lurch in Nathan's stomach.

Zadie was watching. This time it was more of a giggle as she ventured, "You haven't got any glasses, have you?" Nathan shook his head slowly. "Here," she said, sitting down by his side and taking off her back-pack. She removed the thin waterproof from its top and produced a flask and two enamel mugs, delving again for a small lunch box and opening it to reveal cold chicken, tomatoes and paper napkins. "Now, is that better?"

"Yes," said Nathan through a mouthful of bread and cheese or, at least, that was what it vaguely sounded like.

Chapter 4   Strange Bonds

Lunch was leisurely and they lolled in the sunshine. Nathan had found the miniature cigars that were the last element of his bartering produce with the acquaintance on the Spanish trawler earlier in the day and he was enjoying one whilst lying with half-closed eyes and twirling the spent match in his fingers. Zadie had sat up. "This is a strange place," she observed. "Those caves look an unnatural shape … and so does that rock by the cormorant."

"Yes," said Nathan. He didn't need to open his eyes; he knew the place well. "What you are looking at is an old mine – a very old mine – maybe 2,000 years old, or more. De la Beche records it as a thin vein of lead on the 19th Century Geological Survey but the green staining near that cave suggests there was also copper – and it's likely there was tin too."

"How do you know?" asked Zadie.

Nathan reached for his rucksack and opened a side pocket, taking out a small pouch containing two objects. The first was a silvery-grey, shiny cube and he passed it to her. "It's galena – lead ore," he went on. "That area about twenty feet away is the spoil from the old mine and years ago I was sifting through the fragments when I came across a heavier one. That was inside it when I broke away the surrounds." It was the first real specimen that he had found and it had stirred Nathan's passion for Geology. Reaching into the pouch again, he brought out the other item. This time, it was slightly encrusted and had a more brilliant lustre to it in places. It was also an odd shape, rather like a truncated cross with a bulge around the intersecting arms. He handed it to Zadie and took the galena back. "That came from the cave below where we are sitting – you can't see it from here. It's tin," he explained. For a while, he talked about the cave with the green staining. It was inaccessible – a dark, irregular cleft with the swell vigorously rushing in and out of its deep water even on a calm day like today.

He closed his eyes and remembered an exceptionally low tide when he had tried swimming out to it to search for any fragments of the copper ore that he was convinced was there. It had been an evil current; his hammer had snagged in some very deep weed; and he had been overwhelmed by a sense of ancient menace. He had abandoned the hammer and had been very glad to get back to near where they were now. There was an old Cornish litany that his grandmother had muttered over his bedside when he was a child – 'From ghoulies and ghosties and things that go bump in the night, good Lord deliver us'. Nathan reckoned it had given him nightmares more often than sleep, and that place epitomised all his irrational fears.

Zadie gave the specimen of tin back to Nathan and said, "Show me where you found that, then."

"Do you really want to see? It's dark, wet and narrow," he replied.

However, the sun was shining and the wine warmed from the inside. It wasn't a particularly dangerous place and she was moderately insistent, so ten minutes later they had packed up from lunch and made their way a short distance along the cliff top, moving from comfortable grass to loose fragments of rock that shifted beneath them and clattered down the cliff. He stopped and thought better of making a condescending enquiry about her climbing ability; instead, he found his voice moving into its more professional tone, measured and clear. "The cliff is solid here – good rock. Don't stray to the left as it is crumbly and will come out in your hand. There are a series of hand and footholds about four feet apart. Come down backwards and slowly; and try not to step on my fingers. I'll be about six feet below you and it's eighteen holds down to a flat ledge."

He lowered himself carefully over the edge. This was the most dangerous bit with the rucksack apt to swing and unbalance him if he took it too quickly. "OK, I'm far enough down for you to start now," he called up, watching as a pair of light walking boots appeared over the cliff edge, followed by a bottom, and by a back-pack. She had found the first foothold and was seeking for the second with her right foot. "Six inches down and to your right," he called clearly. The boot moved and found it. Nathan ducked as a small volley of stones clattered down on him. That was foolish, he thought; leading from below he should have at least put a cap on to protect his head. Still, it meant that she had relinquished her grasp on the last of the loose rock beyond the cliff top and now he could see strands of hair blowing like golden thread in the sunlight. "The holds alternate from left to right rather like a ladder with only half a rung," he called to her, as they worked their way slowly and carefully down. Nathan could hear the incoming tide swishing and gurgling hungrily in the deep inlet below; the sun was half way to the west now and white horses were cantering at the island of Gulland a couple of miles offshore. "Sixteen, seventeen, eighteen," he counted to himself. That should be it; and he moved his foot out from the cliff face seeking the ledge. There it was. It was reassuring to get a full foot down flat on the rock and he stepped to one side, taking off his rucksack and watching her finish the climb. She was struggling to find the ledge with her shorter limbs. "You'll have to trust for it," he said, near enough to her now not to have to shout. But her reach between her top left handhold and the ledge her right foot was seeking was insufficient. This was proving trickier than Nathan had thought and the longer she was stuck there the more likely she might start to panic or start shaking and lose grip. "Listen," he said with command; "when I say so, let go with your left hand and swing down and out with your right foot. Do you understand?" A clear, "Yes," came back. Good, her voice didn't betray any fear and she was still acting logically. A gull wheeled below. "Ready. Now," said Nathan calmly.

The left hand let go and the right foot came down and out; the right hand left its hold. It happened in an instant. She was fractionally too slow moving her left foot out of its hold and as she did so it pushed her body weight outwards so that, landing on the ledge, she was going to swivel and topple over. Nathan reached and grabbed whatever he could – a bit of thigh with his right hand and her shoulders with his left arm – dragging her back towards him. He could feel her heart beating against him and the flat, shallow breath as he held her there until they slowed.

"OK if I let go now?" said Nathan after a while.

Zadie nodded. Slowly, he released her.

"I'm sorry," he said, "I shouldn't have asked you to – "

"You didn't," interrupted Zadie defiantly, "I asked you to show me." He stood, trying to judge the emotions. "And anyway," she continued, "it's a lot easier going up – you can see the holds in turn."

He moved apart and put his rucksack down again a few paces along the ledge where it was at its widest. She followed and looked around.

"Where's the mine, then?" she asked.

Nathan stepped aside. Behind him was a dark hole about five feet high and half that in width. Zadie gasped.

"Well hidden, isn't it?" he said, and she wondered how he had ever found it.

He explained how the earliest mines were often small and the cliff faces would have been the easiest places to spot the veins of copper, tin, or lead. "This was an adit, driven horizontally into the rock, following the vein and kept as narrow as possible as it was worked by hand. Every extra inch of width or height into the unwanted slate here was an enormous effort for no return. Rock without value would have been tipped over the ledge here and into the sea below. Ore would have been taken up the way we came down in wicker panniers on the boys' backs whilst the men worked in the mine. Probably, there would have been an elementary wooden ladder, lashed with strips of hide, hence the regular nature of the holds which would have supported it. At the top, the ore would have been broken and the pieces they wanted carried up the valley for smelting. That's one of the reasons why there is so little original woodland left in Cornwall," he ended.

Zadie saw a whole community at work opening up in front of her. Tin and copper would yield bronze. The Bronze Age gave way to the Iron Age. It was her territory and she revelled in picturing the domestic and social organisation that would have been a part of such a venture.

"Can we go in this?" she asked, looking into the opening.

Nathan had been anticipating the question but was still not ready with the answer, although her eyes and voice sparked with interest. There were green and white flecks in her irises, he thought, like the Atlantic on a stormy day, and he was feeling a number of strong undercurrents pulling at his emotions

"What's it like in there?" she continued.

That was easier. He could answer that without commitment. It was just fact.

"This adit goes more or less straight for about twenty feet and, after that, there is a gap where the sea has eroded it from below. At low tide there is sometimes some light there and a drop of about ten feet onto rounded, slippery boulders. Beyond the gap, there are another few feet before the passage pinches out and stops. It must have been where the vein ended," he said.

"Is that where you found the piece of tin you showed me?" asked Zadie.

"No," replied Nathan. "It was down in the gap."

They were locked in eye contact. He was unwilling to be drawn further on that particular story and she thought that he was being protective.

"Look," she said finally, "I've done enough pot-holing to prefer being in there in the dark than working my way down an exposed cliff face."

Still he hesitated. Voices intruded against the breeze – a family by the sound of it. He wasn't the only one to know about the sanctuary of Polgodoc. He didn't want to get caught down here, and he certainly didn't want their voices attracting children to try to climb down to them. They would have to go up, or in, and rapidly.

A stone clattered down and narrowly missed them. Nathan held up a finger to his lips to warn Zadie to be silent and quickly extracted a battered cloth cap from his rucksack, motioning to Zadie to put her own cap back on. He mimicked carrying the rucksack in front of them and disappeared into the hole, stopping after a few feet. There was very little light from the entry with the two of them blocking it off.

"Talk quietly," he whispered. "They've got children who will get bored soon and want to go away. I'll show you the end of the adit and then we can go back and get out."

She seemed pleased and moved more smoothly in the dark than he did, sensing the uneven floor and pools intuitively. The sound of lapping waves reached them from below and there was the faintest glimmer of light.

"There is a three foot gap here," he explained quietly. "You have to half jump, half step across, then duck because the ceiling has a lower point in it."

She realised now why he had put a cap on and wondered at the risks taken by the early communities that she knew from intellectual study. He threw his rucksack across and leapt neatly, turning to catch her back-pack before pushing them both further into the narrowing passage. She stepped nimbly and ducked just far enough so that only her cap brushed the rock above. The rock floor sloped back towards the gap and was slippery but he had a good handhold in a kind of dry socket in the wall and, reaching with his free hand, he guided her fingers onto the same grip so that they closed over his.

What happened next was an accident, but probably one waiting to happen. In the confined space as they each jostled to gain a secure footing, her lips brushed across his in a gentle caress. Stars of light and silvery streaks seemed to waver in Nathan's eyes and emotions churned.

"Did you see that?" said Zadie, "Did you see that!!"

Nathan was struggling to think straight but said, "What?"

"Did you see the silver streaks?" she repeated more urgently.

He was now greatly confused and thought that the word 'rock' was appearing in the conversation. With an effort he concentrated on Zadie as her hand tightened on his.

"Listen," she said, "I've got an idea."

He was half way through mouthing, "What?" when her lips caught him full on his lips and her free hand made sure there was no accident on this occasion. Nathan stared in amazement, as they parted and he spluttered for breath. It seemed as if the rock itself was aroused by her passion. Silvery-grey veins were spreading outwards from where their hands still held together. Splitting and growing and widening, they emanated light with a lustre beyond anything that he had seen and illuminated the drips of water into each pool and crevice. Rather than the diamond prisms of dew in the sunshine, the water droplets split again into myriad shades of silver upon silver and the veins grew thicker and thicker.

Hardly daring to believe what he saw, Nathan half whispered, half mouthed, "Mother Lode," to Zadie and so, so slowly he reached out his free left hand to touch the great irregular vein of silvery light stretching from floor to ceiling. All the book-learning fell away and he found himself looking at what the old miners had dreamed and dreamed about; what they had sought beyond every peril and danger – an intrusion of pure tin straight from the igneous masses as they had cooled. Ancient beyond ancient. A huge vein, two feet wide or more. Find this and all the other veins would lead off it. Follow this and there was fortune after fortune. Suddenly, he understood their fears, their hopes, their persistence, their endurance. Why had he never found this before? This was the reason for the adit mined with such hard work. Why had this lode not been worked?

Then his fingers touched it. It was real, hard, extant; and the rock itself seemed to greet his touch. It was almost like finding an old friend, a part of his existence that he didn't know was there. Her fingers reached close to his, sensing the thrill that was tingling through his whole being and, as they made contact with his, the light changed, pulsating down the veins towards one central place. There, and there alone, was a small, dark gap in the iridescent illumination; a kind of carved recess.

"Nathan," said a voice almost in the wrong century, "put that piece of tin you found in there."

It was the first time Zadie had called him by his name and, whether for that or any other reason, he felt disinclined to argue. The pouch came easily from the rucksack and after some small hesitation he pressed his most prized trophy into the recess, holding it there with his fingertips. Three things happened in close succession. The light stopped pulsating down towards the recess and produced a steady, contented glow. Meanwhile, the tin appeared to be losing all its tarnish and the pieces that had given it a malformed shape. It shimmered, almost molten, but remained cool to Nathan's touch.

"Do you see?" said Zadie. "It's a link. The rock is accepting it."

He thought that perhaps his earlier talk of a dynamic, living landscape had gone too far but he held on to the tin as the mother lode widened further and split. Opening beyond it was a passageway of smoothed black rock, etched into visibility by faint trails of silvery light. Rough hewn steps curved away to the left, beckoning to some inner instinct yet laced with a lingering primaeval uncertainty. Silently they responded to the invitation, stepping slowly forward, their packs anomalously modern to the ageless ancientness of clefted rock. As they moved, the tin in Nathan's open palm seemed to call light from the veins ahead, drawing them on, whilst it faded from those behind. Suddenly, there was a dull, solid clunk. They stopped. The entrance had closed.

Zadie tugged at his hand.

"Come on," she said. "If we can get in, we can get out. I want to explore this cave."

Nathan was less certain. This had moved well beyond his reality but he was drawn irresistibly by the mother lode. Holding Zadie's hand, they moved down the steps, sloshing gently in the silvery pools. They must be below sea-level now, he thought, as they moved down and left again. Still the light led them, and the passage arched open into a cavern. Light spread across it and up it and round it, and round again – veining after veining, luminous as the most brilliant night sky.

They spoke in hushed tones, awed by what they saw. The mother lode ran along the floor of the cavern, splitting and circling around a flat mass of black slate of much higher quality than the cliffs they had come through. Smaller veins shot off to the right and left and there were basin-like pools into which drops of water plinked, scattering their silvered diamonds. Once, Nathan had followed a meltwater stream beneath a glacier snout in Iceland; that had seemed an ethereal world – a cacophony of synchronised plinks and symphony of iced light, varying infinitely in its intensity as he had looked through it to the unseen world above. But this was older, older by far, and different in essence.

"It could almost be a place of sacrifice," whispered Zadie, speaking from the ghoulie and ghostie end of Nathan's spectrum and he shuddered at the thought. "Look," she said, "there are rock pools for washing and archways beyond that raised black slab in the centre."

"That's the highest grade slate I've ever seen," said Nathan, circling it cautiously before running his fingers across it in admiration.

It was not entirely flat; in the centre were four similar protrusions facing inwards towards each other and rather like a lion or a sphinx with a strange cleft just behind the head. Actually, it couldn't be a lion as there was no mane – more a lioness, lying but alert, with head raised and paws stretched out in front. It didn't look as if they had been sculpted but their similarity and positioning made a natural origin unlikely. Moreover, there was some familiarity about the shape that was worrying Nathan.

Zadie laid her hand on his and a gentle resonance began to echo around the cavern, softening the plink of water. As they watched, the clefts in the black lionesses began to glow, each to a different colour: silver, orangey-red, translucent blue, and white. Nathan looked at the tin in his palm. It was cleaner and more lustrous. It was also more sharply etched. The rectangular cross pieces were clear and connected by a circle of slightly smaller size, leaving four holes between the intersection of the rectangles and the circle, rather like a full moon separated and split into four quadrants. The surfaces of it appeared to have some kind of intricate design on them and, as it lay in his hand, it radiated the same silvery light as the cleft in the nearest lioness.

"Zadie," said Nathan quietly, "your instinct was right about the entry to this cave. What do you say now?"

"Well, my great Aunt used to say, always put silver with silver," she replied enigmatically.

Nathan regarded the piece of tin. It looked the right shape. The slab was pulsating now as if requiring something urgently but he was hesitant.

"Use the token," said Zadie.

"The what?"

"The token. The tin token. The rock accepted us because of the token – it is a token of acceptance, a key – it's the right shape – use it. After all, if nothing happens, nothing happens," she added, appealing to his logic.

It was a silly thing to do. There was no meaning in it. There could be no meaning in it. But there was no meaning in being in this cave. Tens of times he had been to the same point in the adit but never seen an entry or the mother lode that was still blazing in his mind. No, not just in his mind; it was blazing in front of him and around him; that was what he could see by; that was what seemed to be urging his hand forward.

Slowly he placed the piece of tin into the silvery recess of the lioness rock and pushed it gently in. The cavern blazed with light – pure and silver. Not like spotlights but great strips of silver illumination dispelling every shadow, and before their eyes the surface of the black slab began to bubble, at first slowly then faster, changing from unreflective black to greens and browns, and ochres and whites. They stepped back. A whole landscape was rising before them: little valleys connecting with larger ones and expanding remorselessly onwards; hills and cliffs; promontories. There was woodland and moor; tracks emerged; and, last of all, small groupings of structures that looked like settlements. There were also gaps – flat black areas that remained at slab height and which showed no sign of bubbling upwards to reveal their secret.

For a long while they examined the 'map' in fascination. Zadie thought that she could identify The Camel Valley and Brea Hill with a settlement tucked in its lee just where she had thought it should be – but there was no estuary, just a wide valley with woodland. Nathan was convinced about Carn Menellis and Tintagel at other points on the map, and a hill the shape of Gulland that looked like it was joined to the mainland. In fact, in many areas there was no indication of a coastline at all. They stood transfixed by the landscape in front of them, and finally it came to him. This was the tin landscape. This was the part where the tin lodes reached. The gaps in the map table, as he now thought of it, were where there were other minerals but not tin.

Zadie thought it was a good explanation but was losing interest in the map as she worked her way around the perimeter of the cavern seeking for artefacts or inscriptions. Nathan picked out the glowing tin from its recess and put it in the orangey-red gap in the next lioness figure. The light in the cavern faded rapidly and the map began to dissolve. Hurriedly, he put the tin back in the silver recess whilst he could still see.

"What did you do?" demanded Zadie.

Nathan explained and looked at her wrist as light blazed again and the map reformed. "That bracelet," he said, "is it pure copper?"

"Yes, I think so. I bought it in South Africa during my GAP year. Why?" she answered.

He hesitated. After all, it would mean destroying the bracelet. "It's just that I think the orange-red recess will work with copper ... and I could probably create something like the shape of the tin with the geological hammer and penknife attachments," he ended rather awkwardly.

Some time later he had flattened the copper on a rock well away from the slab or any of the veins, punched holes in it and created a pretty good approximation of the tin shape. Rather apologetically he handed the remaining bits to Zadie, who was sitting on a plinth leaning against a dry bit of wall watching the proceedings. He debated whether to take the tin out of its recess before putting the copper in the red one and eventually decided to do so, leaving it hovering above the recess in his left hand. The map was sinking back now and, although the blaze of silver had ceased, there was still illumination from the veins of tin.

Gently he fitted the copper in place. Immediately it glowed a burnished orange-red, seeming to fill the recess and reform its shape. It began to bubble and froth and spit. Lines of coppery veins started to glow, mixing with the fading silvery light and working their way down the walls towards the black slab. Nathan stared, waiting for the slab to start bubbling and rising to reveal the landscape that the copper lodes reached.

Zadie screamed.

The echoes of her first scream were met by her second and mingled into her third and fourth. Bonds of copper, pure copper, were rising out of the floor and wall behind her, wrapping themselves towards her and encasing her like a fragile song bird in a cage. As he watched, the bonds became thicker and more numerous. In horror, he saw them begin to draw inwards, reducing the size of the cage. Moment by moment it was shrinking.

"Take it out! Take the copper out!!" yelled Zadie.

"I can't!" yelled back Nathan, "It's become molten!"

"Help! Help me!!"

Instinctively, Nathan ran to her and grasped the bars of the cage that were now crushing in on her body and wrapping around her head and legs. It was like a thick spiders' mesh around some insect unable to do anything to protect itself, or an evil version of some process of mummification. There was an inevitability about the inanimate process that had become animate. He struck the bars, grabbing and holding, trying to bend and lever them. Great globules of golden liquid sprayed around him like the sparks from the molten metal of a blast furnace in the night. His hand seared and burnt. Again and again he pulled and struck at the bars, scattering more globules and ignoring the pain that burnt into him. She was screaming too and trying to push the bars away from her head, screaming in a way that signified utter desperation; that there was no hope; that it was something too awful to even contemplate hope; that there was no help; that there could not possibly be any help.

Fragments of copper fell to the ground in virulent redness and, suddenly, the bars slowed in their contractions. Pulsating and beating, they stood still until, moment by slow moment, they began to thin and retreat back into the veins from whence they had come. Zadie fell forward. She was still screaming, and ripping at her blue top. The nauseating smell of burnt human flesh was almost unbearable. She flung herself at and past him, knocking him over, and dived at one of the pools, immersing her chest in as much water as she could and sobbing ever more slowly.

Nathan realised that his left hand was still burning and plunged it into another pool. The copper light had long gone and the silvery light was almost faded. Soon it would be gone too. Soon it would become dark – total darkness – a darkness where you could not even see your finger in front of your nose; a darkness so deep that you could not keep your balance; a darkness that would bring panic and total disorientation – the bane of all deep miners.

He crawled towards Zadie's breath and found her hand.

"It will be OK," she said. "I've been trapped in a pot-hole without light before. Just don't panic. Your rucksack has matches in it. We'll just have to search for it by feel."

She rolled out of the pool and, as she did so, there was the very slightest sense of a less dark patch in the darkness. Nathan strained his eyes until they hurt and as Zadie opened her right hand he saw the red glow. Soon the glow was strengthening. He could see her hand gripping her gold chain now, and in its palm lay the source of the glow which was growing and turning more coppery. The same light began to flow from discontinuous veins in the floor and ceiling, dull but seemingly unthreatening.

"Let's find our packs and go," prompted Zadie.

After a while, they had retrieved them and they walked together towards the worn steps where there seemed to be a stronger glow. Just as when they had entered the cave, the glow grew before them and faded behind them but this time it was coppery not silver. They passed its strongest point and stepped on down.

"Zadie," said Nathan slowly, "these steps are going downwards."

A dull clunk reverberated behind. They stopped abruptly.

It wasn't totally dark though, and Zadie was moving

forward. "I can see something," she called back, "and I can feel a breeze. I told you that if we could get into this cave we could get out of it."

They moved forward together again and the rock gave way to grass. It was night and a few stars filtered out from the scudding cloud, although there was no moon, and as they lay in a smooth, grassy hollow, resting for a moment, exhaustion brought an easy sleep.

Chapter 5   Tokens

"Coffee?" enquired a voice in Nathan's ear.

A vague thought that he hadn't ordered room service flitted through Nathan's mind and he mumbled, "No," rolling over and keeping his eyes firmly closed. This pillow is uncomfortable, he thought.

"It's cold coffee, I'm afraid. Tried lighting a fire but didn't want to waste your matches," continued the voice.

"What time is it?" muttered Nathan.

"Half past ten by your watch," it replied.

What was room service doing looking at his watch and he reached out an arm for the bedside table. Ow! That hurt. He was awake now and as he opened his eyes a face came swimming into view. It was a pretty face and it was laughing at him. There was gold hair and a cap, and a gold chain plunging beneath a torn blue top that had been pulled together with a couple of safety pins where it was ripped.

Nathan sat up.

"You snore," said Zadie.

His mind was beginning to kick into gear and memories were flooding back.

"Where are we?" he asked.

"You'll be able to work that out for yourself in a moment but firstly drink this," she said, proffering an enamel mug of cold coffee. "No. With the other hand," she commanded.

He took the cup and slurped gratefully, suddenly having a desire for a smoke with it and reaching in the pocket of his rucksack.

"They're here. Sorry. I had one earlier – I was feeling a bit nervous," offered Zadie apologetically.

"That's   OK,   you're   welcome,"   he   responded automatically.

"Oh, and go steady on the matches," said Zadie meaningfully.

Nathan thought that both the tone and the comment were odd. "Why? Where are we?" he asked.

"Drunk your coffee?" He nodded. "OK, time for you to see then."

They strolled up the slope of the grassy hollow and came to its crest. Looking into the morning sun, Nathan saw a familiar landscape. There were the cliffs of Polgodoc; there was the distinctive rock shaped like a house with a chimney; and away to the south was the end of the Marble Cliff leading down to the Lion Rock guarding the mouth of the bay near Trevennick. Of course, that had been why the shapes on the map table, as he now thought of it, had been familiar to him: they were imitations of it. Slowly, and with awful certainty, it dawned on him. He was looking up at the cliffs. And there was grass stretching to their foot before they rose in their distinctive sky-line.

"Am I below water? Are we dead and on the sea-bed?" he asked.

"You're hardly dead if you can drink a cup of coffee … and doesn't your hand hurt?" came back the response. The logic was inescapable and he opened his left hand looking at the great weal across its palm. "It will heal. You were moaning in the night and I put some Arnica on it," explained Zadie.

Nathan turned, looking beyond her across a grassy plain dotted with clumps of small trees and outcrops of rock before his gaze settled on a higher mass of rock rising like the broken dome of a cathedral. "Gulland," he muttered.

"Yes. I thought so too," said Zadie. "It's not a question of where we are but when we are."

"What do you mean, when we are?"

"I was up on the cliffs early," continued Zadie. "There are no fields, no dry-stone walls, no sheep, no cattle – a few more trees but not many."

"No fields, no sheep, no cattle, but – "

"Look, I've been up for nearly four hours. I've had time to

think things through. Would you like a wash and something to eat and then we could talk?" she offered tactfully, continuing, "There's a stream nearby – it's good water – and a pool you can wash in."

The thought of a wash and food became imperative and she led the way, sitting more or less out of sight as Nathan stripped off and bathed. As an afterthought, since his shirt and socks stank, he washed them as well, hanging them on the branches of a small tree where they would dry in the sun and breeze before wandering barefoot back up the slope.

"Hmmm, that's not a bad idea," said Zadie, sniffing at her top. "Pity we haven't got any soap. I've been through your rucksack," she continued in a matter of fact way. "We appear to have half a loaf of stale crusty bread; half a cheese; two large bars of chocolate; 22 miniature cigars; a box of Swan Vestas; and an empty wine bottle … and there's plenty of drinkable water."

Nathan was beginning to follow her line of thought and added, "So we have enough food for about 24 hours unless we find some more."

"Correct," she stated, "although we can probably go another 24 hours without it. After that, we are going to have to try to go back."

If it was anything like the coming, Nathan didn't like the sound of that. She rationed out some of the bread and cheese and half a bar of chocolate and they sat talking as his clothes dried.

"Why couldn't I find that mother lode before?" asked Nathan.

"If you don't know the answer to that, I'm not telling you," replied Zadie.

"Well, what about the map table and the copper?" he persisted.

"You asked me where I'd got the bracelet from and I told you South Africa," she went on. "It wasn't Cornish copper and the rock saw us as aliens, invaders, and reacted." Nathan wasn't sure that he liked the anthropomorphisms here but listened as she continued, "Once I'd dropped the remaining fragments of the bracelet, the bars of the cage began to loosen and dissolve. The

key to the cave is the local stuff. Anyway, I want to go up that hill
and see if there is any evidence of settlement visible from there."

Nathan had a sinking feeling as he fingered the 'key' of
tin in his pocket. He had looked at it when he had washed. He
would tell her on the hill top. It would make no difference now.
They went via his clothes, filling the flask and empty wine bottle
with water before re-stoppering it with the used cork, and picking
their way through the open countryside, moving largely from rock
outcrop to rock outcrop.

"Talk to me," said Zadie, who seemed to be scanning the
ground.

"What about?" he replied, thinking which bits of his life
history he was willing to reveal – not that it would matter soon.

"Sea-levels," came back the unexpected response; "when
would they have been as low as this?"

"Sea-levels?" he echoed in the manner of a recalcitrant
schoolboy caught napping in class when the teacher asked him a
question.

"Yes," said Zadie patiently and repeated her question.

"Well, certainly 20,000 years ago," he replied.

"That's no good ... too long ago ... can't you be more
precise?" demanded Zadie.

"I'm sorry," he muttered and laughed. "Anything more
than 20,000 years old I'm fairly good on but less than that is a bit
recent for me."

She sat down on a nearby rock and pulled what was now
a fairly dirty white cap off her head, shaking her golden hair free.
It was her turn to laugh. "Typical geologist," she said, "anything
that's younger than 20,000 years or moves faster than 1 cm in a
thousand years and you can't tell me about it." It wasn't meant in
malice and he sat near her as they looked westward. A pair of black
birds with red beaks circled nearby.

"What I'm trying to establish," she began, "is what time
period we are in. The clue is the sea-levels. These people – "

"What people?" interjected Nathan.

"The people responsible for killing the deer whose antlers

we just passed; the people responsible for mining the rock…" she paused and he kept silent, "these people knew metals, otherwise they wouldn't have mined. They couldn't have been Iron Age … too recent. Before that was the Bronze Age …" (Nathan shifted uncomfortably) "… but what was before that? Fire and wood were the keys. Think of the cliffs you saw this morning. No wood. Where has it gone? Look around you. How many mature trees do you see?"

Nathan was beginning to follow her drift. "So you think there was a Copper Age or a Tin Age before the Bronze Age?" he said thoughtfully.

"Yes, possibly both," she answered. "Which has the lower melting point; which would produce the stronger metal; which would have been the more obvious ore and, crucially, where were the sea-levels?" she ended.

Nathan let the thoughts run through his mind. This wasn't his area but it had all the intellectual challenge of trying to assemble a geological map from a few diverse drilling cores. She watched as he thought, with interest rather than dissatisfaction. Finally he started, "I think the copper lodes would have been more obvious as they would have stained the surrounding rock green and killed the vegetation. Also, that they would have provided a harder metal that could have been polished." Strange how ornament and armament had both driven technology forward throughout the ages, he reflected to himself. "Melting points I don't recall but both tin and copper ores could be smelted with charcoal from wood. On sea-levels, I'm not certain; maybe a minimum of 12,000 years ago for this low in this area, unless…" he trailed off.

"Unless what?" she prompted.

He paused. "Well, at the north end of Greenaway beach there are pebbles of flint. There's not much but it's there." A long time ago he had surprised a colleague by picking up one of these pebbles and bringing his field lecture to students to a grinding halt. "Flint comes from chalk … and there is no chalk near here … the nearest is much further north in the Bristol Channel."

"So what does that mean?" pursued Zadie.

"Probably that it was washed into a marginal lake by some earlier River Severn and then – "

"What's a marginal lake?" she demanded.

He resumed, "When the great ice sheets advanced 100,000 years ago and sea levels fell, the ice swept down from the north. One sheet came down the Irish Sea and wrapped around the present coastline of the west of Wales before reaching almost to the Isles of Scilly. Inland of it were periglacial conditions – like today's Arctic and Tundra. In winter the ground there would be frozen solid and covered in snow; in summer the snows would melt and the top part of the ground thaw out. As the snows melted, the water couldn't flow out to the sea because the ice sheet blocked its way. So it formed a lake on the inland margin, frozen in winter, water in summer. Into that lake would have flowed pebbles of flint, rolled by the summer meltwater streams from the land beyond Bristol. The ice melted, the sea levels rose, and the deposits were driven onshore as the land flooded. For whatever reason, a few of them were trapped in what is now Greenaway."

"What's the minimum time ago that happened?" she asked again.

He thought hard. "12,000 years," he offered, "…unless…" again he trailed off.

Again she pursued it, "Unless what?"

"Well, it hasn't been suggested … and I don't know the Admiralty charts well enough for the offshore depths … but …" (He was putting in caveats as if presenting an academic paper to his peers but she knew she was getting near the truth now and kept quiet.) "…it could be that the ice provided a wall against the sea. Ice sheets melt from the seaward side and from the surface whilst the landward base is locked on the sea floor … but ice floats and eventually, if the sheet becomes thin enough, it will be lifted off its base. It's been happening in the Antarctic today – great slabs of ice sheet the size of Wales breaking free from the ice shelves and floating into the Southern Ocean; it happens in Iceland when a volcano erupts under the ice cap – huge volumes of water accumulate under it then lift one corner until they flood out."

"Never mind about today," said Zadie. "We're not in today, if you remember. What might have happened here and when?"

"Well, if the last remnants of the Irish Ice Sheet were anchored and stretched between Fishguard and the Scilly Islands, it could have been as recently as 8,000 or 6,000 years ago. Sea levels would have risen beyond it but not penetrated under it for some while. Slowly it would lift and…"

"And what?" Zadie prompted.

"The last barrier that was locked to the sea floor would be unlocked and the last of the ice would float … an unbelievable ingress of water would have occurred under it in a matter of weeks – sea levels would have risen a matter of 50 or 100 metres."

"Until they reached a barrier such as the cliffs behind?" she suggested. He nodded. "So a whole society could have been wiped out without a chance to adapt?" He nodded again.

"OK, let's review what we've got," Zadie began. "A society possibly 6,000 years ago … that's within the reach of legend," she mused, "able to smelt; able to shape wood accurately; having use of the wheel, but not engaged in sedentary agriculture …" she was ticking items off on her fingers.

"Hang on, where have you got the last three from?" demanded Nathan.

"For the agriculture, look around you, or think of the valley at Polgodoc – an ideal south-facing slope for strip lynchets but you can't see any fields or any evidence of them," she explained. "The shaping of wood comes from the rectangular arms of your ancient piece of tin and the wheel is the circle encompassing them, with the hole in the centre as an axle."

"I'd thought of it as a kind of Celtic Cross without its long base shaft," objected Nathan.

"That only adds weight," stated Zadie firmly. "The early priests would have taken over an existing symbol and made it their own, just like bishops' mitres or how the church built over existing sacred sites or imposed new festivals on old ones – like All Saints' Day and All Hallows."

The conversation had come to a pause and she got up,

reaching for his hand and saying, "Come on, now. I still want to go up that hill."

They moved steadily and the rock outcrops ahead showed up as granite rather than slate. For whatever reason the direct course to the hill was becoming awkward and they found themselves veering southwards. Finally, they fought their way up onto a knoll surrounded by holly bushes and with a low plinth of rock in its centre. It was an odd rock, about six feet long by two feet wide and two feet high, and having two distinctly different colours to it. The nearer half was almost entirely dark slate whilst the further side was the lighter granite colour. Scattered around on the ground were fragments of each type of rock, as if they had been carelessly discarded.

After the experience of the cavern, Nathan decided to give the rock a wide berth and not to touch it. Half way round it he found himself brought gradually to a standstill. Zadie, going to the other side of it, experienced the same thing. They tried going through the holly trees but they were densely packed and prickly and only had one opening into and out of the knoll. They tried going past the plinth again together but made no progress. Nathan endeavoured to take a run up and go past it at pace but it was like the opposite of a bungee-jump – he was thrust gently and firmly back by an invisible barrier that yielded for a way but did not allow him through.

"Any ideas?" said Nathan warily.

"There's a recess in each side of the top of the plinth," ventured Zadie.

They examined the nearer one carefully without touching the plinth and looked across at the further one.

"They're the same shape but different colours," said Zadie. "This one nearer us looks like a light socket in the dark rock and the further one is the other way round." She had bent down and picked up one of the rock fragments and was turning it over in her hand. The fragment was a crude version of the shaped piece of tin that Nathan had used in the map table.

"Granite," said his voice over her shoulder, "Same as the

other half of the plinth."

She looked ahead to the hill and Nathan knew what was coming next. "I'm going to put this in there," she said, pointing to the nearer recess and before he could object she had done just that and walked to the far side of the plinth. "There," she said, standing with her hands on her hips in a manner as if to challenge him to dare not to do the same. He walked forward and was brought to a standstill again. She laughed. "Pick it out and put it back in," she said. Nathan did so and absent-mindedly picked it up again as he walked smoothly forward to join her. "Try throwing it back," she said. He lobbed it gently, waiting for it to rebound as it hit the invisible barrier but it went straight through and scuttled briefly along the ground before coming to rest.

"I'm beginning to understand this place," she said. "Look!" She bent down and picked up a dark piece of slate, putting it in the recess in the granite side of the plinth before picking it out again and stepping neatly round to the far side of the plinth. He walked to join her and immediately had his progress halted by the invisible barrier. "Catch," she cried, throwing the piece of slate at him. It was a fairly good reaction catch for a close fielder as it headed straight for his nose. "Now put it in, pick it out, and step round," she instructed. Over the next five minutes they repeated the process until they were both convinced: to move from one geology to another required a key, a pass-stone, a token of acceptance, from the next geology. "Now do you believe there is a society around here?" she said triumphantly. "These keys haven't occurred by chance, even if the geology may be a little too living for your tastes."

"So, where do we go now?" asked Nathan.

Zadie pointed – "That holly clump in the distance, and up the hill." He could hardly argue after her successful display at the plinth and it even seemed as if there was a semblance of a track.

One geology later they were working their way up the side of Gulland, having found a patch of berries on its southern flank and eaten the rest of the bread and cheese. The sun was lowering towards the horizon and tomorrow promised to be a hungry day.

Zadie was quieter now. All the way up the slope she had been scanning the landscape below looking for signs of habitation but the best that it could offer was clumps of trees and the suggestion of tracks that could as easily have been made by animals as humans. It had been a good theory, thought Nathan, but she had pushed the conclusion beyond the facts. He had seen it before in academics who had become fanatics for a narrow interpretation, although there were exceptions – like Alfred Wegener, who had perished on an ice cap in Greenland long before his theories on Continental Drift had been accepted. Nathan sighed. Soon he would have to tell Zadie about the 'key' of tin.

They settled against some curved rocks just below the summit of Gulland and watched the orb of the sun distorting as it cut the horizon, gleaming red as it disappeared behind a great bank of building cloud, scattering its final rays on a small lake below them.

"Listen, Zadie, it will be dark soon and I need to tell you something." She turned her head and he had the fleeting impression that she had been crying. "You know the tin 'token' that we used to get into the cavern?" She nodded. He drew it from his pocket and held it for her in the palm of his hand. She leant across.

"It's very clean, and you can see markings on it," she said.

He paused. It was a long pause. Finally, he said apologetically, "It's the wrong colour … when I fought the copper bars that were forming a cage around you in the cavern, something happened … it changed … it fused the copper and the tin … it's bronze. It can't act as a pass key to the cavern any more – it's an alloy. There is no way back."

She leant her head towards him and said, "Nathan, I know. I saw the light on it when you were washing and I heard you in your sleep. Look, I want to show you something." She bent her head and drew the gold chain over her. At its end dangled a beautiful ornament. In the post-sunset light it was still unmistakably copper – clean cut, etched with markings, and clear as the day it was forged.

"You've seen it before," she said gently. It was identical to Nathan's 'key' but more beautiful by far. He could not imagine having seen it but not remembering. Reading his thoughts, she went on, "I showed it to you in the pub and you said it was a coppery rock. I took it back and cleaned it with vinegar and a toothbrush. In the cavern, when the copper bars enclosed me, all the grot on it was burnt away. It burnt me too. That's why I plunged into the pool. This is what gave us the light to find a way out. And that's why I know there was a Copper Age ... and that there is a way back."

She put the chain back over her head and tucked the copper key away, leaning her head on Nathan's shoulder. They watched the blaze of stars, unsullied by pollution from city lights or vapour trails, and talked late about little things – flowers and gardens, colours and hues, Christmases and summer holidays – before falling asleep. Late on it was chill and Nathan got up to relieve himself. The waning moon was rising over the Lioness Rock on the skyline and he thought he heard the howl of a lone wolf away to the west. The thick bank of cloud was still there but it seemed not to be threatening to bring rain.

Having woken once, Nathan dozed fitfully, his eyes drawn back to the coruscating beauty of the heavens. His mind flitted through continents and time and came to rest half a world away. There, it had been the Southern Cross serene in the firmament above and the great blaze of the Milky Way scintillating with a thousand stars unseen in city light but each clear in the desert night. He had been young and had wandered away from the dying embers of the campfire into the vast emptiness of flat red space, lying amidst the gnarled, dead Mulga trees and gradually being impressed by the huge weight of ancientness – of time weighing down upon him. Those same stars had been looked up to by Aborigines tens of thousands of years beforehand and it might be a hundred years before another human footprint stepped where he was; he had felt infinitely small in the great panoply of nature and Man's unfolding. Later, there had been strange rocks – rocks like the eggs of some giant dinosaur, each bigger than a man, stained red with the desert dust and glowing in the sunrise, almost as if something within was seeking to bridge the barrier of time encrusting it; almost as if it could. Aboriginal myth had it that they were the eggs of the giant serpent that was the personification of evil. That was an old, old place. But this place was young by comparison. It felt almost fragile; teetering on the brink.

Venus rose, and he slept.

Chapter 6   Soloma

Nathan came to full wakefulness but did not move. The long distorted shadow of Gulland stretched out before him as the sun rose behind it in the east. He nudged Zadie gently. They both looked, unwilling to break the spell with speech. First turning pink with the flush of dawn, now crimson, now orange, now yellow, gleaming brilliantly in the reflected rays was a towering wall a thousand metres high, stretching from north to south as far as the eye could see. Battlements of pinnacles rose; clefts of deep crevices opened up; blocks the size of skyscrapers crenulated the skyline; crevasses and seracs joined the detail until the rising sun made them blend into a blinding white. How long they had watched without speaking they didn't know.

"Ice sheet," breathed Nathan in an awed whisper.

"People would pay thousands to see this," said Zadie in equal awe.

"They do, but they can't," he replied. "Some travel to the Arctic or Antarctic to do so but they don't see what we've seen. The polar sun is low and there is no proper sunrise in the summer months – so there would be nothing of the play of colours, or even the detail that we can see now as the sun gets higher. This is something that hasn't been seen for two hundred generations." And they sat immobilised.

In front of the ice sheet was a lake, irregular in shape, wide and long, with isolated islands of ice floating in haphazard fashion. And as they watched further, a huge chunk of ice wall toppled forward with impossible slowness and majestic splendour – the product of ages past, calving to its ending. Great sprays of water rose as an upward waterfall and waves spread from its burying, rippling outwards and rocking the ice islands. They couldn't see the waves break on the near shore of the lake as it was hidden by a low line of hills, but some moments later a groan like distant, tortured thunder rolled over them and, later still, a single swell reached the smaller lake below them.

"About ten miles," said Nathan.

"What?" Zadie asked.

"The ice wall is about ten miles away," he explained, "I was counting and waiting for the sound."

Zadie was impressed. Another thought occurred to them almost simultaneously. She was slightly quicker than he was and knew his rucksack as well as him by now. She already had the binoculars half way to her eyes when he cautioned, "Don't look at the ice – it will blind you."

That hadn't been her intent though. With the early morning light behind them visibility was excellent and Zadie was scanning carefully away to the south.

"Looking for smoke?" he asked.

She nodded. Any settlements would be active by now to make the most of the daylight hours. Eventually she yielded the binoculars to him and he scanned the cliff line southwards as far as he could see, thinking that smelting could also produce smoke, and worked his way back towards the low line of hills and up the shallow valley to the smaller lake that lay below them. At one point, he thought he saw a herd of animals grazing but they were distant and could just as easily be deer.

They decided that they would go as far as the small lake half a mile away and replenish their water before eating the last of the chocolate and heading back. Climbing the hill again would not be necessary as they could skirt round its side, which would save energy. Three quarters of the way down, they were in a thicket of hazel when Nathan, closely followed by Zadie, came to a halt. It was an unmistakable sound floating gently in the breeze towards them … intermittent but clear … light in tone, and somewhat chattery. Zadie was excited as she mouthed, "Voices," and made to move forward but Nathan pulled her down beside him, finding the binoculars again and saying quietly, "Let's just think about this and see what we've got first." Reluctantly she agreed and waited impatiently for the binoculars.

"Two figures," he announced, "One short, one taller. Coming down the low ridge directly in front of us. They will be looking straight into the sun if they look at us and the binoculars shouldn't flash."

It wasn't so much passing the binoculars to her as Zadie grabbing them at the first indication of a willingness to relinquish them on his part. She watched for a long while until the two figures had reached the lake, keeping up a quiet running commentary. Nathan smiled to himself, thinking it was rather like a cricket commentator filling in during some prolonged pause in play. He could see the girls clearly now with his own eyes and the lake was only 200 yards away. The two girls had waded out onto a flat rock in the lake. The water had come up to the older girl's waist and nearly to the younger girl's armpits but they seemed quite at ease in it and were now sitting silently taking things out of two skin pouches. Whatever they were doing they were ready now and the older girl took up a poise like a heron, motioning to the younger one to sit still. It was a practised routine.

"Fishing," said Zadie, at the same moment as the girl's arm jabbed rapidly forward and back producing a flapping silvery fish on the end of a narrow shaft of wood. She passed the whole thing to the younger girl and picked up another shaft. "There's some kind of barb on the end ... but it doesn't flash in the sun ... probably flint ..." (Zadie was back into commentary mode.) "... still used even after smelting was known ... could be harder and sharper and easier to find." The younger girl had neatly extracted the shaft, threaded the fish onto a short piece of sinewy line, checked the tip, and placed it ready for the older girl to use again. Six times this was repeated; it was all done with the minimum of noise, fuss, or movement.

A sense of guilt was beginning to arise in Zadie that she had been monopolising the binoculars for the past 20 minutes and she reluctantly offered them to Nathan, turning to her flask for a drink of water. She was surprised when he almost immediately gave them back.

"What's up?" she said.

"Oh, it's probably better that you look," he replied. "They seem to have finished fishing and the older girl has gone for a bathe … she doesn't have much on," he added lamely. Zadie giggled, deciding that she didn't need to watch either, and offered Nathan some water.

It all happened very suddenly. There was a truncated scream followed by thrashing of water and a continuous high pitched wailing. Zadie was the first to react and crashed through the hazel bushes, running down the slope with a speed that Nathan couldn't hope to match. By the time he had reached the edge of the lake, Zadie was out on the flat rock and had the young girl wrapped against her. He hoped she wouldn't let her turn round. Blood was dissipating in the water and fragments of flesh were drifting away towards the far side of the lake until they slowly sank, leaving little evidence that the older girl had ever existed.

A gentle sobbing came from 20 yards away. Zadie was looking at him from the rock. Comforting the young girl was instinctive to her but she also wanted to get her onto the dry land. She would have to wade up to her thighs. Whatever had attacked was clearly unexpected to the girls and might do so again … and not only did Zadie have the girl, she also had the copper 'key' dangling on the chain around her neck. He had just determined to wade out to the rock himself when Zadie's voice came clearly, "No. You stay there. Watch the water. I'm going to wait until it's absolutely still and then I'll come."

There didn't seem much point in arguing with the logic of this, although Nathan's emotions were doing a good job of trying to do so. If he went to her, it would mean one disturbance of the water on the way out to the rock and two disturbances on the way back; Zadie coming to him would mean just one journey. Idly, he picked up a rock. He didn't see what he could do with it but it felt better to have something in his hand.

"Right, I'm coming now," called Zadie's voice, as she stepped off the rock into the water and steadied herself.

The little girl was hugged around her shoulders, still clasping her string of fish. Nathan didn't watch; he scanned the waters beyond the rock intently. There was a splash. Nathan swivelled – Zadie had stumbled … but she was up now, dripping water and getting the girl back on her shoulders … what was more they were nearly half way across. In that second's glance away, he had missed it and a chill spread through him as he heard his voice, as if distant and detached from him, call out, "Movement! Coming fast … near the rock!"

Zadie was making no pretence at trying not to splash now – she was pushing through the water as rapidly as she could with her little burden clinging quietly. This was going to be close. She was tiring and the floor of the lake was irregular and slippery. The surface movement was round the rock and gathering pace. Nathan hurled the rock in his hand at a point to one side of the creature's line of attack and, for a moment, it veered to investigate the disturbance before resuming its course with renewed aggression. It was still going to be too late. Zadie was not going to make it in time. Nathan jumped into the water and grasped the wet mass of faltering limbs, half dragging, half throwing them onto the shore before flinging himself after them as a wall of water from the frustrated animal's final swerve washed over them.

Water streamed down their hair and faces and it was difficult to tell the tears from it as they remained locked in shock. The little girl was the first to start moving and was tugging at Zadie's hand, still clutching her thread of fish in the other hand.

"I think she wants to get away from here," said a voice that still did not seem to be entirely part of Nathan.

"I'd be rather glad of that too," came Zadie's shaky reply, and they half walked, half stumbled over a low rise towards the hill they had been sitting on and out of sight of the lake, collapsing on the uneven ground as the adrenalin surged and ebbed through their bodies.

*   *   *

Some time later, leaving the others sitting together, Nathan worked his way slowly up the hillslope to where they had left their belongings. Before he came back down with them, he scanned the landscape carefully with the binoculars; if there had been anyone within hearing distance, surely the noise would have attracted them? Nothing: no movement; no noise; no smoke. An intense desire was triggered by the last word. He wouldn't be able to smoke in front of the little girl without scaring her further. He sat and consumed a small cigar and a few pieces of chocolate before packing anything else that he thought might frighten her out of sight and heading back down. He was intensely hungry, despite the chocolate, although the nicotine would stave the pangs for a while, and had calmed his nerves.

The girl was sitting close by Zadie, fingering the gold chain around her neck and looking at the copper 'key' attached to it. Her face had a little mobility now, although the trauma was clear in her eyes.

Zadie's voice was deliberately suppressed and steadied as she said, "You were a long time," half in enquiry and half in admonition. He told her what he had been doing (but not about the cigar) and she said, "Thought as much. There's very little in this landscape. Little food … and that creature was hungry. What do you think it was?"

"I haven't read a lot recently on murderous aquatic animals that inhabit ice-marginal lakes in ancient Cornwall," he retorted edgily. He really didn't want to think about it.

"Well, I've found out several things," said Zadie quietening his edginess, and she went on to describe how the girl was attracted to the gold chain and had fingered the copper 'key' almost with an element of awe. "So she knows gold, she knows ornaments, and she knows copper," Zadie ended, "but we know nothing useful about her."

He was wondering what to do next when the girl detached herself from Zadie and disappeared out of sight.

"Where is she going – I didn't hear anything?" said Nathan, slightly too sharply.

"Oh, probably to the bathroom," replied Zadie tetchily. "Anyway, she's left her fish and pouch, so she'll be back."

"OK," he replied. "Fair comment ... I deserved that. Here, have the last of the chocolate before she returns."

Zadie accepted the peace offering and it seemed that any residual animosity had disappeared as, over the next half hour, the girl disappeared several times, coming back with various objects and assembling them close to Zadie and Nathan. Drawing a sharp piece of flint from her pouch, she slit the fish open, neatly removing the bones and unwanted bits before turning and looking expectantly at Nathan.

"Ah," said Zadie with interest. "This will test your boy scout skills; she's expecting you to light the tinder. Strange, it points to a hunter-gathering society where the men were custodians of the fire. Normally, you would expect the men to do the hunting and gathering," she mused.

Nathan thought quickly as he slipped his hand into a side pocket of his rucksack and extracted the box of Swan Vestas, trying not to rattle the matches. He knelt down with his back to the girl, obscuring her view, and extracted a match, lighting it with as small a strike as possible and holding it to the tinder, making sure that the match burnt down as far as his fingertips before pretending to blow into the little flames.

"You seem to have got away with that," said Zadie, who had been watching both him and the girl. "I think you could step away now and go and sit on the opposite side of the fire from me."

Not willing to argue with her intuition, he did as she suggested, and the girl came forward, feeding the fire and moving the flat stones that she had gathered into its perimeter. "Neat," said Zadie, "all small pieces of dry wood ... no smoke ... good bright flame ... the stones will heat on their surface ... don't know what the holly is for though." Twenty minutes later she found out as, with the fragments of firewood burnt, the girl held the three old holly stems over the last of the flames, burning off the leaves with a crackle and blackening the stems so that they hardened. She sharpened the points of them on the hot stones before pushing the stones close together over the glowing embers and placing the pieces of fish on them. Twice she turned the fish, before looking satisfied, skewering a piece on the blackened holly stem and holding it out to Zadie, who automatically said, "Thank you." The girl stood, beginning to become agitated.

"Try eating some and nodding or smiling," whispered Nathan.

That seemed to work and Nathan found himself the recipient of the next holly-stuck piece of fish. The girl sat looking at the fire.

"Why is she not eating?" asked Zadie.

"Perhaps the children wait for what's left," suggested Nathan.

"Or maybe she hasn't been invited to," countered Zadie. "There seems to be a definite etiquette here."

Nathan paused in his eating, smiled and stretched out his arm, palm upwards, towards the remaining fish. That did the trick. The girl skewered the smallest portion, eating voraciously before the whole process was repeated. Six fish split into two gave twelve pieces which, fortunately, left no difficult question of division.

Thinking of some of the groups he had seen eating on holiday, Nathan asked slightly maliciously, "Would you like to explore the difference in meaning between civilised and primitive societies at the meal table?"

Zadie pulled a face before replying, "It's interesting though. There is a strong gender division. Possibly a matriarchal society as she went to feed the woman first."

"Or possibly you were the food taster, just in case there was anything wrong with it – sort of disposable," provoked Nathan.

"I'm not going to rise to that," said Zadie, laughing with him for the first time since before the lake, "but there are some other interesting things. For instance, she doesn't seem worried that we are speaking an unknown language to each other and – most interesting of all – she has taken no interest in our clothes".

Nathan bit off a reply about women and clothes and instead observed, "She is probably still very shocked – and I think that she holds you in some kind of respect ever since you showed her your copper 'key' – it's almost as if that means that we are acceptable."

When they had finished the meal, the girl buried the fish bones in the centre of the fire and pushed the stones so that they overlapped. To a casual glance there had never been a fire there.

*   *   *

In another context it would have been regarded as a game of charades. Zadie began it. With a mixture of pointing and miming they had established that the girl's name sounded like, "Soloma," or at least she responded to that. Soloma had grasped 'Nathan' and 'Zadie' much more quickly. They had also established a nod for 'yes' and a shake for 'no'. Zadie had tried to investigate where the girl lived, miming sleep, and it looked like the answer was 'no fixed abode' as she had spread her hands and arms outward and turned on the spot. Now Zadie was on a different track, trying to find out where Soloma wanted to go. Nathan joined in, miming walking and pointing in various directions, but Zadie was better at it than him and the girl seemed to respond more quickly to her suggestions.

"It's not you," said Zadie, taking a break from the mime. "There's a definite gender division in her society and she's used to learning from older females, although the meal showed that the sexes come together from time to time."

It jarred in Nathan's mind. That was a possibility. "Seasonal movement," he said, surprising Zadie.

"What?" she said.

He explained his thoughts slowly, sorting them as he did so. "This near that ice-sheet, the land will only be open for a few months in summer … it will be frozen and snow covered by October – that's why there's no evidence of settlement and food is scarce. The men have gone, and left the women to forage here. When they come back the deer and other animals will be forced inland and there will be food where they can capture it."

"So, where have they gone?" said Zadie doubtfully.

"I think they spent the spring and early summer mining and smelting at the cliffs and have taken what they found overland to the south to trade – movement would be impossible in winter."

Zadie considered the suggestion carefully. It had some merits and would explain the lack of current activity in an area that she was convinced was a smelting society. But it would suggest a knowledge of trade routes and degree of organisation over a wider area far in excess of anything that she had imagined for a 'Copper Age'.

They gave up the debate and went back to establishing in which direction Soloma wanted to go to be reunited with her kin. They were not making much progress with the family bit, but three times now Soloma had pointed resolutely at the cliffs rising in the east. Indeed, Nathan thought she was pointing pretty exactly at Polgodoc.

"Well, it's noon," he said finally, "and we all seem to want to go in the same direction, so we may as well make a start. If you go in front, Soloma will probably lead you," he ended.

He could see Zadie toying with the idea of wanting to explore nearby but Soloma had tugged gently at her hand and she seemed amenable to following. Skirting the southern flank of Gulland hill they came to good water in a tumbling stream and drank, lapping it from their hands, before moving on to the nearby holly clump. Soloma had run ahead and was standing by the plinth with three granite pass keys that she had picked up from the ground nearby in her hand. "This seems perfectly normal to her," observed Nathan, as Soloma put in the key, skipped to the far side of the plinth and threw it back on the ground as she waited for them to follow her.

Half way across the granite section they rested and drank again. Soloma had disappeared and returned with a small cupped hand of berries which she put on the thrift beside them. Her eyes were gaining in expressiveness now. It was gnawing at Nathan that after the next plinth they would have to decide what to do with her and he could see Zadie thinking the same. He excused himself with a jocular, "Just going to the bathroom," although the merry tone was superficial, and wandered off behind a clump of yew trees.

As he returned around the yew trees a glint of afternoon sunlight bounced off a rock some ten yards away. He hesitated, and looked across at the others. Soloma was sitting happily caressing the copper 'key' in Zadie's hand. Smiling, he wondered if she thought of her as a surrogate for the sister that she had so recently lost – at least, he had assumed it was a sister. He glanced to his left again. It was definitely a glint of golden sun on dark green and there was the tiniest hint of speckled red. He felt himself drawn to it. If it was what he thought it was, it had no business being here – it would change the whole geological map of Cornwall. Once, he had spent an entire fruitless week abseiling down the cliffs of The Lizard in South Cornwall seeking a good specimen of it; one of the few specimens of Cornish rock that he didn't have. And there he was. His feet seemed to have carried him the ten yards without him noticing it and he was standing, looking down into a saucer shape of polished rock – deep, dark green with small blotches of equally dark red and containing pebbles as big as seagulls eggs of the same material. "Serpentine," he breathed. "Those specimens would be worth a fortune," his mind said and, as he looked away to his left, he saw six pillars of the same rock crowning a low rise in the landscape.

He stood transfixed, slowly reaching out his hand towards the basin. Out of the corner of his eye he saw movement and, at the same moment that he touched the basin in reverence, a mobile bundle of small girl running at full pelt threw itself at him and knocked him backwards. He was up as quickly as she was and they both stood looking towards the rise as dark green fire, speckled red, sped along the ground. Her hand was pulling urgently at his. He couldn't understand the words but they were pleading, desperate. The first pillar began to change shape, dissolving in front of their eyes. First a head appeared; a back and tail grew from it; legs and claws emerged – all mottled the same green and red. The creature turned and moved, settling its eyes upon the girl.

Something black and red flew across Nathan's line of vision and his gaze snapped. At last, he turned with the tugging hand, yelling to Zadie, "Run! Take the bags! Get to the holly trees!

Get to the plinth! Get beyond it!"

It was uphill and a struggle. There was snarling to the sides and behind them now, and still the little hand pulled him on. She could have got there herself, he thought. Zadie was near the holly but something had streaked in front of her, scattering rocks with its paws. She had made it into the hollies but now the thing was circling back to block their path.

They had failed by no more than twenty yards. The six beasts, like dark green and spotted red hyenas circled them. Nathan held a small branch in his right hand and Soloma's trembling palm was pressed into his left. There was a solemn menace in the creatures circling, almost a ceremony. Soon they would turn and face and strike. It would be over just as quickly as at the lake. They tried edging up the slope towards the entrance to the hollies but the rapid outbursts of snarls from that direction halted their attempt. Five times round the beasts had paced. How much longer would they hold off? Soloma was cringing now and her grip was slipping. She was on her knees and, as her hand finally left his, the animals stopped circling and bent their eyes upon her. Their malevolence was palpable. Saliva dripped from ill-coloured fangs, open in anticipation; and they edged forward together, a solid circle of living evil intent upon its prey.

"No!" cried Nathan. "No, you shall not have her!"

A crackling brand of dry holly landed in the ring and Nathan grabbed it, jabbing at the nearest beast which howled in reluctant retreat. The fire was fading rapidly but then came another brand, and another, until there was a kind of guarded avenue of burnt and burning leaves through which they could edge their way foot by foot closer to the holly. One beast was still directly in their way but suddenly a flaming stem landed right on it and its tail ignited. The sight was hideous as the fire spread through its fur from tail to nose and with a ghastly howl the creature bounded away. A few yards from them it appeared to vaporise and an avalanche of small rocks scattered down the hillslope. They stood rooted to the spot. "Move! Move now!" cried a voice, and they thrust their way past a panting Zadie who was laying more smouldering brands across the entrance to the holly ring, barring it to the remaining animals.

The animals were still there – he could smell their evil breath and hear their snarls just the other side of the holly, and Zadie was running out of matches – she did not dare set the whole holly ring on fire or they would all be incinerated inside it. It was their only slender protection.

"There are no pass keys!" she screamed at him, "They're gone! Nothing!"

Soloma had shot straight to the plinth when they had entered the holly clump and had thrown herself on the ground looking for the dark slate tokens that would let them through the invisible barrier to the next geology. Now she was clawing at Zadie, tugging her towards the plinth. A ripping of branches suggested that the animals were acting in unison, trying to tear a hole in the holly barrier. Nathan backed away and felt the plinth behind him; Zadie was there too; and Soloma was standing on the plinth ripping at Zadie's top until finally she had the chain in her hands and plunged the copper 'key' into the recess. Holding together, they moved through to the far side, as Soloma yanked the key out with the chain, and they staggered down the slope beyond the holly ring and collapsed for the second time that day. The pool in which Nathan and Zadie had washed was below them and the dark slate cliffs of Polgodoc rose above the gentle green slope in the near distance. Echoes of snarlings reverberated from the cliffs.

Chapter 7   **A Dark Time**

They were lying near the pool. Zadie and Nathan were in a soft and earnest conversation. Soloma was curled up in an exhausted sleep.

"We can't take her," Nathan was saying, "she belongs here."

"We can't leave her," argued Zadie. "You heard the echoes of those howls, and it will be night soon. What were those creatures anyway?"

"It," said Nathan. "There was a single mind driving their actions. Whatever it was, it was unutterably evil. It wanted me to give it the girl as a sacrifice."

"Well, there: do you want to leave her to that kind of fate?" she continued.

"No, but would she be any better in our kind of society? Wouldn't it be kinder…" and his voice became silenced as he looked at the small, peaceful form curled up near them. "OK, we'll see if she wants to enter the cave and take it from there," he ended, and he could see the smile of satisfaction on Zadie's face.

"Besides which," ventured Zadie, seeking to cement her success in the argument, "we owe her. If she hadn't used my copper 'key' we would never have escaped from those animals."

It was a valid point that he couldn't deny. "Strange that she should know to do so. After all, she used the local tokens at the other plinth," he commented.

"Yes, I've been thinking about that," replied Zadie.

"And…?" prompted Nathan.

"I think that the copper 'key' is a master key acceptable to all the plinths – and probably your tin 'key' was too, before it became bronze. They are much more finely made – and they seem to convey some indication of reverence, or respect – a kind of status giving free passage over the land. Probably, there were only a few of them." Zadie continued speculating over the key and the common tokens and who would use which, but Nathan's mind was running over a different problem.

There was an hour's light left as they headed up the grassy slope towards their best guess as to where they had exited from the cavern. Five dark clefts in the cliff base looked like possibilities. "Pity we didn't mark the spot," said Zadie, without acknowledging the impossibility of having done so, or any reason for doing so, in the confusion of their original exit. Nathan stopped pacing along the foot of the cliff and looked at the girl, who was waiting patiently.

"Give her the key," he said.

"What? My key? The only way out?" snapped Zadie.

"Yes," said Nathan softly.

Zadie was fighting with her emotions in a way that Nathan hadn't seen before and after a long wait she bent her head slowly forward, lifting the gold chain over the hair that was flaring equally gold in the sunset and pressing the copper into Soloma's hand, before pointing at the cliff.

Soloma walked from cleft to cleft and stopped in front of the third from the left, waiting for them to join her. They walked in file up the irregular floor to the dim ending of the cleft, Soloma holding the copper in her hand, and touching the rock where it barred their way. Nothing happened. Zadie reached for Nathan's hand in alarm, and suddenly there was a glow, spreading steadily from floor to ceiling and widening. The copper lode mirrored the dying rays that stabbed at it from the great, flattened orb of the sun setting over the ice sheet to the west and it shimmered like a living flow of burnished, blood-flecked copper, pulsating slowly towards the darker recess in its centre. Zadie grabbed the chain from Soloma and pressed her precious key into the recess in the wide, copper vein. Slowly, it opened in front of them and they stepped through into the passage that sloped upwards towards the cave.

Coppery light spread in front of them and contracted behind them. A solid clunk of closing rock brought a sudden halt to their step but they moved on and into the cavern. Nathan veered towards the large black slab in the centre of the cavern but Zadie pulled him on, following the glowing veins on the floor. Soloma seemed at ease but didn't look like she knew the place or could guide them out of it.

"Wait," said Nathan. "You don't know which exit to take."

"I'm following the richest glow, just like we did before," said Zadie.

"Look," he replied, "the only place I thought I saw copper at Polgodoc was in that evil cave where I nearly drowned. I don't want to emerge below water and, if we did emerge in it above water, there is no way we could get out safely." She paused and retraced her footsteps, making to hang the chain back over her neck. "No. Don't do that," he said urgently. "Keep it in your hand – we need light."

"What do you mean?" she asked.

"When we came in," he began, "I had the tin in my hand. The light led before us and closed behind us … and the mother lode blazed straight at the slab. After the copper attacked you, it was only when you rolled out of the pool in the darkness and opened your hand that we had any light. Please, Zadie, listen."

They were standing in a triangle – Soloma demurely waiting, Nathan nearest where they had entered, and Zadie beyond the slab towards the deepest coppery glow. "Just as there are a number of entrances, there are a number of exits," he went on carefully. "We came in by tin and we are trying to go out by copper." He had her full attention now. "If we don't choose the right exit we'll either be underwater or under a collapsed cliff. Firstly, I want to mark the way we came in." He lowered his rucksack and reached to the bottom before retreating several steps into the darkness. Zadie thought she heard a slight clink before he re-emerged. "Now, at least we can get out to where we were," he said without encountering argument. "We want an exit that curves up and to the right and is wide enough for us to walk side by side," he continued. "When we reached the cavern, the mother lode of tin blazed straight at the map table and beyond it. Now think. Was it the short side of the rectangular slab, or the long side?" he said firmly.

They looked each other in the eyes for a long time before she dropped her gaze and stammered, "I ... don't ... know."

Nathan moved across and put his arm round Zadie's shoulders. There were tears in her eyes now and she seemed just about all in. "It'll be alright," he murmured. "Just hold on a little bit longer ... and try to keep your hand open." Soloma nestled against her, drawn by the emotion rather than the words, and gently held her fingers across Zadie's so that they wouldn't close completely over the copper and extinguish the rapidly diminishing dull red glow.

If he could have asked her to lean on the slab with him to activate it and place the copper in the back of the Lioness, he would know which way to go. The weal in his left hand where he had held the tin throbbed as a reminder. But she was in no state for him to ask her. Instead, he bent down to Soloma and whispered, "Keep her safe," and, as he stepped into the almost total darkness, he thought he saw a small head nod once.

Ten paces from the narrow side of the slab. Arms outstretched and still the dullest glow behind him. There was the wall. One opening – too narrow; a second but it was going down: work back to the fading light; get back to the slab ... seven paces, eight paces; and the faces came into view. As Zadie's hope was fading so was the last light from the copper. It would be gone entirely in a few moments; already he could see no further than his hand. His feet found his rucksack and he searched for the side pocket, feeling carefully. The box of matches slid into his hand and he shook it gently – hardly a rattle. Gingerly opening it a finger's width, he felt two matches and shut the box again. He turned at right angles to his previous attempt and paced, counting to himself. The darkness was total now. That must be the wall he could feel. One entrance ... right size, bearing right ... no, now it was straightening. Carefully back down. He was losing orientation in the dark. Second entrance ... bearing right ... going up ... staying right. He risked a match and a few feet in front of him he caught a gleam of silvery-grey from floor to ceiling. This was the right exit and he turned, nursing the match and going as far down the passage as he could before it burnt the tips of his fingers and the last bit fell spluttering to the floor, extinguishing its brief light. Now he worked by feel, very slowly sliding his feet forward, searching for each step and holding his arms out sideways, running his fingers along the edge of the passage. The contact between his fingers and the walls vanished and he shuffled forward two more foot lengths until he was sure he was on the floor of the cavern. A gentle sobbing reverberated around it, although there was no light to orient the echoing noise. Don't be distracted by the noise, he thought. Be confident. Twelve paces straight ahead. Ten, eleven, twelve ... the noise was nearer but still no contact ... thirteen ... was he taking shorter steps, or had he veered off course? Fourteen ... his foot hit something solid. He moved it from side to side. It must be the base of the slab. One sideways pace. Two sideways paces, and there was something soft. Reaching down into the darkness, he felt a small hand grasp his. Something brushed against his wrist and he realised that Soloma was trying to pass him his rucksack. He slipped it on and the little hand moved Zadie's closed fist to him. Nathan followed the arm with his touch and turned, lifting Zadie under her shoulders in the total blackness; her abandoned hope had taken with it the will to move. Soloma's hand and arm reached around her waist from the other side and he squeezed it in thankfulness.

It was better to speak into the darkness than to be overcome by it and he found himself saying, "Soloma, it's twelve straight steps to the wall. It's difficult carrying Zadie and we're only shuffling, so it'll be more like twenty or thirty. We want the middle passage. It may be wide enough for all of us." He was trying to line up each footstep in front of the previous one and was keeping count, "twenty-six ... twenty-eight ... thirty ..." Surely it must be soon? Nathan flailed into the darkness with his free arm. Nothing. "Thirty-four ... thirty-six," and his toe hit the wall. Feeling to the left with his free arm, he could just touch the edge of an opening. Had they veered to the left, or to the right? He was stronger than

Soloma and guessed it would have been to the left as a result, but he didn't want to risk it and reached across squeezing her hand twice in a downwards direction before lowering Zadie to the floor. Soloma seemed to understand and, as far as he could tell, was crouching with her arm still round Zadie.

There was one match left in the box in his pocket and he had both hands free now. He would have to risk alarming Soloma. He found her tangled matt of hair and ran his open palm down in front of it over her forehead saying, "Close your eyes for a moment." Whether it was the tone or the gesture, she didn't jerk away as he struck the last match and a blinding glare burnt into his eyeballs, causing him to nearly drop it as he moved it away from him and sought to scan the wall. The passage he had touched the edge of looked too small but he couldn't be sure. There was one six feet to the right that looked larger. Beyond that he couldn't see. There was no telling which was the middle passage. The match was gone … and the darkness returned. There was no use in waiting for his eyes to become accustomed to it as they wouldn't see anything. It was a simple choice – left that he could feel the edge of with outstretched fingers, or right that he had glimpsed as wider.

It was more a choice of chance than a finely balanced decision and, uncertainly, he opted for the right hand of the two. If it didn't curve to the right, he might recognise the fact. He reached down and found Soloma's hand, squeezing it and pushing to the right, then lifting Zadie under her shoulders again. They side-stepped until they sensed a passage was in front of them. Not much time now; she's fading, he thought, and stepping up they moved awkwardly forward, brushing against the side of the passage. Another step, and another … it seemed to be curving … or was it straight? His foot caught on an irregular step and they fell forward. Water splashed on Zadie's face and Nathan's hand felt the very smallest sliver of wood crumble under his touch as he pushed them out of the shallow pool on the floor. A thrill of certainty tingled through him. Whether it was the effect of the water on her face or Nathan's returning hope had communicated itself to Zadie, she seemed to be making an effort to move with them now. She was less of a dead weight. That was definitely a step from her; and another.

Six more steps and Soloma must have touched the rock face first. Suddenly, there was a blinding silver light and they staggered and fell forward together. A solid clunk reverberated behind Nathan, so close that he could feel the vibration on the sole of his boot. But the light continued to shine silver in front of him and, as he looked, he saw the waning moon reflected in the puddles in the floor of the adit at Polgodoc. There was the sound of the sea, and the smell of salt air, and the distant noise of sheep.

Zadie opened her eyes and said weakly, "Nathan, I was in a very dark place."

Gently he reached across and unwound her closed hand. He lifted out the gold chain and lowered it over her head, tucking the copper key out of sight beneath the once blue top and saying, "We've all been in a dark place," as he wiped back her hair and kissed her on the forehead.

"Thank you," she mouthed, and her eyes fell on the little form that was brushing the tears from her cheek.

The reflected moonlight entering the adit meant that Nathan and Soloma should be able to cross the gap fairly easily; a semi-inert Zadie was a different proposition. There was the cliff to face too, but he would worry about that later.

Soloma's sight was good and she skipped across the gap without Nathan needing to warn her. The sea was sloshing noisily below it and he thought it must be high tide, as a corner of his mind started thinking of times and days. Soloma disappeared out of the entrance and came straight back, sitting silhouetted against it, waiting. Zadie was moving each limb in turn, flexing them and bringing her knees up and down to her chest.

"I think I'm strong enough now," she said, "but you'll have to go first."

Nathan had come to the same conclusion and was glad to see that her mind was working logically and sequencing what lay ahead. Beckoning to Soloma, he passed the two packs over the gap to her and she disappeared outside with them, returning in time to see Nathan making his large step across the chasm. He turned to face Zadie, who was partly crouching and had clearly decided to jump. She did so before Nathan was ready. One foot landed but the other missed and slipped into the dark gap with her body following. Nathan grabbed and there was a tearing sound as stitch by stitch the seam in the blue top was unravelling; an elbow slithered by beneath the ripping garment and he scrabbled after the slipping arm, locking both hands around its wrist and pulling. He grabbed again, grasping her under the armpits and falling backwards, hauling her with him, and landing awkwardly with her body on top of him.

"Thanks," said a remarkably stable voice, "I told you I was strong enough."

Nathan winced, "Yes," as Zadie shifted to get up and stuck her knee painfully into him somewhere near his stomach, and narrowly missed his head with her foot.

They sat on the ledge outside the adit for a few minutes, breathing in the air and drawing comfort from the simple sounds. Although the sun had set, there was still a surprising amount of light reflecting from over the north-west horizon; it was that kind of twilight when the sun had gone and the moon was clear but the stars were not yet showing. However, they couldn't linger … there was barely enough light to climb by and there certainly wouldn't have been without the moon.

Nathan was standing looking at the climb. He thought that he would take the two packs up first, come back for Soloma, and down again for Zadie. It would be a good forty-five minutes' effort, even if it all went well, and he retrieved his watch from the rucksack, and explained his thoughts to Zadie. She nodded. That way she would have the greatest time to gather her strength. Stuffing Zadie's pack inside his own rucksack made it a bit unwieldy but it was the best way to leave two hands free for climbing. Launching forward, he made the big reach to the first hold and he was there on the rock face: left hold … right hold … up like a ladder; he was climbing, and a tremendous sense of freedom washed over him.

Nearly there now. An agitated cry came from below. This wasn't the point at which to look down. He'd have to reach the top first. Over he went. He had the rucksack off rapidly, flinging it onto a solid bit of rock back from the cliff top, and was just about to look over the edge when a small head of black hair virtually flew over it and beamed a huge smile at him. He didn't know whether to be angry or to laugh. That made matters simpler. He pointed to the rucksack and Soloma sat happily by it as Nathan returned to the cliff edge. He peered over it and was shocked to see a very dirty white cap that said, "Pull me over the last bit will you."

Chapter 8 An Ending and a Beginning

They had stepped lightly together up the valley and were washing off the grime from their face and hands as best they could where a small spring bubbled out in greeting. Zadie was talking, "You were about two thirds of the way up and she just flung herself at the cliff. I jumped after her. I've never seen anything go up a rockface as fast as Soloma … took me a bit longer," and she laughed. Nathan felt a sudden rush of admiration for Zadie. It had taken a lot of courage to make that first leap on her own after her experience coming down the cliff. She must love the girl very much.

Normality had opened like a door for two of them and closed for another, and they talked much about Soloma as they walked along the deep lane with the scent of honeysuckle piling up in great pools in the still night air. It was almost overpoweringly normal in its impact on their senses. Soloma was grasping Zadie's hand.

Later, Zadie asked, "What time is it?"

"Just after 10.15pm," he replied.

"…and what day?" she continued.

"If I've got it right, tomorrow will be Friday," he answered.

"That's what I thought, too," she said as an owl hooted in the distance.

Nathan feared what was coming but still asked, "Why?"

"I need to have cleared up and be out of the flat by nine-thirty – it's a Friday to Friday let..." and, as she paused, Nathan was thinking that she could stay with him, but the voice went on, "…I have a lift with my friend – the one you met in the pub – to a meeting at 2pm in London. You'll be fine, you know."

He had always known it would come to this but it didn't make it any easier.

"How far are we from Padstow?" came the voice again.

"Not far – about fifteen minutes," he answered, thinking that he needed to turn off the lane in the opposite direction in a few hundred yards more.

Their footsteps hadn't slackened and they stood with one stile to the left and one stile to the right. She looked in the moonlight at the faded lettering on the wooden sign guiding walkers and read, 'Padstow ½ mile'.

"It's fairly straight and will bring you out near the top of Fentonluna Lane," he began automatically. "How will you get across the estuary?" he asked, stalling.

"Oh, I'll get a taxi round – I've still got my cash card," the voice continued.

"But how will you explain things to your friend?" said Nathan, seeking to buy time.

She faced him now and said, "So long as I'm back before the pubs close she won't notice today and, as far as the rest, I think I'll just say that I met a nice guy in a pub and went away with him for a few days – it was all very exciting – and I don't remember much about it. After all," she added mischievously, "it won't be too far from the truth." She was smiling, and stepped forward, placing the little hand in his. "Look after her," she said, bending to kiss the dark hair. She kissed him too, and stepped up onto the stile and waved: "I'll be back; I'll find you."

Nathan stood for a long while before turning and clambering over the stile that would lead to Trevennick. The little hand walked obediently beside him but after a while it stumbled. He bent and picked up Soloma, resting her against his shoulder. Soon she was asleep.

It was nearer midnight than 11pm when he reached his bungalow. It was in darkness but the front door yielded to his touch as he had never developed a habit of locking it. He didn't really feel like turning on a light and he knew the house well enough to negotiate the obstacles without having the need to do so. Soloma was still asleep and there was no need to wake her – tomorrow would bring sufficient challenges. He laid her on the sofa and sat in the old armchair nearby. Perhaps he would make a cup of tea soon, he thought; but he fell asleep, dreaming of strands of golden sunlight streaming from behind a white cloud floating in a pale blue summer sky.

END OF PART ONE

Part 2

**Turn back, O man, forswear thy foolish ways;
Old now is earth, and evil mars her days.**

(after Clifford Bax)

Many waters shall not quench love.

Part 2

Chapter 1   **Chaos at the Bungalow**

A crash of thunder rolled through Nathan's dreams, quickly followed by another crash and the slow splintering of wood, as if some great tree was yielding its boughs one by one to the lightning strikes of the storm. Water was rushing and gurgling and his subconscious mind took him back to Pentire with squalls seeking to loosen the fragile grip of his pained right hand wedged in the rock, and the drop two hundred feet to waves grasping hungrily at its base. There were words too – strange words – almost laughter mocking him in his inability, and sounds – sounds like chicken squawking. Yes, that was it. Chickens. His chickens: his chickens in the garden, greeting a new day.

His eyes were open now and he moved his head. That was a mistake. Pain flooded through Nathan from a neck locked uncomfortably from its lolling overnight in the old armchair. That woke him fully and he moved his eyes, rather than his head, to watch a copper bowl half-roll, half-slide from the bright surface of the kitchen floor onto the carpet of the room where he was sitting. A slender arm retrieved it whilst a straggle of black hair and half a dark eye protruded round the door jamb.

It must be admitted that Nathan had seen his kitchen in a better state. Soloma had clearly woken before him and had been attracted to the light streaming in through its east-facing windows, to the chickens foraging noisily outside and, above all, to the copper utensils hanging or stacked above the old, cast-iron range. In an attempt to reach these she had pushed the rather decrepit kitchen stool over towards them but it had collapsed under her weight and now lay in its constituent parts on the floor, amidst the coppers that she had succeeded in dislodging. It gleamed in the early sunlight – not least because she had discovered how to operate the kitchen taps and was sitting gleefully turning them on and off and watching the water cascade over the edge of the old, cream-coloured sink.

As he slopped across the wet, stone floor in his socks, picking up pans and utensils, Nathan was glad that the boiler had been turned off for the summer and the little girl had not had to contend with water from the hot tap. Soloma was still sitting on the draining board, looking at him inquisitively, as he pulled the plug out of the sink and let the water gurgle away. She was a quick learner and, as he opened the back door to the verandah, he saw her putting the plug back in and pulling it out again, whilst turning the taps on and off and lapping water from her cupped hand. Instinctively, she preferred the cold tap for drinking, he thought idly, as he squelched onto the dry wood outside and sat in the rocking chair to peel off his socks and squeeze them out before hanging them over the rail of the balustrade to dry. His bare feet had found a laceless pair of well-worn gardening shoes by the time Soloma appeared at the door and looked out in interest.

Well, they would have to eat; better search for some eggs and pick a few vegetables, his mind told him. He beckoned to her to help. She had a sharp eye and was as good as he was at telling the freshness of the eggs and they soon had half a dozen in one of the copper bowls, before Nathan went into the vegetable patch to gather some beans and carrots. Maybe he would add some early potatoes. It would be an odd breakfast but there was no bacon or bread left, so they would have to make do.

Soloma was watching the chickens, which were watching him, as he gathered the vegetables, and he nodded encouragingly to her. What happened next was unexpected. Perhaps he should have been aware that Zadie had already established a nod for 'Yes' and a shake for 'No'; however, he wasn't being more than politely encouraging, as he thought, and he was enjoying the practical task of picking the vegetables whilst thinking that the Californian poppies on the dry-stone wall were even better than ever in their virulent shades of orange and lemon.

Five chickens were quick enough and escaped with much noise to the top of the old shed with its tumble-down roof. The sixth was unlucky, catching a claw in the netting over the raspberries. Soloma had it by the wing-tip and with an increasing crescendo of noise a mobile cacophony of small girl and large chicken rotated through the vegetables towards the far corner of the garden, where they became ensnared in the pile of rotting down waste that provided Nathan with a steady supply of good manure. It was a fairly competitive outcome for a while as hair, feathers and muck flew into the air, until a final screech was followed by silence and Soloma emerged with the bird. She had wrung its neck and was sitting against the mesembryanthemums plucking it expertly before looking around for a sharp stone.

Nathan retreated inside and removed the sharp kitchen knives from their drawer by the sink, putting them high in the top cupboard. Soloma's society must have been very hard up for meat and he didn't want to find out how well she could handle a sharp, carbon-steel knife on the local farmers' fields. He also had a very bad feeling about the chicken. It was not so much about its death, although the speed with which events had unfolded had been something of a shock; it was more about what might follow. A decade ago he had been leading a trek in Nepal and the sherpa had asked by sign language whether they would like chicken to eat for that night's supper. He had nodded and was surprised to find the cook boys carrying live chickens up the mountainside in the pannier baskets strung round their heads. That evening the chickens had been slaughtered and chopped up before being added to the usual rice and lentils as a special treat. It had been hard going eating the meal and not giving offence to their hosts but he had finally gagged on it when a chicken head and eye had surfaced out of the feather-covered lentils.

Soloma appeared at the kitchen door, stinking badly and dripping muck and chicken blood in equal proportions into the somewhat shallower lake that still composed the kitchen floor. She was beaming excitedly, thoroughly pleased with her work and offering her prize to Nathan. He was relieved to see that the head and bowels of the chicken had gone, along with most of the feathers and the claws; it was also skewered through with one of the stakes he had used in the garden. Soloma looked towards the little lounge in which they had slept and Nathan nodded reluctantly, gathering a box of matches from above the kitchen plimsoll-line and following the trail of blood and muck. The fireplace was laid up, as it always was, and the copper dogs were a suitable support for the improvised spit. Nathan made no attempt to hide the matches from Soloma as he lit the fire and she didn't seem to cringe from the 'magic'. Soon the first flames were burning off the remnant of chicken feathers and Nathan reckoned he was safe for half an hour or so as he returned with some kitchen mitts to prevent Soloma using the cushions to turn the spit. Goodness knew how he would explain to his rather observant neighbours having a fire at 9 am on a day early in August. Meanwhile, Nathan cleared up and cooked the eggs and vegetables, putting them on two plates. He decided to risk (blunt) knives and forks.

It was a strange kind of meal, when it was eventually ready. The aroma of the food – and the chicken did smell exceptionally good – mixed with the smell of muck heap. Soloma adapted to the fork well after experimenting on the carrots and beans and watched Nathan cutting his potatoes with a knife but decided to eat them with her fingers instead. Of the chicken, there was little left. Hardly a usual breakfast, Nathan reflected, and now there was the problem of getting Soloma – and her clothes – clean.

The bathroom was off the little, stone-flagged hallway. Nathan ran both taps until the bath was half full, although since there was no hot water it made little difference. After some sign language, Soloma seemed to grasp the idea of having a wash and Nathan shut the door to go and hunt out some small but brightly coloured long socks that had once been used to hang up by the fireplace for Father Christmas, along with one of his smaller flannel cricket shirts and a sleeveless sweater. He could hand wash her clothes and hang them out to dry, he thought, as he paddled back down the hallway to the sound of running taps and saw that the rather nice, old, hand-woven rug was soaking up most of the incoming tide from under the bathroom door. Life was becoming a touch difficult, he observed to himself, as he placed a clean towel and the clothes on a chair by the bathroom door.

Some time later, Soloma was sitting in the sun in the rocking-chair on the verandah, admiring her (wet) Father Christmas socks and stroking the flannel shirt. Nathan had made a cup of tea, using the electricity while Soloma was in the bathroom, and was contemplating what help-lines were available to him. He needed to visit the shop to buy some basics and, equally, somehow he needed to obtain some Cornish tin – or else the cave at Polgodoc would be forever closed to him and he could never return Soloma to her own people, which was becoming a growing necessity in his mind. He couldn't hide her in the bungalow for ever and once term started again questions would be asked about a child that was not at school. And he certainly didn't fancy using an inauthentic lump of tin to try to gain entry to the cave after Zadie's experience with the South African copper. A pity she had gone back to London, he thought with mild irritation. He needed a woman to help with this girl. If the start of the day was anything to go by, he wasn't going to manage.

Chapter 2   Mabel

As Nathan stared over the tops of the runner beans with their scarlet flowers towards the chickens that were still sitting in shock on top of the old shed, the word Mabel came into his mind. Aunt Mabel. Of course, she might help – and she wouldn't ask awkward questions either. Not that she was a real aunt; Nathan didn't possess any of those. She had known him since he was a boy and she had known his grandfather. She had helped him in the past, particularly when there had been that little run-in with the local constabulary one May Day in Padstow and a constable had ended up in the harbour, rather muddy and wet. Not that it had really been Nathan's fault – he had just been in the wrong place at the wrong time but he had needed somewhere to hide out whilst Her Majesty's Customs & Excise Officers had taken a peculiar interest in his whereabouts. Aunt Mabel had lost her husband in the war and was old now but she still had a bright mind and lived where she always had in a nicely secluded farmhouse a mile or so inland from Trevennick.

It was after noon and Nathan thought he would take a chance as he went inside to the phone. Soloma looked like she was not going to attack anything else and the kitchen floor was drying nicely, along with her clothes on the line. The hall carpet was dripping in the sun. He picked up the heavy bakelite receiver and put his fingers in the holes as he dialled.

Nathan was caught by surprise as the phone answered after only two rings and a warbly voice said, "Trevennick 226." Mabel had never adjusted to adding the new digits onto the front of her old number.

"Is that you, Mabel?" Nathan enquired superfluously.

"Well, there's no one else here, dear," came back the retort.

"Mabel, you shouldn't say that – it might encourage

someone to rob you," began Nathan, getting sucked into a conversation that had occurred before.

"But Nathan, dear, it's only you and Lucinda who phone and, anyway, I don't have anything worth stealing," she continued. "Now, how are you? I haven't seen you for ages."

The conversation was not going well and Nathan looked at his watch. Of course, he thought, the phone was on top of Mabel's drinks' cupboard or, to be more accurate, her store of cider bottles. She would already have had a couple and escaping from Mabel – or her equally loquacious but fractionally younger friend Lucinda – with less than an hour's conversation when they had been at the cider was nigh on impossible. He sighed to himself and decided to plunge straight into the matter.

"Look, Mabel, I've got a girl…" he began.

"Oh, that's nice, dear. Is she pretty?" interrupted Mabel.

"Well, yes … I mean, no … well that's not the point," responded Nathan.

"Oh, it always was in my day," observed Mabel.

"She's a young girl," stammered Nathan.

"Oh, you want to be careful about that, Nathan dear. They can lock you up for that kind of thing nowadays."

"She's not a girlfriend!" exploded Nathan.

"Well, why didn't you say so?" admonished Mabel.

Nathan ground his teeth. Hadn't he been trying to do just that? He would have to invent something quickly here. He didn't like lying to Mabel but how could he explain Soloma's presence?

"She's a distant niece," lied Nathan. "It's just, I've got to go away for a few days and I was wondering…."

"You're not in trouble again are you, Nathan? You know the last time you had to go away."

Nathan recalled the occasion well but he was hoping that Mabel wouldn't insist on going through the whole story.

Instead, she said, "Would you like her to come and stay with me then?"

"Thank you," said Nathan, sighing audibly with relief, "that would be most helpful."

"Oh, you know me; I like to help you," finished Mabel. "So you'll want to be round in a few minutes?" she added astutely.

"Fairly shortly," replied Nathan.

"We can have a nice chat then, dear," ended Mabel, putting the phone down promptly but not without a slight chink of bottle on glass escaping to the receiver.

The rocking chair was empty when Nathan emerged onto the verandah and Soloma was sitting on top of the dry-stone wall on one side of the garden, eyeing the cows in the field beyond and munching at a bunch of carrots that she had pulled from the vegetable patch. Apparently, she had decided that the leaves were not for eating and had discarded most of them. Nathan beckoned to her as he folded her old clothes off the line into a cloth bag, and she jumped down to see what he was doing.

In front of the shed was a garage – or at least something that had once passed for one. Nathan pulled open the wooden doors with some difficulty, their faded green paint flaking to his touch, and they stood looking at the old, beige landrover with its drop windscreen and open top. His eyes veered to the numberplate – NP 180 – and he recalled purchasing it from an elderly farmer up on the moor, slightly before the age at which he was legally allowed to drive. It had been old even then and if it had not been for the number plate it would not have had the same attraction. Only a small legacy had allowed him to obtain it. Over the years he had replaced most of its parts, although the seats and chassis, and some of the bodywork and the dashboard were original, along with quite a few of the unseen parts. There were no seat belts as it pre-dated the requirement for these, and the engine was started via a pre-ignition heater button on the floor near the gearshaft. The folded down windscreen obscured the missing tax disc. Ever since the garage had closed on the main road it had been difficult obtaining an MoT for the vehicle. Prior to that, the mechanic had lived in Trevennick and they had made the usual barter arrangements, the last service costing four laying hens and a case of something obtained from a Scottish trawler berthed briefly in Padstow. Now the mechanic had moved away and, without an MoT or tax disc or seat belts, Nathan felt vulnerable to every passing police car. It was possibly not helped by his knowledge that one of the twin fuel tanks contained red diesel from the farm next door.

The key dangled in the dashboard, as usual. He opened the door and pushed the pre-ignition button whilst Soloma delighted in climbing over the side and standing erect in the passenger seat, before jumping out again and hiding amongst the runner beans when Nathan started the engine and edged the vehicle out of the garage. Several minutes later she was back in the landrover looking sternly to the front and resolutely refusing to sit down. "Boadicea in her chariot," said Nathan to himself.

There was only half a mile to travel up the village road before crossing the main road and getting onto farm tracks and it would be fair to say that the oncoming traffic slowed and gave way in generous fashion, as if Nathan and Soloma, or the vehicle, were celebrities. Altogether fine, he thought, until they start talking about her standing there in a flannel cricket shirt later tonight.

He looked across at her silhouette, swaying easily as they drove the rutted track to Mabel's and maintaining a magisterial presence, and realised for the first time that she would not be a child much longer. Soloma pointed at the sheep and vaulted the closed passenger door as they slewed to a standstill by the low stone farmhouse, its windows looking down the valley to the little bay and the vast ocean beyond Trevennick. Nathan exited the vehicle by more orthodox means and was greeted by Mabel's pair of white geese. He had lived in terror of these for many years. Provided he gave them some attention they were fine, but if ever his attention was fixed elsewhere they would nip him nastily on his calves. Rome could have had no better guardians against unwanted incursors, he thought, as he cautiously approached the door, suddenly aware of a problem that he should have foreseen – Mabel would expect Soloma to speak English. He paused, trying to construct a passable story, but two things happened simultaneously – Soloma ran forward and, grasping the lion knocker, wrapped it hard on the oak front door – and the geese, neglected for a moment, attacked from the rear.

"Nathan, have you been neglecting my geese?" came a voice. "You know how they like to greet you. Now how about introducing me to your niece?"

Nathan waddled forward carefully, aware that he was being followed by much hissing, and thinking that Soloma had already been embraced by Aunt Mabel and didn't need a formal introduction.

"I'm sorry, Mabel," he began. "It's been a bit hectic recently," he said (honestly). "This is Soloma. She's a niece … from France … distant relatives," he lied.

Mabel had not been out of the parish for thirty years. There was little chance of her discovering his deception.

"Oh, well, she's very welcome, wherever she's from," continued the sing-song voice. "Now, she doesn't seem to be wearing her own clothes, so if you will just bring her bags in from your landrover we can make her more comfortable," with which command Mabel and Soloma disappeared inside.

Nathan stood uncertainly. This was a mistake, and the geese attacked in unison, nipping nastily. He had a cloth bag with a few clothes in it but Mabel wasn't going to accept that these were all that Soloma possessed. He could lie and say that he had left the rest at the bungalow. Ouch! The geese had attacked again. That was the trouble. One lie led to another lie, and the geese seemed to know full well when he was contemplating deceiving Mabel. Warily he walked back to the front door, bag in hand, one goose accompanying him on each side. The door was ajar and he shut it behind him with the distinct suspicion that the two geese had taken up position on either side of it, awaiting an unfaithful egress.

Mabel and Soloma were in the kitchen as Nathan entered sheepishly, his calves hurting.

"Look Mabel," he began, "This is all I've got. It's difficult to explain, and I don't think I can."

She looked at him with a clarity in her blue eyes that he had not noticed before and said slowly, "How long do you need, Nathan?"

"Two or three days," he replied awkwardly.

"Then you had better go. I will look after her. Do what you must but don't be too long," she ended abruptly.

Suddenly, he found himself the wrong side of the front door with Mabel's geese hissing him towards the landrover and watching him off the premises as he drove down the rutted track, discontented both with himself and how he had handled the situation.

Chapter 3   Wilf

The rotted wood on the bottom of the garage doors broke off as Nathan closed them and the chickens continued their mute disregard of his return. He left the landrover outside on the collection of half-weeds, half-flowers that the slate fragments permitted to grow on his drive and set about collecting objects from inside and stowing them in the vehicle. Most of them seemed to go 'clink' as he lowered them into the hidden compartment beneath the passenger seat. The bungalow seemed peculiarly empty without Soloma's presence and he mooched around, unable to settle. He would leave early in the morning when it was still dark – that way there was less likelihood of being stopped.

Wilf had not exactly been a friend – more an acquaintance with whom there had been a degree of mutual respect. He was a large man with more muscle than fat and had worked in the Cornish tin mines until they had finally closed, defeated by the increased production costs of hard-rock mining and cheaper production costs from the alluvial deposits in Malaysia, combined with cheap labour in Bolivia, and government policy. When the last job had gone at the Wheal Jane, he had found work at the Camborne School of Mines. There he had encouraged a generation of students, passing on a substantial amount of his knowledge – and keeping some vital segments to himself.

The A30 had been quiet and Nathan worked his way through the back roads of Carn Menellis to find a spot where he could watch the occasional traffic without being obvious. It was soon after 7.30am when he spotted his quarry and drove up to the improvised car park in the shadow of the old Cornish beam engine. Trevithick had been responsible for so much of this industry and had never received the acclaim of Watt or Boulton or Newcommen, he thought to himself, but nor too had those who preceded him and whose lives and deaths only the landscape remembered. Once, late one evening, Wilf had started talking about some of the forgotten names and places – about the mines that had closed; about the disasters; and about the lure of the Mother Lode – but then he had clammed up again.

He was silhouetted against a doorway – not that there was much spare doorway – replacing mining lights and tags when Nathan looked in.

"Morning Nathan. Took a while from where you were parked, didn't you?" came the deep voice.

"Yes," said Nathan.

"Got a new field trip then? Want to see some real bits of mines?" There was a vague interest in the voice.

"No. Personal."

Wilf paused in his work and looked at Nathan for the first time. "OK. Ten-thirty then … where you were parked."

"am or pm?" asked Nathan and Wilf laughed before saying, "Let's start with am."

Nathan walked slowly to the landrover. So far, so good. There were two mining museums nearby. Carthew was OK for quartz and other impurities found whilst extracting China Clay amongst the spoil heaps once known as the Cornish Alps but it was no good for tin. He would head down to Redruth and see what they had on display there.

Two hours later, having found nothing interesting, he was back where he started and Wilf's slightly younger landrover drew up behind him.

"OK, Nathan. I have thirty minutes … the new bosses in Exeter are tight on time. I've got the dogs … let's walk and you can ask me what you want," stated Wilf.

Nathan had been thinking about this carefully and, as they walked over the pitted and pock-marked moor, the golden flowers of gorse marking out the spoil heaps from the old workings, he replied, "I have three, possibly four, questions."

"Firstly, I want two lumps of Cornish tin."

"Secondly, I want to know about the old mining techniques and where they were first carried out – not the 19th Century stuff but the really old start to the tin industry."

"Thirdly, I want to know about the bits of Cornish history that don't add up in the mining of tin. The things that are peculiar, unexplained, undocumented."

There was no point in being less than frank with Wilf. His response would either be very negative or, at best, enigmatic. It looked like it was going to be the former and for five minutes they walked on, with Wilf occasionally whistling his collies, before he stopped and faced Nathan, saying, "Where are you staying?"

"I'm not yet. I could go into Camborne or Redruth and find somewhere."

"No. Don't do that," Wilf replied. "Your face and your vehicle are too well known. You still haven't got a tax disc on your landrover and you probably have red diesel in its tank. What's more, if you ask those questions in a Camborne pub there are several sets of ears that might be interested to hear. Go up on the moor and find a B&B. I have half a day owing – I'll meet you where we did that old survey. I'll be there at ten-thirty." And with that he strode off at a pace faster than Nathan could match.

Finding a B&B in mid-August, even on the moor, proved not entirely easy and he booked for two nights just in case, frittering the rest of the day away browsing through antique shops in St. Austell and Looe, looking for old artefacts and books.

The next day dawned murky with low cloud obscuring the landscape and, as Nathan worked his way upwards with map and compass, he could well have been walking back in time. Each stone loomed as a sentinel to the past and each animal cry, dampened by the fog and distorted by the wind, echoed of legend. Surprisingly soon the triangulation pillar revealed its cold, grey finger pointing towards the equally cold heavens and Nathan settled in what little lee he could find. It was strange how time stretched when vision was obscured. It seemed like an hour, although in reality it was only fifteen minutes, until he heard heavy breathing labouring up the opposite slope and a figure magnified by the faint light through the cloud gradually diminished from grotesque giant to the semi-normality of Wilf.

They walked down the slope a while until they found more shelter, the overhanging granite rocks dripping in front of them from the encompassing cloud.

"Strange places, some of these rocks," observed Wilf. "No metal ores visible here and yet someone took a huge amount of effort to create this opening."

"Did you know the weather would be like this?" asked Nathan as they settled down.

"Yes, but I didn't think it would be as bad as this," replied Wilf. "However, it helps to answer your second question. This is what it would have been like on the higher moors much of the time for the early miners – nothing much to see above ground … and even less underground – no wood, no fire, no warmth. Two hundred metres lower and we'd be below this cloud but we'd also be out of the metalliferous zone. The best place for them to mine was at the cliffs by the coast … better visibility and better access … and easy to get rid of the spoil," and he ran some of the decomposed granite through his fingers – growan, he called it. "The most obvious stuff went long ago … maybe two thousand years or more – tin, copper, lead – anything where the cliff showed a distinct colouration … small groups of extended families passing on skills from generation to generation and working their way along a stretch of cliff or land, enlarging and squaring off the weaknesses that nature had exploited. Of course, iron tools were the key – that's when they were able to move up here and tackle the harder rock. Prior to that they could only split it with fire. Much of the metal ended up in the Mediterranean – mined in the gloom at great risk and ending up in the sunshine at great profit." He paused and laughed, somewhat unhappily. "Want a bit of chocolate?"

The clammy cold was penetrating now and Nathan accepted it gratefully whilst the voice went on, "The trade routes were much better organised than we give them credit for. Each journey would have been as short as possible – and time consuming: North coast to South coast – a few days here; a week where you come from. Then the worst journey – across the Channel to Britttany – and on down through France, passing from trading group to trading group, increasing in value at each exchange, until it finally reached a Mediterranean port and linked with the Phoenician trade routes. Might have taken a year from smelting in Cornwall to shaping and use in the eastern Mediterranean."

"And the old priests followed the flow of wealth back along the trade routes?" Nathan ventured.

"Yes. Although there was never any real wealth here … only hard work and an abysmal standard of living. Life was often very short and very nasty. The story's a bit like that chocolate you've just eaten," he said, rising abruptly and stamping and flapping to get some circulation returning.

He talked about the missing pieces in the Cornish story as they walked down through the cloud. It was strange stuff; part legend, part fact, and much speculation. Druids and priests melled with disappearances and breakthroughs; with old families whose lines were extinct; with treasures lost and times of isolation; with plague and hardship. They were below the cloudbase when he changed topic.

"You said you wanted some tin. If you want tin, why don't you go out and buy a chunk? There's thousands of tonnes on the spot market."

Nathan retorted, "It's Cornish tin I want."

"Well, there's plenty in the gift shops and probably the antique shops and museum shops."

"You know as well as I do that is not pure tin and it's unlikely to be genuinely Cornish. What I need is two chunks of pure unsmelted tin, this size," Nathan said, making a circle with his thumb and finger.

"That big, and not smelted, it would have to come from near a mother lode. There's nothing out of Geevor or Wheal Jane, and there's not been a decent mother lode found in Cornwall since the 1890s … and they got too greedy … followed it out under the sea bed and mined too near it; worst mining disaster in Cornish history … hundreds died when the sea broke through. They say you can still hear their cries from the cliff top when the wind is in the north."

"I just reckoned," said Nathan, "that maybe someone who had worked in the deep Cornish mines most of their life might have come across some chunks of tin that didn't quite make it to the crusher …."

They paused to face each other. He could have overpowered him easily and torn each limb casually apart if he had taken offence but Nathan met his gaze until they both looked away down to where the two vehicles were parked no more than a hundred yards apart.

"I could give you some tin and say that it was Cornish. Even if you put it under an electron scanner for a fingerprint, there would be nothing to match it against," Wilf stated.

"There would be the background Radon reading," countered Nathan. "Besides which, this is not that kind of request."

They both leant on Nathan's landrover.

"OK. You've not told me the whole truth but you've not told me lies. I may be able to help but I don't know when," said Wilf, and they fell to haggling over a down-payment as watery shafts of sunlight finally began to penetrate the over-lying gloom.

"By the way," Nathan asked after they had reached a suitable compromise, "is that library of yours down at the School of Mines still open to outsiders?"

"Depends," grunted Wilf. "They might give you a visitor's pass. Only, this time leave your jacket outside."

"Why?" asked Nathan, looking slightly embarrassed.

"I suppose if I was to mention a small book entitled, 'Notes on an original geological survey of North Cornwall by De la Beche', with some hand drawn maps in it, it wouldn't jog any memories?" continued Wilf. "Used to be the only two 19th Century copies in the library – and now there are none on the database."

"OK," said Nathan, "so where's the other one?" and this time it was Wilf's turn to look sheepish.

"What do you want, anyway? The library's not great on historical stuff before 1850."

"I was after some offshore surveys – sea-bed – bathymetric material."

Wilf seemed on the brink of saying something further but

changed his mind, observing instead, "Yesterday, you said you had a possible fourth question for me."

Nathan hesitated, "I was going to ask you what you knew about Serpentine."

Wilf fixed him with a steady stare and answered, "Presumably you don't mean its geological history, location or chemistry."

"No. I was thinking more about it's place in Cornish legend, actually."

"Look, Nathan, I don't know what you're up to. This isn't your usual line of research. Serpentine has always been on the dark side of legends – sacrifice, murder, extinction, disappearance, destruction: Gwenhallion died for it; Arthur's crown was lost for the lure of it; the monastery at Padstow was sacked for rumour of it. Don't you go seeking it – leastwise, not the old stuff – modern's different."

"I get the message. You don't like it?"

"I'll say no more, except this: you aren't the first person to ask me for Cornish tin recently. It was a city gent a few weeks ago … smart suit and shiny black leather shoes, all bespoke … didn't like him, nor did my dogs … let them jump up with their muddy paws but he didn't turn a hair."

"And did you give him some Cornish tin?" asked Nathan.

"I gave him some tin," said Wilf meaningfully, "and for a good price," with which he picked up his down-payment, swung it over his shoulder, and marched off towards his landrover. Nathan thought he heard, "Take care," as an aside over the retreating shoulder and was deep in thought as he got into his own vehicle.

Chapter 4   To Little Vennick

Whether or not Wilf had phoned ahead Nathan was not sure, but the library accepted his researcher's card and gave him access to their database. They also asked him to leave his jacket at the counter.

There was little material on offshore surveys and certainly nothing geological. The inshore navigation charts were detailed for the Camel Estuary and close to the coast but lost interest after depths of fifteen metres or so. The admiralty charts were better for offshore work once he had converted measurements from fathoms but the submarine contour interval he could construct was too coarse to give an accurate impression of the sea-bed. Surprisingly, his best information came from a German survey dated 1938 and he printed off a copy of the area around Gulland, whilst wondering about some of the annotation and the reasons for conducting it. A polite cough behind him indicated that the library was about to close and he was proffered his jacket. He wouldn't be surprised if Wilf checked what he had been looking at, he thought, as he took several wrong turns on the dark moor roads back to the B&B.

The next morning was bright and clear, and Nathan was still mulling things over as he headed back along the A30. If he had not been preoccupied with his thoughts he would probably have spotted the police car sitting on a bridge over the dual carriageway near Zelah. As it was, it was a casual glance in the battered wing mirror that alerted him to a blue flashing light turning round and accelerating down the slip road. He was spared trouble by a lorry with Polish number plates deciding to overtake a caravan with German ones, and the consequent general snarl-up behind him. As he turned left, then right at the top of Zelah Hill onto a very minor road, he glimpsed the flashing blue lights screaming down the outside lane of the main road and diverging from his course; there were another two miles until it could next turn off the A30.

Nevertheless, he plotted his way back along minor roads through the villages named after saints – Newlyn, Mawgan, Eval, Merryn. It had added nearly an hour to his journey when he turned onto the rutted track to Little Vennick farmhouse and ground to a halt on the loose slate that served as a drive. He parked away from the building where the vehicle was hidden from any view and walked cagily towards Mabel's door.

He paused, looking left and right and doing a complete rotation, peering towards the door to see if the cunning enemy were planning a late ambush as he reached for the knocker. Nothing. Not a sound. Not a hiss. Not a movement. Never had Nathan known Mabel's geese fail to greet him in their inimitable way and he became concerned for the old lady, running the last few steps and flinging open the door without knocking. It had probably not suffered such a presumption in years and cannoned into the brass umbrella stand behind it, which disgorged its contents of walking sticks just in time for Nathan's feet to become ensnared by them and for him to go sprawling onto the carpet which, in turn, slid him head first into the cider cabinet supporting the telephone.

It was into this situation that Mabel opened the kitchen door to the hallway and said, "Is that you Nathan?"

Several minutes elapsed as Nathan re-arranged the hall furniture back to something like its original shape and then followed the sound of laughter through to the kitchen. Mabel was sitting alone.

"Look, I'm sorry … there were no geese and I was worried for you and … I tripped … and, where's Soloma?" he babbled, as Mabel raised a quietening finger to her lips.

"Don't be concerned," she said. "I'm here, and I'm perfectly alright … and the geese were getting old."

Nathan had a sudden apprehension that Mabel's geese had met the same fate as his chicken and was opening his mouth to speak when Mabel pre-empted him.

"Nathan, there's someone who wants to see you."

A figure bounced round the far door and pirouetted in the middle of the kitchen. The pretty frock was dated – probably 1950s in style – but suited her and flared outwards with the motion. Her black hair was clean and silky, held in place with a copper hair band; clean white socks and a leather pair of shoes completed the picture as Nathan gasped and burst into spontaneous applause and laughter. Soloma took this as a sign to repeat the performance and he rose to kiss her gently on the head. Mabel was slightly watery-eyed as she rose and he kissed her head too as he put an arm round her and she said, "Let's go into the sitting room: there's a lot to discuss."

The sitting room was a small formal room, immaculately kept and a period piece. Anti-macassars were draped over the two wing-back chairs and coloured cut glass was in a corner cabinet. A few silver-framed photographs adorned a mahogany table, upon which a maiden-hair fern sat in a porcelain pot. An ancient box of scrabble with wooden tiles was wedged against a copper log bucket and a solitaire board with old fashioned marbles was in the middle of the rug in front of the fireplace. The fire had been lit at some point recently and there was a distinct smell of descending soot mingled with some form of food. The standard lamp in the corner had tasselled fringes dangling from its shade and the walls were covered in a faded green, Georgian-stripe wallpaper. Someone had turned the Scrabble board over and the wooden tiles spelt out names – SOLOMA, LUCINDA, MABEL – and there was another that he couldn't make out.

Nathan had never been invited into this room before and he stood, waiting to see where Mabel would sit. She chose one of the wing-chairs and Nathan occupied the other one while Soloma played with the marbles, occasionally going over to finger the silver-framed pictures. It felt like cucumber sandwiches at the vicar's, and he wasn't looking forward to the conversation.

Mabel fixed Nathan with a watery stare. "She's not French, you know. I was parachuted into Normandy in the war to translate for the Resistance. My French may be a bit rusty but she doesn't understand it."

Nathan was uncertain whether to be more amazed at the thought of Aunt Mabel dangling on the end of a parachute or embarrassed at his fabricated story and mumbled, "I'm sorry."

They talked for a long while, Soloma pausing and looking up like the old dog had done when it had heard a word that sounded familiar but with an interest in her eyes that showed an intellect processing the words and phrases and beginning to make sense of at least a few of them.

Finally Mabel ended, "Anyway, dear, Soloma and I have had a good chat. Lucinda came round too, and she brought some clothes. There are some more in a case, and the original ones in your cloth bag. I've taught her to use the loo and to wash with soap, and she's not afraid of electricity. She's very bright, you know, and learns quickly. She has a smattering of English now. Keep talking to her. Perhaps, just don't leave any sharp knives around the place."

Nathan grimaced and thought of the geese, albeit they had given him such a hard time.

"Look, Mabel, I have a favour to ask." Her non-response encouraged him to continue. "Could I leave my landrover up here, and we could walk back to Trevennick? It's a nice evening –"

"What have you done, Nathan?" interrupted Mabel.

"Nothing. It's just that I think the number plate was logged by the police on the way back from Camborne and they may make a few enquiries. It's out of sight up here," he added lamely.

"Did you see Wilf?" she asked, and his nod seemed to reassure her. "Well, if you are walking you had better get on your way. It will be nearly dark by the time you are back."

She ushered them into the hall before disappearing. Shortly, she came back and whispered to Soloma, who seemed to understand that it was time to collect her new belongings and re-emerged with a small leather case with faded brass fittings. It wasn't much bigger than a modern attaché case but the faded labels on it betrayed its heritage – a stylised image of a Catalina flying boat with the legend 'Imperial Airways' across it, along with several old hotel stickers and one that read 'Peninsula & Orient'. The leather protective caps on its corners were scuffed but in other places the patina still shone through where it had been lovingly opened and handled. Nathan sensed that it was a particular piece of Mabel's history that she wanted to pass on to the little girl. Mabel hugged her as they stood together, not much different in height, and then moved apart.

"Nathan, you might find this useful," she said, offering him a small leather bound book. "I've marked the pages," she added, "and … you are welcome to use my house – whenever you need it. Now, take care of her, and off you go."

Nathan murmured, "I will. Thanks." He called out, "We'll come back and see you at the week-end," before they turned and plodded down the lane and into the setting sun.

Soloma was carrying her case like a treasure and delighting in her new clothes. Nathan was cheered by her as they cut across the main road and followed a back path to his bungalow but he felt weighed down by guilt and the seeming acceleration of time. He wished he knew more about Mabel. Perhaps he would go back there tomorrow. Soloma would like that.

The chickens were already roosting when they arrived at the bungalow. He laid up a fire and lit it – more for company than warmth – as Soloma reached up to the light switches and explored the rooms. Mabel had also taught her to open drawers and he could hear the sound of further exploration. He made a bed up for her in the other bedroom and put her case on it, opening it to discover that Mabel had put pyjamas on top, and finding big brown eyes watching him carefully. He left her for a while and settled in the armchair to watch the flames, reaching for a bottle of cider from the cupboard nearby. He was close to nodding off, with the unopened book on his lap, when there was a clink from behind him and a small figure dressed in bright pink pyjamas was carrying two glasses from the cupboard towards him. She put them by the bottle and looked meaningfully at him. He laughed. Hardly surprising if Soloma had been with Mabel and Lucinda for two days, he thought. He poured a small amount into each glass and they sat there, sipping slowly and watching the dying fire.

Chapter 5   Of Letters and Rocks

There was no noise from Soloma's room when Nathan woke and he dressed quickly, nipping down to the village shop and retrieving a couple of pints of milk from the crates outside. He left a note saying that he had taken them and asking for some bread to be put on one side for him to collect later. It would go on his account.

Several cups of tea later, there were still only small noises from Soloma's room. He knocked and opened the door to find her sitting in front of the mirror brushing her hair with a small, silver-handled hairbrush. She had laid her clothes out on the bed. She pointed to each of them, looking expectantly at Nathan, who realised that she was asking what to wear. Yes and No, nods and shakes, and some basic colour words seemed to be making the beginnings of dialogue, if not conversation, and Nathan found himself beginning to talk in a simple running commentary as he went through the morning tasks.

The vegetable patch was suffering from providing two persons with some rather peculiar breakfasts as well as other meals. Soloma had taken great delight in carrots and laughed every time the somewhat mis-shapen orange roots emerged from the dark earth. Her routine was to take each to the garden tap, turn it on to wash off the soil – causing further delight – and sit and eat it from tip to top before throwing the feathery green leaves away and repeating the process. The raspberry patch had also suffered depredations and it was a good job Nathan had not said yes to the white skirt. Meanwhile, he was halfway along the line of potatoes that he usually reserved for October. The chickens had developed their own strategy and one remained on the shed roof watching intently and squawking if Soloma moved suddenly, whilst the others foraged, pausing frequently with heads cocked to one side for sounds. The supply of eggs had sadly diminished and Nathan was in danger of having to buy some at the shop.

Soloma had taken to luke-warm tea. She sat and slurped quietly, watching Nathan gathering half a dozen thin slates and wiping them down. The rest of the morning was spent scratching letters and numbers on them, and on the others that Soloma fetched and cleaned. They worked their way through sounds with Nathan muddling up the slates and Soloma sorting through them, putting them back in order. It was a remarkably successful time and they both enjoyed it. Soloma had gathered more slates and engraved them in a different style, using straight lines rather than curves, and was triumphant when she finally put seven of them in order to spell ƧOLOⱮA, as Nathan prompted the sounds.

After lunch – Nathan wondered vaguely what the carrots were doing to Soloma's digestive system – he left her by the armchair, engraving yet more slates. It looked like numbers this time but only using single strokes so that 4 was rendered |||| and 5 appeared as a strange symbol _\|// , until he recognised it as a stylised hand. He thought about locking the doors but finding the keys would take time and he didn't see the point really; she seemed happy enough and he wouldn't be long since the shop was only five minutes away.

Once there, he found it both busy with regular holiday-makers stocking up on their accounts – gin, tonic, cider, clotted cream, baps, expensive meats, more tonic water – and that he had rather more to buy than he had thought. By the time he reached the counter, his basket was rather full.

Kelvin's cheery voice greeted him, "Hello, Nathan. Thanks for the note. Haven't seen you for ages."

It was a staccato kind of conversation that punctuated the lifting of each item out of the basket. As a self-admired source of village gossip, Kelvin would continue in this vein and Nathan would endeavour to give away as little information as possible.

He was doing quite well until the voice continued, "Seen smoke from your chimney recently. Unusual that, in August. Trouble with the electricity? Oh, eggs! Has the fox been at your hens then?"

"No," said Nathan, "they're just off laying at the moment."

"Wouldn't be surprised if a fox scared them. Old farmer Trevelyn, he lost two sheep up on the moor a few days ago. Talk of a new big beast on the loose."

Nathan was paying attention now. He didn't like the sound of that, nor its timing. Kelvin had that sixth sense of a successful shop-keeper and gossip of recognising when his customer's interest had been twinged and was taking the items out of the basket more slowly as he continued, "Yes. Strange thing was the bones hadn't been gnawed. Ah! Roast chicken. Barter economy broken down for the summer then?"

"It's not up to its usual standard," Nathan admitted.

"Oh, ice cream … and a bottle of wine. Anyone would think you were entertaining, Nathan. Is that it then?"

"Just the bread, please," said Nathan.

"Ah, yes. I'm afraid there was only granary and wholemeal left. Hope that's OK?"

"Fine," said Nathan, thinking that they were the most expensive and that almost certainly Kelvin had sold everything else before putting the last two on one side for him. He felt them surreptitiously as Kelvin asked him to sign the account. At least they didn't feel like yesterday's bread, he thought, as he trudged back up the hill with his bags, wondering whether Soloma was still engraving slates or was sitting on the dry-stone wall eyeing the cows.

Soloma had not been idle whilst Nathan had been out. She must have been watching for him from the old, stone wall and ran in through the kitchen just as Nathan reached the sitting room and came to a halt, putting the bags down and observing the scene. Slates were lined up across the floor, and beside them were two other lines of rocks. Behind the armchair the drawers of the cabinet containing his collection of Cornish rocks stood hanging at an improbable angle. Each rock had been washed (copiously) to bring out its fresh colouration and the carpet squelched under him. Soloma was standing excitedly pointing at the rocks and fingering some of them.

"Pretty rocks," said Nathan, kneeling down beside her and feeling the water through his trouser knees. She must have thought they were like the marbles at Mabel's and Nathan rolled one of the slightly rounded specimens of greenstone across the carpet, knocking it into a lump of purple phyllite by accident. Soloma got up and recovered the rocks, putting them back. That was odd. Nathan moved a few more rocks. The same thing happened. Then he muddled up half a dozen specimens. Same again – back in the same order. Soloma was very definite about this, and quite excited. Whichever way he changed them, she changed them back – and there was one rock that she kept settling by. It was a piece of white coral that Nathan had found many years ago at the back of a rather crumbly cave of poor quality limestone near Harlyn. He had only gone into the cave as a result of a dare from some of the village boys, and he certainly wouldn't fit into it now. The rock didn't really belong in the collection according to the texts, and he had never written about it, suspecting its authenticity even though the location of its finding was virtually inaccessible.

Nathan was standing, trying to work out the logic in Soloma's order. "Definitely not by colour," he said aloud, "nor by shape; nor by size." What did that leave? If this was a piece of university work, what would he expect his students to do? His mind started kicking in – 'stratigraphic column'. He looked again. Were they ordered by age of formation? It was close, but not a perfect fit. He muddled up some of the younger and older rocks, and waited. Soloma re-sorted them accurately, even though the distinctions were unclear except to a professional eye. He was close to something here. What would he do if he was sent a random collection of rocks: identify the geology; look at age; find the location; map the outcrops? Then it hit him blindingly clearly: "map it!" This was something to work on and he rolled all the rocks into a heap, leaving the piece of coral to one side. Maybe he could make a game of it.

He sifted through and took an angular piece of granite that had come from the moor inland, then he pointed to Soloma. She took a piece of quartz that he had picked up from near the same site. He selected a medium grade slate from nearby, then she chose something green and purple from the Trebetherick collection. They seemed to be working their way from inland towards the coast and he went for a pebble with quartz veining that had come from Greenaway. She snatched it away with a laugh, and substituted the darkest piece of high grade slate. That was from Delabole. That didn't fit. He took it away again. She put it back. Then he remembered the map table at Polgodoc. He left her choice in place and went for a black pebble laced with quartz. That seemed acceptable. She chose a granite pebble and he put another dark one after it. Strangely, it was only a part-rounded chunk of limestone from the cliffs near Trevennick that she would allow for the next choice. She insisted on placing the piece of coral some distance away from it and sitting by it. Everything he tried in the gap was rejected. "How can there be a gap in the rocks?" he said aloud, and moved the coral closer. She moved it apart again.

Eventually they left the agreed sequence alone, a kind of geological cross section from inland to out at sea, and he bundled the remaining rocks into the drawers, only one of which was too splintered to shut. They would have to have the ice cream now, as it had thawed and was beginning to leak through onto the parsnips; just as well he hadn't put it in with the bread. So supper turned out to be a kind of back to front meal, starting with ice cream and ending with raw carrots and cider.

Nathan rolled back the carpet and decided to light a fire to help dry things out, no matter what Kelvin might speculate. Having wiped the floor dry, he spread out maps and charts and spent time trying to match up Soloma's cross section to them. A while later, he retreated to the armchair opposite her and very carefully examined a small book that had the name 'De la Beche' on its cover, and a map printed largely in German.

Chapter 6 News

It was the middle of the next morning and they were arranging slates into sounds on the back verandah in the sunshine, when there was a solid knocking and a cry of, "Nathan!"

He held his finger up to his lips to Soloma, who was kneeling with the piece of coral dangling around her neck on garden twine, and said, "Quick! Hide!" It was a command that he had taught her in case of unwanted visitors and she shot off into the runner beans while he crunched round the side of the house.

The village postman was stooping near the front door, about to place a letter under the large piece of slate which he had turned over so that the word 'Post' was uppermost.

"Morning, Nathan," he began, "Letter from your girlfriend."

Post was highly unusual for Nathan and the front door had been built before the days of the Penny Black. Somehow, Nathan had never got round to adding a letter-box.

"Morning, Martyn," he responded. "I don't think that's right."

"Well maybe it was a brief acquaintance," Martyn continued, "definitely female writing; says 'Do Not Bend', so probably contains a photograph; post-marked 'West London'; and you clearly didn't introduce yourself very well."

"Assuming you haven't opened the envelope, how can you possibly tell all that?" asked Nathan, his heart rising nonetheless.

"Don't need to open the post to tell what's in it," replied Martyn. "Don't know what you'll do when I retire next year!" Anyway, have a look for yourself."

Nathan had to admit that Martyn had a point. The neatly written envelope was addressed simply to:

Nathan
Trevennick
North Cornwall.

It had no postcode and, whatever was said of The Royal Mail, he had never found its local delivery lacking in initiative.

He said, "Thanks," in genuine gratitude and was about to disappear round the side of the house when Martyn spoke again.

"By the way, who is the little girl?" Nathan paused and Martyn continued, "Saw her on the wall watching the cows when I was delivering to the old farm … and Kelvin was talking about you making some peculiar purchases."

Martyn had been the village postman for as long as Nathan could remember, and he claimed that his grand-father had delivered telegrams of 'the old Queen's demise'. He was much more discrete than Kelvin and Nathan took the warning, saying, "Thanks, Martyn; just a distant relative come to stay for a few days' holiday and enjoy the coast."

Martyn nodded, accepting that he hadn't been told the whole truth, before casting a parting comment over his shoulder, "Can't imagine you being seen with a bucket and spade on the beach!"

Nathan crunched slowly round the side of the old cottage, twiddling the envelope in his fingers. Deliveries of post were unusual to him and Martyn always left them under the slate at the front door. Today, he had made a point of knocking and calling out. He trusted Martyn and the events disturbed him.

He had hardly rounded the far corner when a voice said, "What?" pointing at the envelope.

"Very good!" responded Nathan approvingly, as they sat down to open the envelope together. It contained two photographs and a short note.

Soloma grabbed the first photograph and said excitely, "Zadie!" and Nathan realised that this had been the mixed up word on Mabel's Scrabble board.

"Yes, it's a photograph of Zadie," Nathan commentated.

"Let's see what she says."

The piece of A5 paper was folded in half and had been written in haste, without a salutation. It read: 'Think you might want/need these. Hope to be down next Wednesday. If this letter finds you, so will I. Love, Z'.

As with many communications, its brevity opened up an increasing number of questions. Although it had been addressed to him, at least part of it was to Soloma. Which part was to whom was rather important and Nathan found himself paraphrasing and amplifying as he read to Soloma, ending, "Well it looks like Zadie will be coming soon."

That afternoon he decided to go for a walk along the cliff with Soloma. They would take the back path to avoid the beach but there were enough people around for them not to appear out of place once they reached the cliff top. Besides which, if Martyn knew there was a girl staying at the bungalow, there was a good chance that Kelvin would find out soon. It would be better to be seen in public than be thought to be secreting someone away.

It was a lovely walk and they revelled in the sunlight and air. There was a peculiar clarity to the Cornish light when the air streamed in from the north-west; it had attracted the water-colour artists to St. Ives in the 19th Century, and photographers ever since. Now, each moment was a perfection of natural expression that the professionals could only seek to capture in poor imitation. The waves were well-formed and rolled into the little bay below, each laden with its surf boards and ending lapping the ankles of excited toddlers; sandcastles and kites competed with dogs, frisbees and beach cricket as Nathan and Soloma progressed slowly along the path above; and the sound of children playing mingled with the cries of wheeling gulls as the sun's rays played on cloud and water.

There was a rock that Nathan knew as pulpit rock, its rounded high back towards the sea and its seat towards the land. Sheltered there, Soloma sat looking out along the cliff line past the sphinx like silhouette of Porthmissen towards Polgodoc, and a much shorter distance the other way down to the lion rock that guarded the bay. She seemed particularly at peace, alternating her view, while he stood and felt the solid greenstone cliff tremble slightly with each onslaught of a thousand miles. He looked down to the rock. It was not a lion, more a lioness, as it had no mane. Behind its distinctive head was a deep cleft, making its back a separate entity. Water swelled around it. Many years ago he had been shown how, at low tide, to access the lioness' head and back. It had involved an exposed overhang, swinging up over the swirling waters of the outer rock before landing on its angular back. The flat, sloping surface of the rock there had been etched by eons of salt weathering and insolation into little valleys and intervening heights, knolls and depressions, miniature cliffs and half-formed embayments. He looked at Soloma. She was looking out towards Gulland and then beyond, fingering the coral on the garden twine.

"Let's go, now," he said, holding out his hand.

The sun cast their lengthening shadows from behind. A solitary kite flew below, and a farmer's dog greeted Nathan like a well-known friend as they made their way back towards the bungalow.

They were mid-way through supper when there was a hammering upon the door. Nathan looked up uncertainly and mimed to Soloma to hide herself. He could hear a female voice calling, "Nathan!" It sounded distressed but not threatening as he opened the front door into the dimly lit hall.

"Lucinda!" he gasped. "What are you doing here? Are you alright?"

"May I come in?" came the reply and, as he hesitated, she said, "It's alright, I know about Soloma."

"Of course. Come in. It's a bit messy. Come and sit in the armchair. Mind the rocks and the carpet."

Lucinda negotiated the obstacles without tripping over them and she sat down with an exhausted sigh, closing her eyes.

"We've got some supper in the kitchen," Nathan said, "would you like to come and join us and have a glass of cider?"

A tired voice, close to tears, answered, "Yes. I think I would. That would be most kind."

And so they sat down together – Lucinda wrapped in her own thoughts; Soloma struggling to master the delight of seeing her again and the anxiety projected by her mood; Nathan wondering why there should be such a late call. He poured three glasses of cider, and Lucinda burst into tears.

Between sobs, she said, "I came round earlier … but you were out … I only got back from the hospital at three … it's all been so sudden …."

"Lucinda," said Nathan gently, "what's happened?"

"Mabel. It's Mabel. She's dead. Died this morning. Martyn told me she didn't look well when he saw her at the beginning of his round: he often used to look in on her. I went up there soon afterwards and found her asleep in her chair … the one that looks down the valley. Except, she wasn't asleep …" the voice trailed off.

Without understanding the words, Soloma had put an arm round Lucinda and buried her head on her shoulder slightly more quickly than Nathan had reacted. Together they tried to comfort the old lady who was too proud to give way to the tears that needed to flow.

Two hours later they had returned, in the quite dark, having walked Lucinda home and turned on the lights for her, promising to come back in the morning.

Chapter 7   Zadie's Return

It was nine o'clock when Nathan rang the bell at Lucinda's but there was no reply and eventually they found a note. It looked like she had been crying as she wrote and it said simply, 'N, Have gone to claim the body. Will phone later. Love, Lucinda'.

They walked slowly back to the bungalow and had just gone back inside when there was a rap on the door. Nathan yanked it open, expecting to see Lucinda, and found Martyn, who said, "Just wanted to say how sorry I was about Mabel."

Nathan stepped outside, shutting the old oak door behind him, and observed, "Gather you were the last person to see her alive."

"Yes," said Martyn. "Got to give evidence to the coroner. She seemed kind of pre-occupied … not as with-it as normal … and her geese weren't there; they usually come and eat the breadcrumbs from my hand."

There was a long pause, during which Nathan thought that he would never offer Mabel's geese breadcrumbs on his hands, and then realised that he neither could nor would have the opportunity to visit Mabel again. He was close to tears.

Martyn broke the silence. "Look, I've another package for you … think it's rocks, probably from Wilf … post-marked Camborne … got your surname this time – Nathan Peters – but not the right postage. Says you owe £2.68, but I'll sort that out with the office. Here you are," and he thrust the package into Nathan's hands before turning and departing with a stumble.

He couldn't find the words to reply and he went back inside, saying, "Just rocks," to Soloma as he put the package down on the pile with Mabel's old book and Zadie's letter.

Soloma was on the wall looking at the cows when the phone went. Nathan answered promptly and heard Lucinda say, "They have agreed to release the body without an investigation, and I've fixed the funeral for 2pm next Thursday; it'll be the young minister who stands in during the holidays. I'll tell young Martyn the Post, and he'll tell those who need to know. 'Fraid I'm going to be fairly busy organising things but I do want to talk with you – here – after the funeral." Nathan expressed his thanks for the call and offered whatever help he could give.

It was Saturday. All being well, Zadie would arrive on Wednesday. That would help with the funeral, as he was determined that Soloma should have the opportunity to go. There was so much to tell and he had no contact number for her: 'Zadie, West London', wasn't going to get far with Directory Enquiries, and he didn't doubt the superiority of Martyn's postal delivery to that of the metropolis.

He threw himself into life over the next few days, spending the mornings working with Soloma on sounds and words and verbs and nouns, and the afternoons walking. She would sit at the pulpit rock for as long as he would let her. Once, they walked to a chandlers in Padstow and he filled his rucksack, although he didn't stay long because of the way the foreign seamen were looking at Soloma. Another time, they walked inland to Little Vennick, but it was a forlorn visit. The door of Mabel's farmhouse was locked and, as he tried to explain that Mabel wasn't there any more, Soloma had reached up to the big lion knocker, its commands echoing unanswered from within. At least they could walk now without fear of being seen.

A few condolence cards were left by the front door. He didn't know some of the names, or why they should be addressed to him. Indeed, one wasn't: it read, 'To Nathan and the little girl – we loved her too. May she rest in peace'. Even Kelvin had a sympathy card when he went into the shop; and he wasn't asked any questions.

In the evenings, they spent time cleaning the bungalow from ceiling to skirting, before lighting a fire. Soloma was working on engraving words now, while Nathan had cleared up the rocks and maps and was trying to make sense of two things. One was the book that Mabel had given him. The chapter that she had marked was entitled: 'Cuneiform & Runes in Ancient Cornwall'. It was old and undated, and there were some obvious inaccuracies in it, but it traced the elements of cuneiform writing that had penetrated Cornwall along the trade routes from their Phoenician origin and the runes used by the Nordic invaders who had come the other way. Together they had mingled to create some of the distinctive Celtic imagery, half word, half picture, in stone and metal. Some, as did the author, called it peculiarly Cornish, and he could see generic fragments of the illustrations in Soloma's slate engravings.

The other occupation was the second photograph sent by Zadie. The first had been confiscated by Soloma and was carefully propped against the mirror in her room. The second was strange. It showed what appeared to be some kind of very simple sketch, or characters, on a creamy white background with a light brown stripe across it. There was a suggestion of a smaller, darker circle in one corner. For the umpteenth time, Nathan tried to match it up with some form of cuneiform inscription or Soloma's engravings, but got nowhere.

Wednesday dawned and they set to clearing up outside before making the beds with freshly washed and ironed sheets. Nathan had recovered a moth-eaten sleeping bag which he hid behind the sofa, intending to offer Zadie his own room. He put out Soloma's nice frock and laid up the table before saying to her that he was "going down to the shop." She nodded and continued washing her hands under the taps.

Nathan had taken a while at the shop, not least because several villagers had wanted to talk about their memories of Mabel, express their condolences, and apologise that they could not be at the funeral. He was not really surprised at this and had not counted on there being more than a handful coming, although Lucinda, Martyn and Kelvin were a powerful enough combination to make sure that everyone knew.

Outside his front door he put down the bags and opened it quietly. There was a sobbing coming from inside. No, it was more of a retching, and a smell of sick was permeating through the house. He ran through the sitting room and found Soloma in a heap under the kitchen sink. There was sick by her side and she was vomiting again into a mess of tablecloth and crockery and cutlery that had been pulled from the table. The empty bottle of red wine that he had left to breathe had come to rest in the debris and, remarkably, there were still two glasses half full on the far side of the table. Good, she hadn't drunk the whole bottle then, thought Nathan, as he rolled her into the recovery position and checked that her tongue wasn't blocking any further vomit.

It was at this moment that a voice from the front door called out, "Hello. Anyone at home?"

It wasn't exactly the meeting that he had desired with Zadie but it said much for her that she didn't flinch from mucking in, and two rather messy hours later they had Soloma cleaned and sleeping peacefully in her bed. They took turns to look in on her whilst tackling the kitchen and consigning much of Nathan's best crockery to the bin. By the time they were satisfied that the little girl was out of danger it was truly dark, and they sat talking late into the night.

"How did you find me?" Nathan asked.

"Oh, easy," said Zadie. "I went to the village shop and said I was writing an article about rocks and was there anybody in the village who could tell me about the local ones."

Nathan smiled. "So what are you doing for work?"

"I'm off to Cyprus for a six month excavation in a few weeks. It should be a nice winter out there, and I might even find some Phoenician pieces."

And they fell to talking about Soloma, and Mabel, and the funeral the next day, and then Soloma a bit more. In the end, they both fell asleep in the armchairs and didn't wake until the chickens were clacking noisily at the new day.

Chapter 8   A Funeral

The little church nestled in the valley with its stubby, short steeple of heavy, local slates pointing diffidently heavenward and the dry-stone wall enclosing a sloping graveyard. The wrought iron gates had been pinned back for the funeral and Nathan saw that someone had put a bunch of freshly picked scabious on the ledge under the old lych gate. He trod the uneven path to the sheltered porch and pushed open the heavy door, hewn from some unsuspecting oak, already old 800 years before when it was made by some forgotten craftsman. There were seven pews on either side of the aisle and a short transept that was more an obligation to the cruciform plan than a feature of significance. Beyond was the squared apse with its altar table and big brass candlesticks framing the narrow stained glass windows. To the left was the old septagonal preachers' pulpit, with its wooden steps up and sounding board above.

Lucinda had been before him and put out some orders of service on the pews. They had agreed not to follow the coffin in and he settled in the second pew back, leaving the front one for her. Ahead of him was the great lectern, its wings spread rather than furled. It was old – cast in bronze rather than Victorian brass – and the sunlight caught the copper in it. At some point its eagle's head had been damaged and replaced with something that looked more akin to a seagull's head – presumably more familiar to the local artisan who undertook the work. Around the dark plinth at its base the faded letters of a verse from Isaiah would be just visible he knew, without needing to look.

This had been the church that his grandfather had preached in each summer when Nathan had come to stay with them as a boy in the bungalow and the local minister had been on furlough. In those days there had been morning and evening services and the kneeling hassocks that he glanced down at had still seemed freshly embroidered in honour of the Coronation. His grandfather had drawn a full congregation, and a strange one. Once, he remembered an elderly couple driving down from the moors in a horse and trap and tethering it outside, largely blocking the lane for the duration of the service. They had sat bolt upright throughout, except when they knelt to pray, and had put two silver sixpences in the collection plate. Since their home was distant, they had been invited to Sunday lunch at the bungalow, before attending the evening service and driving back in the twilight. Nathan had been terrified of their propriety, although usually he enjoyed the strange visitors that dropped in to the bungalow during the summer.

One service stuck in his mind. Normally he was excused the evening service, being deemed to be too young and left with his grandmother, but on this occasion he had been scrubbed, brushed, and dressed up to go with her. Some had come on foot a fair way and he had sat at the back of the full church with her and was made to shake many hands, some gnarled and crushing, as the congregation greeted his grandmother. He had felt like an exhibit. The sermon had seemed interminable – stretching from Adam to the archangel's last trump – and he had nearly finished the second fruit pastille (sucked slowly, not chewed) when his grandfather had taken the big, gold pocket-watch that had been given to him by his father out of his waistcoat, unbuttoning its gold chain and laying it over the edge of the pulpit so that it dangled in front of the congregation.

"You do not know the hour," the slightly quavering voice had said with the utmost conviction so that it carried into every corner of mind and building; and he had reached beneath the pulpit for a dandelion with seeds on it and, raising it to his face, he repeated, "I tell you" … (puff) … "you do not know" … (puff) … "the hour" … (puff), scattering the airy white seeds so that they floated through beams of light dissembled by the stained glass into their constituent colours and drifted in changing hues across the heads of the upturned faces as he caught their eyes one by one. In the tangible silence, he had sat down and the organist had struck up, 'The day thou gavest Lord has ended, The darkness falls at thy behest …' and, as the congregation launched into the hymn, his grandmother's hand had led him out through the old oak door and the small graveyard. She had been singing quietly as she went "…while earth rolls onward into light…" and as they reached the wrought iron gates she was on the last verse "…like earth's proud empires pass away." He had fallen asleep almost as soon as they were back at the bungalow but had been distantly aware in his dreams of voices talking late.

The door creaked open with a practised reticence that no touch of oil could dispel and Lucinda entered with the young priest who was looking after several parishes over the summer. The young man apologised that the churchwarden was away and that there might not be an organist, so they had chosen a couple of well-known hymns. He took the arrangement of flowers that Lucinda was carrying and placed them on the altar table before helping the undertaker to set up the trestle in front of it and cover it with a dark green drape. Lucinda sat in the front pew and turned to Nathan after a few moments silence.

"Nice flowers," he said. "Are they from your garden?"

They were an unusual mixture of gladioli and crocosmia and old-fashioned fragrant roses, but they worked well together and the arrangement had been constructed with love.

"Yes," she replied.

"How many are you expecting?"

"Not many," came the response. "Look," said Lucinda, "come and see me soon."

"I will," said Nathan, and then they fell to their own thoughts. He looked at the cover of the order of service which said simply:

Mabel

Died 26th August 2006

Occasionally, the door creaked, and Nathan moved along the pew as Zadie and Soloma slid in beside him. Lucinda turned and kissed the little girl. There was a particularly loud creak and Nathan looked round, surprised to see a dozen or more faces scattered through the pews. There was the old farmer and his wife who kept the cows that Soloma liked to watch in the field next door. The wife smiled briefly, uncertain whether it was proper at a funeral, whilst the husband kept his face unchanged. His wrinkles showed the battering of the years and the dark suit that he was wearing had also taken a battering, its black cloth having that greenish tinge of age and the high triangular lapels speaking of a brief period of fashion in the 1950s. Nathan wondered if he had been married in it. There were the Trevelyns over on the other side, and the farmer next door to Little Vennick, and several other elderly faces that he knew by sight; Martyn the Post was there with his wife. There was also a young man, more brightly dressed, probably on holiday – and there in the back pew was Wilf, dressed as Nathan had never seen him in a tie and what passed for a jacket. That explained the loud creak then, as the pew had objected to its unexpected burden. It looked like they had found an organist as well, as he glimpsed the shock of long, white hair settling on the organ stool at the back of the church and the long fingers, slendered with age, reaching out to touch the stops.

The priest was at the door and the congregation stood slowly. He processed down the aisle reading 'words of comfort' from the prayer book but with a formality that deadened love and hope. Behind him came the pallbearers with the wooden coffin and its brass fittings, a single red gladioli and a card on top. Nathan was taken aback by how small the coffin was when they set it on the trestle. He recognised the pallbearers – local farm-hands, any one of whom could have tucked the coffin under his arm and carried it alone.

The minister began the service, seemingly perplexed as he looked up and the organ began its introit to 'Crimmond' and the congregation sang 'The Lord's my shepherd' with more heart than he had imagined. He spoke briefly but well when it came to the eulogy and Nathan recognised some of the comments that Lucinda must have assembled. Soon, they had risen and were singing again, the organ gathering in throat and feeling:

> 'Abide with me; fast falls the eventide;
> The darkness deepens; Lord, with me abide
> When other helpers fail, and comforts flee,
> Help of the helpless. O abide with me.'

The pallbearers had the coffin on their shoulders now and were slowly turning to follow the priest …

> 'Swift to its close ebbs out life's little day;
> Earth's joys grow dim, its glories pass away;
> Change and decay in all around I see:
> O Thou who changes not, abide with me.'

… and, as they drew opposite Nathan's pew, they paused to adjust their feet. Soloma reached out to stroke the coffin, then stood on the pew, and gently placed the piece of white coral strung with garden twine next to the red gladioli on its lid …

> 'I need Thy presence every passing hour;
> What but Thy grace can foil the tempter's power?
> Who like Thyself my guide and stay can be?
> Through cloud and sunshine, O abide with me.'

… Lucinda had exited her pew to follow the coffin and Soloma stepped forward to go by her side, instinctively holding her hand. It seemed entirely natural that Nathan should grasp Zadie's hand as they stepped out and followed them …

> 'I fear no foe, with Thee at hand to bless;
> Ills have no weight, and tears no bitterness;
> Where is death's sting? where, grave, thy victory?
> I triumph still, if Thou abide with me.'

… The congregation were following as the bearers

stooped awkwardly beneath the low, arched doorway, built when
malnutrition and uncertainty of life had rendered five feet a good
height for an adult …

> 'Hold Thou Thy cross before my closing eyes,
> Shine through the gloom, and point me to the skies;
> Heaven's morning breaks, and earth's vain shadows flee:
> In life, in death, O Lord, abide with me.'

They had ground to a halt and the bearers were manoeuvring the
coffin around an open grave. Nathan was surprised, as this was an
old-established family area, and he looked at the headstone of the
opened grave. It read:

> Captain David Vennick
> Born November 1st 1919
> Died 1941
>
> May he find peace in God

He could glimpse a plaque of dull, discoloured brass beneath the
thin covering of earth.

They were all assembled now and the priest took a breath to
begin the burial, when suddenly the organ burst into life. It wasn't
a dull, muted, plaintive sound but a deep throbbing that could
be felt as much as heard as, one after another, the great sixteen
foot pipes came into play, like a creature released from decades
of incarceration and indifference, and stop after stop opened up,
moving from one crescendo to another. The old raven fluttered
from her sanctuary in the large yew tree nearby, her head feathers
greyed with age, and alighted on the spire, while the seagulls
wheeled in silence and a voice, clear and powerful, intermittently
drowned by the music, carried to them:

> "And did those feet in ancient times
> Walk upon Cornwall's mountains green?..."

And they stood, waiting … and there it came again …

> "And was Jerusalem builded here
> Among these dark satanic mines? …"

And again …

> "Bring me my bow of burning bronze …
>
> … Til we have built Jerusalem
> In Cornwall's green and pleasant land."

And they waited longer as the organ reached and over-reached itself to its final crescendo and the silence reverberated around the little churchyard.

A gull squawked, and the young priest bowed his head and began.

After the burial was over Lucinda was talking to the farmers by the Lych gate as they returned to their daily tasks. Wilf had given Nathan a hug across his shoulders that left his bones objecting, and told him that the tin was OK and that he didn't owe him anything. His parting comment was, "Be careful." Meanwhile, Zadie had taken Soloma back to the bungalow and Nathan found a tall, elderly figure with flowing white hair down to his shoulders and an equally impressive moustache by his side.

"She thought a lot of you, Nathan. Don't let her down when she needs you. And … I'm glad I missed you."

It all sounded a bit rambling and Nathan wasn't paying full attention but he thanked the old man for playing the organ, and turned away from the grave.

After a few paces, he found the priest rushing up in his everyday clothes and saying, "Where did you find that organist? He was brilliant; wonderful."

"Nothing to do with me," answered Nathan. "Try Lucinda. And, thanks for the service."

He glanced again at the grave and plodded back up the path. They had all gone now, he thought. So had Mabel.

His hand was on the wrought iron gate when an unfamiliar voice said from beyond it, "Excuse me, could I have a word?"

He was a young man, casually dressed and clean shaven, with a small Maple-leaf emblem in his shirt lapel. Nathan recognised him as having sat in the back left pew at the funeral.

"So, why were you at Mabel's funeral?" he asked.

"I'd hoped to meet up with you," came the answer. "You are Nathan, aren't you? And you are interested in rocks?"

Two nods were sufficient response.

"Look, I'm trying to trace my family history. I'm flying back to Canada on Sunday. I know it's a bad time, but if I could just have a few moments …" continued the stranger.

Nathan sighed and gestured towards the bench by the church gate, moving a few empty cans before sitting down.

"OK, what do you want?"

The stranger began, "My name is James Heal and I believe my father lived in North Cornwall … and that he knew someone called Nathan before he left for Canada … I've been working my way from village to village, asking."

"I never knew anyone by the name of Heal," said Nathan contemplatively. "Have you tried checking the parish registers?"

"Yes. Every one I come across; but there are gaps, and I'm not sure that Heal was the original name."

There was something vaguely familiar about the stranger and Nathan asked, "What was your father's name?"

"Mark," replied the young man.

Nathan thought for a while and then observed, "He would have had to have married very young for you to be his son." He thought again and asked a question that would be less unusual to a foreigner, "Can I see your passport?"

The young man reached into a pocket and passed it across. Nathan flicked it open to the personal details. The picture was younger and more evocative of the face he had in mind and, as he scanned the page, he probed further, "Exactly what do you know about your father's arrival in Canada?"

"Not a lot," replied James. "He was young, maybe eighteen. He bought a farm in the Prairies and married a local girl. She was young too and I was born to them before either were twenty. My mother died in childbirth with the second child … we were too remote and couldn't get help in time. My father continued with the farm, but it was too much for him on his own and he became ill. I was in my teens and tried to work it myself. Eventually he became delirious. There were moments when he seemed sanguine and he murmured about Cornwall, and rocks, and Nathan. I sold the farm to fund myself through university and I have a degree now. I came over here for an interview into a research post, although the part-funding for the flight was the biggest attraction."

Nathan was still sitting silently. If he was wrong he could hurt this young man greatly and so, after a long pause, he responded, "James, was there any particular place name that your father mentioned when he was talking about Cornwall?"

Now James paused before replying, "Yes. There were several. There was something about a Lion rock, and a coral cave – and somewhere called Polgod. I've never been able to find any of them on a map."

Nathan sighed again. "And what do you make of your middle name, James Curgen Heal?" he read out loud.

"Only that it was a family name of my mother's."

Nathan began slowly, "I once knew a Mark Curgen. He was younger than me but left school at age fourteen to work on the farms around here. There wasn't much money in it and he falsified his age to emigrate to Canada on a free passage. His parents were elderly and lived in the village. She was a Curgen, and I never knew his surname. I don't think he came from around here as he spoke with a thick accent. You'll find the Curgen graves just up the slope from the Vennicks," he added.

Somewhat unwillingly he gave his phone number, and watched the young man go back through the gate to the graveyard before he headed off quickly to the bungalow. Perhaps he should have said less or more to him: there had been other reasons for

Mark to leave, and his old parents had died heartbroken within two years of his departure.

Zadie looked enquiringly as he came in and he said, "Tell you later." Soloma was twirling in her frock and he smiled as he bent to kiss her.

"We've got some kind of dinner together," said Zadie.

Later, they sat talking, with Soloma curled up in front of the fire until Zadie carried her through to bed. It had been a long day and Nathan was snoring while Zadie was still in mid-sentence. She let him rest and turned to reading for a while.

Chapter 9   Iglos

"This book is amazing," said Zadie the next morning, "and so are these slates of Soloma's. There's so much that is original, and you can see it coming through in the traces of what is left today. Look at the figure for 5, for instance, and the lack of an F or U. I'm going to copy some of these runes onto slates and see what she makes of them."

"Zadie," said Nathan softly, "she's not a living experiment: she's just a little girl," and they both stopped and leant on the kitchen sink, watching her picking and washing carrots. "That's unusual. I think you might be about to get a surprise breakfast."

"Why?"

"Well, normally," continued Nathan, "she picks and eats them one by one, but she's got a handful now. In fact, you might be about to get some raspberries and eggs to go with them. Do the best you can," he chortled, "I'll put the frying pan on for the eggs and make you a cup of tea – Soloma likes one too," and sure enough, a few minutes later it looked very much like Soloma was trying to teach Zadie how to eat a raw carrot from tip to top. Nathan had the eggs frying and asked in mock seriousness, "Do you think there is a rune for raspberry?" as he put two cups of tea on the table and slurped from his own. Soloma said, "Thank you," and Nathan replied; he had learnt a little of Soloma's language as they had made words together and talked about common objects.

Zadie was impressed and pushed the raspberries to one side of her plate before tackling the egg and asking, "So what other words do you know?"

"A few dozen or so," said Nathan: greeting and farewell; a few commands like give and stop; and a smattering of nouns – water, sky, cloud, food, girl. Look," he continued, "it's a lovely morning. Let's go for a walk and then you can spend the afternoon exploring the sounds and words with Soloma."

They took the back paths to the cliff top and Soloma was enjoying trying out words on Zadie. It was almost the end of the season and there were spaces in the car park as well as the beach below. Waves were curling majestically, seeming to hover at an impossible angle of curl before propelling the body surfers forward. A creamy froth of bubbles next to the cliff marked the line of an evil undertow that dragged out past the Lion rock. It wasn't long before Soloma was seated on 'pulpit rock', looking along the cliffs and out to sea.

"She seems very content," said Zadie. "What's she looking at?"

"Yes," said Nathan, answering the first comment, "she would sit here for hours if you let her." After a while, he continued, "I think she's looking out towards her home. She looks along the cliffs until she sees the chimney rock at Polgodoc, then out to sea to Gulland, then beyond, then back round to the Lion rock; then she starts again."

"Come," said Nathan to Soloma in her own language, and soon they were walking back through the last of the ladies' slipper and long-dried, tassel-heads of thrift to the bungalow. Nathan was glad of the chance to spend some time clearing up and assembling various items that he had obtained, or had in stock, while Zadie sat on the verandah exploring slates and sounds with Soloma. Nathan noticed without particular regret that the book on cuneiform and runes had found its way into Zadie's possession. He didn't mind but would like to have had time to peruse some of the other chapters in it; the one on oral myths, legends and traditions had caught his eye as a chapter heading.

That evening they were in the sitting room. Soloma had pointed firmly at the open grate and said, "Fire," to Nathan in a manner that suggested he should lay one up for their guest. Now she was feeding it economically and carefully to make sure the wood blazed well but was not consumed too rapidly. Nathan had brought out a cider bottle and Soloma had appeared with two glasses and, somewhat hesitantly, with a third. He nodded at her and smiled.

"I have to go back tomorrow," Zadie was saying. "I have a preliminary team meeting about the archaeological dig on Sunday and then about two weeks before we are off. I'll be away six months."

"She wants to go home," said Nathan blankly. "She's pining for it. Look at the way she sits up on that rock and looks out to sea."

"Maybe," said Zadie.

"Besides which, she can't go with you, and I need to be in the university department in two weeks. She can't stay here on her own. Mabel's dead and, anyway, a child around in term time but not at school starts raising questions …"

"What about Lucinda?"

It was Nathan's turn to say, "Maybe." He went on, "I tell you what. We can walk into Padstow with you in the morning for you to catch the coach – I need a few things there – and I'll go round to visit Lucinda in the afternoon and see what she says. But I'll need a contact number to let you know."

They discussed the details further and the conversation ended with Nathan saying, "…and so if she does want to go back, will you help me take her there?"

"Yes," answered Zadie with the very slightest hesitation. "By the way, where is there?"

"I'm not entirely sure. It's beyond Gulland some way. It must be before the ice sheet – although the rock that she was particularly interested in was a white coral, and the nearest piece in that direction is in the Caribbean."

"Hmm, could take a while on foot," observed Zadie laconically, "and not exactly in the right direction for Cyprus. I suppose it would mean going back through the cave." It wasn't so much a question as a rather reticent observation on Zadie's behalf. "That cave has resulted in me being nearly strangled by copper bonds; being burnt; nearly being eaten by wild animals; and nearly losing my mind."

"Yes," said Nathan. There wasn't much else that he could say.

"I'll take her on my own, if I need to, and if Lucinda hasn't got a solution, but if you do come you might want this," and he rummaged in a package that Martyn had delivered some few days ago, although it seemed an age past, and produced two lumps of silvery-grey shiny rock. He gave one to her.

"Tin, I suppose," she ventured.

"Yes," he answered, "and it's Cornish."

"Are you sure about that?"

"As sure as I can be. Sure enough for me to use the other one, anyway. After all, I haven't got much choice, have I?"

"But you will try Lucinda first?"

"Yes, I will."

"And you'll text me?"

"Ah, probably a message. I don't think texting is an option," he said, pointing to the bakelite phone with its metal ring of numbers.

"Well, if we have to do it, make it Tuesday. Time is running out." As if the matter was settled, she changed topics and asked, "What did you make of the photograph I sent you?"

"Oh, it was very nice," Nathan stammered, caught off guard. "Actually, Soloma has it on the dressing table in her room. She recognised you straight away."

He felt he was digging a hole for himself. A face looked round from the fire and smiled.

"No," pursued Zadie. "What about the other photograph? The one with the writing on it?"

Nathan looked blank. He had thought that it might be an inscription but hadn't been able to make out any letters. He reached behind him, unearthing it from beneath the discarded package from Wilf and De la Beche's book.

"I couldn't make out any writing," he admitted honestly, "and I didn't make anything of the stone it was etched into either."

Zadie dissolved into laughter. "Have you tried looking at it in a mirror?"

"A mirror?" he echoed.

"Yes. It's a silvery thing that shows a reflection of people – or objects."

"No." Then, rising to the bait, he objected, "Why should I look at it in a mirror?"

She was ready for him before he had finished. "Because the letters are from my copper key. It's what the token burnt onto me. That's why I plunged into the water in the cave. It's a reverse image. And, incidentally, that's not stone in the background – it's my flesh."

Nathan sat in bewildered silence, looking at Zadie and contemplating the depth of the hole into which he had lowered himself.

"Here. Let me show you," and she plucked the photograph from his hand and held it in front of the mirror over the mantelpiece, waiting for him to join her. Soloma stood up as well, as they copied out the cuneiform writing:

IGLOS

MENEVR

They were still looking at it when Soloma pointed and said, "Iglos!"

Half an hour later they hadn't managed to gain any real meaning of the word from Soloma. Clearly, she recognised it and it made her happy. The best they could do was something connected to birds in the air. Questions led to diverging lines of thought and no further progress. Eventually, all three embraced in a hug before retiring to bed or, in Nathan's case, the moth-eaten sleeping bag.

Chapter 10　　　An interview with Lucinda

Footpaths were often shorter than roads in Cornwall and it was barely thirty minutes before the three figures were climbing over the style near Fentonluna Lane and heading down towards the harbour at Padstow, where Nathan bought three pasties. They munched them for a late breakfast as they walked slowly towards the car park by the old railway station and Zadie's ten o'clock coach to London. She waited until the last minute before hugging them both and boarding.

Her parting comment to Nathan had been, "I'll pick up your message tomorrow evening and come down overnight on Monday, if I need to: the coach arrives at 8am and I'll be at Polgodoc by nine, ten at the latest."

He had nodded and waved as the coach drew away, before heading down the quay with Soloma to a camping store and making a few purchases. Prices were coming down rapidly now and there were very few customers.

The walk back was leisurely and it was just after noon when they made their way past the church to Lucinda's house. Rain was in the air and the clouds were scudding across but it was warm enough out of the wind and Nathan reckoned it would hold off until tea time. "Pull," he said to Soloma, pointing to the chain hanging from a pewter bell in the porch of Lucinda's house, and Soloma did so, delighting in the noise and repeating the action several times until they stepped back from the porch and watched for movement. It was a much bigger house than Nathan's, solidly built of fashioned slate with stone mullioned windows inset and two pairs of chimney stacks at either end, crowned with their tent-like arrangement of sloping slates to deter seagulls from depositing directly down the chimney and aligned so that the prevailing wind would not suck all the warmth out of the house during the winter months. Nathan wondered idly who had built the house and when, as he looked across the ample slate drive towards the white-washed garage and then around the garden. He knew that the garage would contain Lucinda's ancient Austin Cambridge, complete with roll-down hood – a rare convertible; what was even more surprising was that it continued to survive Lucinda's driving and the occasional dry-stone walls that had apparently leapt out in front of it to dent its honour, quite apart from other road users. Perhaps it was so distinctive that they automatically gave deference to it and the still attractive features of the elderly female behind its wheel. The garden was large – large enough for a dozen holiday cottages if ever it was 'developed' – and was Lucinda's pride and joy. Even now, it was full of colour and scent: hollyhocks waved at him from the corner of the house; the big patch of sedum beyond was beginning to turn russet; achillea flaunted their heads of faded gold the size of dinner plates in the lee of the wall; and climbing roses still bore witness to the last of the summer, cascading their blossoms in fragrant nonchalance.

"Come on," said Nathan, grasping Soloma's hand. "Maybe she's round the back."

As they rounded the corner they saw Lucinda's still blond hair between an impressive bank of gladioli. She was sitting in the intermittent sunshine, out of the wind, at a wrought iron table on which there was a bottle of cider and two glasses.

"Expecting company?" called out Nathan.

Soloma ran over to her as she exclaimed, "Nathan, dear, do come and sit down; I've been wanting to see you. No, I wasn't expecting company – it's just that it's Saturday: Martyn used to visit Mabel at the beginning of his round and bring her down here in the post-van. I guess I'll get out of the habit eventually."

Nathan smiled at the thought of Mabel bouncing down her rutted track in the post-van and kissed Lucinda in a social way before saying, "I think you did jolly well at the funeral; the flowers were just right … and so was the organist: I wasn't expecting that."

Lucinda offered Nathan a glass and for once he wasn't in a hurry and didn't decline. Soloma looked over hopefully and

Lucinda chuckled and retreated inside, re-emerging with another glass and half-filling it.

"Actually," she said, "I was surprised to see him. I thought he had been dead twenty years. We used to call him Goldilocks when we were young – he had golden blond hair down to his shoulders. Martyn must have known where he was and given a message to him. I haven't heard the organ played like that since your grandfather preached; I thought we would be singing without music." Turning her gaze to Soloma, she added, "That was lovely of you to put the coral on the coffin, dear."

Soloma looked across and smiled.

Lucinda was in loquacious mood, although it appeared from the bottle that she had only recently poured a glass of cider, and Nathan found the conversation flowing in disjointed fashion with only short responses needed from him. He was waiting for an opportunity to ask about Soloma and he decided on an indirect approach, as Lucinda paused to sip her drink.

"Lucinda, what do you know about Polgodoc?"

The reaction was unexpected as she put down her glass and looked straight at him.

"How do you know that name?"

"My grandfather," he said. "I've always known the name."

"Well," she said slowly, "perhaps he was wise. There's not many that use that name; very few now."

"Why is it not on the Ordnance Survey map?" he questioned.

"Because we didn't tell them when they made the maps."

"Who is we?"

"The old families; much older than Prideaux Place. There are only two left now, but then there were more. Some were not from these parts, some were. It goes back a long way."

"What's so important about a name?"

"It's not just the name, it's the place." She was considering him carefully. "What do you understand by it, Nathan?"

He had over-stepped the mark and was feeling awkward.

Shortly, he answered, "Pol means the place of ... and Godoc I took to be some old saint or family group, so 'the place of Godoc'. Look, I didn't mean to cause offence. I'm sorry."

"You don't need to apologise, Nathan. Clearly your grandfather didn't tell you everything. Listen: it can also mean 'the place possessed by'. The old saints adopted older names. So, 'Petroc' could mean 'possessed by Peter', or 'Peter's possession', or 'in allegiance to Peter' – not in terms of worship but more of pledging ... and 'oc' could be singular, unlike 'ick', as in Trebetherick, which could refer to a group."

"I'm not entirely following you."

"In very simple terms, 'Polgodoc' can be rendered 'the place of god's possessions', or 'the place possessed by god'. I shouldn't tell you this, Nathan, but soon you'll be the oldest family in the village."

His mind was racing to digest several pieces of information at once. Lucinda's interpretation of 'Polgodoc' was unsettling and he determined not to tell Zadie about it until he had time to think it over. Instead, he pursued the latest unexpected statement.

"I don't understand you, Lucinda. There are no Peters in the graveyard. I've checked the parish register and there are no records of my father, or any other Peters. How could I be here longer than you?"

"Names change. Mine is Lucinda Venn, as you know. It was not always so. People come and go ... not many ... and sometimes it skips two or three generations ... always when times are difficult – you'll know the time; you'll see." She seemed to be rambling now and said, "Peters was not always your surname – at least, not your original one. Your great-grandfather changed your grandfather's name when he was younger than Soloma."

"Why? What was the original name?" interjected Nathan.

"There was a rift between the families – I'm not sure why – it was before my time. The original name was Petrocks, or Petrox. Spelling was a bit haphazard then, and it didn't matter so much as everyone knew everyone. You'll find the Petrox' graves in the higher part of the cemetery ... the opposite end to the Vennicks'.

If you look in the register you'll find your grandfather's baptism recorded."

His mind whirled and he stammered, "Why didn't my grandfather go back to the old name? Why didn't he stay in the village?"

"He went into the church and the vacancy for this living came up while he was still in ordination. There was nothing else local and he took a parish in the Midlands. But he came back each summer and kept the bungalow. His son – your father – met a local girl there and they married. Mabel and I went up to the wedding … some awful town producing motor cars and straw hats. They visited here seldom. He might have settled but your mother was a city girl: it was too quiet for her and didn't have the things she wanted – always new things and new fashions."

"I've never seen a picture of the wedding," said Nathan, "at least, not since I was little."

"Nor have I," said Lucinda. "They were all lost in the fire when your parents died. You were in Australia at the time. Then your grandfather died from the shock of it all. It was weeks before you were back."

"I know," said Nathan slowly. He recalled how he had been working his way through some very ancient geology west of Alice Springs. He had tuned to the World Service to try to hear the previous day's football results and the crackly tones of the BBC voice had come through on the battered radio, 'This is an urgent message for Nathan Peters. Would Mr. Nathan Peters, believed to be travelling in central Australia, please contact the nearest police post. This is the end of the urgent message.' And the crackling voice had faded again. It had taken him two days to reach an outback police post, and another day before the officer returned and could make any sense of his presence. There had been the kit to see to and the landrover to return, and a long rail journey on The Ghan to Adelaide; after that, a further journey to Sydney and a re-arranged ticket home with no funds. The funerals had long been over and he had ended up coming down to the bungalow as there was nowhere else for him to stay.

"Mabel and I went up to sort things out," continued Lucinda, breaking into Nathan's memories. "We had to stay in some tacky, modern hotel for a week. We tried to obtain your grandfather's body for burial in Trevennick, but the nursing home wouldn't release it to us. At least he had put the bungalow in trust to you. Just as well, or it would have been sold to meet your parents' debts. They weren't insured or anything. Don't you know any of this?"

"No. Not really. I gleaned bits and pieces from the lawyer, and Martyn said the odd thing," he answered. "You and Mabel did an awful lot. You must miss her. Did she grow up in the village with you?"

"Yes, I miss her," replied Lucinda, "but I didn't know her until I was in my teens. She was not from these parts. In fact, her arrival caused quite a stir in the village ... she took up with David Vennick ... the war was coming and they wanted to get married. His grandfather didn't approve and threw them out of the big house. They moved into the farmhouse at Little Vennick, where she's lived ever since. All that's left of the estate now," she added, "grandfather left the rest to the church: they kept most of the money and built the organ as a gesture for the village."

She was quiet now, and Nathan asked, "Did you know David Vennick, Lucinda?"

"Yes," and the eyes filled with tears as she went on, "he was my brother."

Soloma had refilled Lucinda's glass and was sitting by her. It was some time before Nathan broke the silence again.

"Lucinda, I'm sorry; I knew none of this."

"There was no need for you to do so," replied Lucinda, regaining her composure. "Anyway, what are you going to do about Soloma? You'll be back at work in a few days, and she can't stay on her own."

"I was going to ask your advice," answered Nathan honestly, "I wondered if – "

"Of course, she could stay here," interrupted Lucinda to the unfinished question, "but there will be questions asked as to why she is not at school ... and, does she really want to?"

"I'm not sure. I think she might be pining."

"…for home?"

"Yes," he said deliberately, meeting Lucinda's penetrating gaze.

"I tell you what, Nathan. Why don't you sit here a while and we'll gather some flowers and take them over to the grave. I'll see what I can find out."

"Do you understand her, then?"

Lucinda smiled. "Some. Not as well as Mabel, but some" … and it seemed like a secret had been exchanged, if not several.

He waited as the little girl and the elegant old lady pottered round the garden. Soloma was doing most of the selecting of flowers and Lucinda was snipping them neatly with her secateurs and laying them carefully in a straw basket that hung over her arm. They went through the private gate into the graveyard next door and Nathan could see their heads bobbing amongst the graves. The old raven was watching from the church roof.

It was a while before they came back and Nathan was thinking that he might go to the morning service, and look for the Petrox graves afterwards. He had much to consider from what Lucinda had said and was still lost in his thoughts when he was surprised from behind and Lucinda sat down beside him. Soloma went off to smell the flowers.

"I think she wants to go back, Nathan," said Lucinda. "There was quite a bit that I didn't understand, and she kept saying, 'Zadie come,' along with something about a lake."

"Zadie was the girl with me at the funeral."

"I guessed as much."

"She didn't say anything about where home was, did she?" asked Nathan.

"Not exactly," replied Lucinda, "and, by the sound of it, you know much more about Polgodoc and what lies beyond than I do."

"You never explored with Mabel, then?"

"No. Not allowed. It was a one way door for Mabel, and for any adult who chose to come here. Something special was needed

to go the other way. Hasn't been done for two generations until….
Anyway, I think a child could." She thought for a while, stretching
her mind back over the bedside stories that her grandmother had
told her, and then added, "The only thing I can tell you is that
Mabel loved white coral."

Then she rose, saying, "Wait here a moment."

It was quite a time before she returned, carrying something
small but heavy. It was rectangular and about the size of an egg
box.

"Here," she said, placing it on the wrought iron table.
"Mabel said that if anything happened to her, you were to have
this. It took me a long while to find it up at Little Vennick."

He picked it up. It was certainly heavy for its size. It
looked like it might be made from half an inch of solid smelted tin.
There was a slight indent running all the way round it and no sign
of any hinges.

"Do you know what it is?"

"No – only that it was important to her," replied Lucinda
and, not for the first time that afternoon, Nathan felt that he wasn't
being given an entirely full story.

"Anyway, take it back with you and look after it. Soloma's
coming now and I must start thinking about supper," said Lucinda,
almost as if an interview had ended. And they found themselves
ushered out of the garden and walking the short distance back to
the bungalow.

Chapter 11   An Unexpected Challenge

The promised rain had blown through overnight and he decided against church; it would be too confusing to try to explain the service to Soloma. So they went for a long walk: up to Little Vennick; across the high fields with their distant views of the moors towards Bodmin; along the ridge with its glimpses of the estuary; and down again until the open cliff-top that led to pulpit rock. She was looking out to sea again and he said, "Soon, Soloma. Soon you'll be going home."

He had left a message for Zadie and it was much later that evening, after Soloma was asleep, when he picked up the tin box and turned it over, examining it carefully. There was nothing on it to indicate age or purpose, nor how to open it. He tried tugging, to no avail, and reached for a slim letter knife made from ebony wood. Slowly, he worked his way round the slight indentation in the sides of the box until he felt, rather than saw, a slight movement; it was another ten minutes until the indentation had opened to the thickness of the knife, and ten more before he gently prised off the lid.

Nathan gasped quietly. Inside was a wooden container made of some wood that he didn't recognise – possibly holly – beautifully polished and split into four compartments, each solid but with a fashioned recess. Three of them were empty and small pieces of India paper fixed to their bases had the faded lettering Sn, Cu, and C in them. In the fourth was a beautiful stone, the very slightest bit opaque and with a bluish tinge to it, if it had any colour at all. At one end it had a small ring and a fine chain running through it. From the lack of tarnish, he knew before touching it that the chain would be gold, and he lifted it gently out of its cradle, peering at the label Aq beneath and resting it in the palm of his hand. It was a long while later that he put the lid back on the box and went to bed. He would dearly love to have spoken with

Mabel.

The next day was to be Soloma's last and they didn't stray far from the bungalow since the weather was in unsettled mode with a series of fronts streaming in from the Atlantic. Late in the afternoon he was packing things into his rucksack from various parts of the cottage and garage, when he became aware of Soloma standing behind him, watching. He stopped and looked at her, and reached under his bed for the old cloth bag. They took it through to her room and he stayed with her while she lifted out the clothes that she had first been wearing when Zadie had rescued her in the lake.

"Yes," said Nathan, "Tomorrow you are going home. We will have to start early. Zadie is coming too."

Soloma seemed settled as she ran her fingers over her old clothes and looked in the leather pouch at the sharp flints. Nathan didn't know how much she had understood but reckoned that the combination of the clothes, 'home', and 'Zadie coming' had gone a fair way. He lifted Mabel's suitcase from under the bed and pointed to Soloma, saying, "Hide your new clothes." When he looked back in, Soloma was changed and the new clothes neatly folded into the case with the pink pyjamas and silver hairbrush on top. He shut the case, putting the leather shoes by her and saying, "Keep these."

It was very late that evening when the phone rang. Nathan thought it would be Zadie saying that she was just leaving to catch the overnight coach and was surprised to hear an agitated Lucinda.

"Nathan, you don't listen to the television, do you?"

"No. I haven't got one of those. What's wrong?"

"It's the news. It was on the national news, as well as the local."

"What was, Lucinda?"

"Oh, it's very sad. Two little girls have gone missing. Aged 9 and 11. They were camping with their parents and went off to play nearby. Didn't turn up by supper time, and now it's dark early, of course."

"That's very sad, Lucinda," said Nathan, wondering why

she was so agitated. It was awful but these things happened. Maybe they would be found in the morning.

"Where were they?" he asked.

"That's just it," came the reply, "They were our side of Padstow."

"I'm very sorry, Lucinda, but I don't think I can help. There are others who would be much better at searching and I'm taking Soloma back in the morning."

"I know. That's just it, dear. She told me. Don't you see? They'll be mounting a full scale search operation at first light – coastguard helicopters; door to door enquiries…"

Nathan had gone very silent.

"Nathan, are you still there? I can't hear you."

"Yes, Lucinda, I'm here. I'm beginning to see the problem. A girl with no history … matching the age, and possibly appearance … enough people having heard things to interest the police in her … nowhere to hide … even Mabel's wouldn't be unsearched … and trying to get along an open cliff-top in the full view of a search and rescue operation. Yes, I'm beginning to see the problem."

"Good," said Lucinda's voice, "I thought you would. I just thought you ought to know."

"Thanks, Lucinda."

"Give Soloma my love, then … and, good luck."

The heavy clunk of the receiver echoed the heavy feeling in his heart.

He lay down, seriously thinking about waking Soloma and going now. The problem was he had no means of contacting Zadie. Perhaps he could leave her a note. That would look good though: 'Dear Z, have taken S; please follow!' What if it was found, or what if they had a night search out and were spotted? He was tossing and turning, worrying at the possibilities in his mind, until he unintentionally fell asleep.

A clatter of low helicopter blades passing overhead woke Nathan. "Blast!" It was seven o'clock already. He looked rapidly out of the window. At least the low cloud and rain showers might reduce the visibility and deter the dog-walkers. Suddenly, he felt a horrid pang as he thought of his wishes and the two missing little girls. Soloma and he would just have to take their chances.

They were out of the bungalow in fifteen minutes – and it looked like it. They cut through Lucinda's garden – she wouldn't mind – and climbed over the stone wall at the bottom, over the log spanning the stream and out of the wood and up a field, keeping to the landward side of another wall. Nathan blessed the builders of these big, old, dry-stone walls. His mind was racing ahead trying to think of lines of sight. It was also nagging away, pestering him with worry as to whether he had put everything he wanted in the heavy rucksack. They paused in a square, stone sheep pen. It was a high point and he could just make out the rescue helicopter moving very slowly up and down the Camel estuary in the distance. With the binoculars, the dots on a field near it separated into figures walking in a line towards the estuary; closer to them, there was a clutter of vehicles and more lines assembling, working back towards where the campsite was, covering the nearest ground first. There were dogs too.

No matter how his mind raced and worried there was no getting away from the fact that there were two, long, exposed sections ahead with no cover, easily visible from the sea or cliff path. Despite the urgency, he spent fully five minutes scanning the path for movement and looking for any sign of boats before he said, "Come on!" and they walked hurriedly across the open ground. Twenty minutes later they had made the comparative safety of a tangly thicket. He was breathing heavily and there was a curious look in Soloma's eyes.

"Fifteen minutes on the next stretch," said Nathan to her, "but there are sheep in the field. Let's hope they don't get spooked," and they moved more slowly trying not to disturb the grazing animals. They were half way across when he looked back and saw the roof of a distant landrover moving towards a gate in the wall behind them. Two minutes and it would be there. Another landrover was following. It was the coastguard one with its blue light on top. Nowhere to run to. They would be caught in the open. They moved more quickly. The animals were noticing them and had started moving too. That was a dead give-away. The first landrover was at the gate, stopping; figures were stepping over to open it. And then the rain came. It was heavy and horizontal, and he exclaimed thankfully as it soaked them – and cut the visibility – its blanket of condensing molecules wrapping them in obscurity. Wet and somewhat shaken, Nathan led Soloma into the first of two deep, narrow valleys before turning off into the hidden valley of Polgodoc.

They sheltered from the wind, visible only from the sea now. Soloma was playing with a discarded flip-flop, and he looked at his watch. "Eight-thirty," he said out loud, "Zadie should be here by nine," and they settled down for an uncomfortable wait. Several times he was convinced that his watch had stopped. Every moment dragged and he could feel his nerves increasingly on edge. He struggled to force his heart-beat down, sweating profusely. Each sound jangled and he started peering round the rocks to look landward. He couldn't be seen, but nor could he see. Soloma was becoming edgy now, catching his emotional state. Nine o'clock came and went and the watch crawled on to nine-fifteen ... nine-twenty. He had his binoculars out – not that they told him anything that he couldn't see with his eyes – and was looking every thirty seconds now. It was becoming a distraction, and he only caught the sound at the very last moment. It was a distinctive guttural throbbing, strengthening in the gusting wind.

"Soloma! Hide! Cave! Quickly! Cave! Hide!" he cried in alarm.

Soloma hesitated for a moment then plunged over the cliff, her black hair flying and, turning to bring his binoculars to bear on the pair of cormorants fishing below in pretence of an ordinary bird-watcher, he could feel his heart hammering in panic as the big, yellow Sea King lumbered slowly round the headland that had been shielding them from unwanted view. Had she understood? Had she made it in time? Would she stay put?

It was a magnificent piece of airmanship in the elderly helicopter – holding steady in the gusting wind barely ten feet above the wave tops that it was flattening with its downdraught and less than thirty feet from the cliffs. They must have called up every plane and pilot that could still fly; he hadn't seen one of these for years. The two spotters, harnessed in the open door, were searching the cliffs foot by foot and they saw him immediately. Nathan lowered his glasses. The machine was moving very slowly now, almost stationary, and he could make out the faces and expressions quite clearly. One of the figures seemed to be mouthing something at him and held his hands apart, as if in enquiry. Nathan waved an acknowledgement back and gave the thumbs down signal. Still the helicopter paused. At last, it was moving again – slowly, very slowly – resuming its foot by foot search and lingering a long while at the chimney rock, until it lumbered like an ungainly, airborne sea-lion round the next headland. He could still hear its throbbing, although he was beginning to hear the loudness of his heart-beat over it, when a voice said behind him, "Where is she?"

He spun round.

Chapter 12   **A Crown of Gold**

"Zadie!" he cried, and hugged her in relief.

They broke apart and Nathan said, "She's hiding in the adit. At least, that's where I hope she is. She would only just have reached it in time as the helicopter came round the headland."

"I saw it," said Zadie. "I was waiting until it had gone before turning off the main path. Sorry to be late, but Padstow's murder: all the traffic is being stopped in and out, and the drivers questioned; they're starting a big cliff-top search – with dogs."

"We'd better move," said Nathan, "Will you follow me down?"

She nodded, eager to see Soloma, and he lowered himself carefully over the cliff edge, feeling for the first foot and hand holds. They were slippery from the rain and the heavy rucksack was being battered by the wind. He paused, waiting for her to follow. Then he was off, and counting …sixteen, seventeen, eighteen … that was the last … step out and find the ledge, and turn cautiously with the rucksack. He stood, waiting. She was moving much more smoothly and had her hand and foot holds the right way round this time. Good … that would avoid such an awkward last step. At last she was there beside him.

"Dogs," she muttered, as she moved past him along the ledge, "Distant. Only heard them once."

There was a tremendous screech of delight. When he stuck his head into the narrow entrance to the old mine he could see Soloma and Zadie locked in embrace. There wasn't sufficient width for them to be side by side and Zadie's head was brushing the ceiling. Nathan pushed his rucksack in ahead of him on the uneven floor and was blocked from joining in the embrace by it, having to content himself with calling out, "Good girl!" and being rewarded by two sets of teeth flashing in smiles at him.

"We can't stop. We'll have to go on in the order we're in

here. Zadie, keep a hand near her at that gap, and watch your head when you jump," he called out.

If Zadie had misgivings about the place, it didn't show at first, and she prompted Soloma towards the dark, blank ending of the adit where the early miners had apparently given up their pursuit of the tin lode. Nathan was aware of progress in front of him. He had the best view with the light behind him and, although it was very dim now, he glimpsed two figures skip lightly in one case and half-jump in the other. He lobbed the rucksack across and it was Soloma who grabbed a buckle as it slid on the floor towards the water sloshing in the bottom of the chasm and dragged it into the furthest part of the recess. Nathan leapt and ducked and found the handhold, his fingers closing over Zadie's, and steadied himself. The sound of a dog echoed nearby and he was searching urgently in the confined space for the pocket that contained Wilf's chunk of tin. But Zadie was already hesitating with the other piece in her free hand and, whether for the love of the little girl or the joy of their reunion, the blank wall of rock had burst almost immediately into life. A great silvery vein stretched and widened before them, pulsating towards the small recess at its heart. Whatever hesitation Zadie had after her experience with the non-Cornish copper was overcome by Soloma taking the tin from her hand and thrusting it into the socket. The mother lode widened further and split, revealing the curving passage beyond, and they slipped through while it was still opening fully. The silvery veins were beginning to trace ahead along the walls and ceiling of the passage as Zadie and Soloma took a step forward.

However, Zadie's mind was beginning to throw dark nightmares of becoming unhinged in blackness, and she felt her fists balling up and her body tensing. It was as well that Nathan had determined not to tell her of Lucinda's interpretation of the place, or the old lore that no adult could return through it. Her first step slowed but she drew confidence from Soloma holding the tin in her open hand beside her and found her fears of entering a dark place in her mind diminished. The silvery light wasn't as glorious and majestic as the first time Nathan and Zadie had entered but it was light enough to see by. As Nathan reached back to drag the rucksack after him, he distinctly caught a half sentence blowing in the wind, "… fetch a rope, then …" Two steps later there was a solid clunk behind him. The rock door had sealed them in.

The other two were well into the cave of Polgodoc when Nathan reached the last step of the curving passage. He was still rummaging in his rucksack and they spun round at the hiss.

"Nathan, what are you doing?" demanded Zadie as he stuffed an aerosol can back in his pack.

"Nothing; just a dab of fluorescent paint," he answered guiltily.

Zadie took two steps towards him and, after a significant pause, contented herself with, "I'm not sure the rocks will let you get away with that."

"Alright, but this time let's check our bearings and count exits before we do anything else," he replied.

They took them from the massive slab of pure black slate in the middle of the cave. There were five openings on the side that they had come in on, facing the long side of the tabular slab, and they had come through the middle one. There were three facing the other long side of the slab, and the middle one had an empty bottle by it.

"Right, so that's agreed then – in middle, out middle."

"Yes," said Zadie, "Now, let's go."

He appreciated something of her dislike for the place but was still standing by the slab, opposite her.

"I want to use the map table."

"No."

"I want to see if Soloma can point out her home on it. It may save a lot of time," continued Nathan.

"You are not putting your bronze key, assuming you've brought it with you, in there. It's not tin and it's not copper. We'll probably all be attacked by both sets of rocks. I want to get out of this place."

"It may save time and danger," he reiterated. "Besides which, you have the copper key. You know the rocks accept it."

There was an intense struggle going on in Zadie's mind. Logic fought emotion, and fear was in conflict with love. Somewhere, curiosity was also rippling beneath the surface.

"It wouldn't take long," he chipped in to the battle.

Soloma edged from a neutral position very slightly towards Nathan and that small, physical movement finally seemed to tip the balance.

"Very well."

She came grudgingly to join him, reaching beneath her tunic and producing a gold chain, from which hung the copper token. It glittered in the silvery light and Soloma stood next to her, looking admiringly at it. The thing had always reassured her and, to some extent, comforted her.

Possibly thinking the same thoughts, Nathan said, "We still don't know what 'Iglos' means."

Soloma's gaze had been concentrated on the four lioness-like protrusions in the middle of the slab and she raised an arm, pointing and saying, "Iglos," and again; "Iglos there."

Zadie and Nathan looked at each other and the unspoken thought flashed between them. They might not understand what she meant but Soloma would not knowingly take them into danger.

"What do we do, then?" asked Zadie.

"Well, last time I think we were both leaning on the slab and it started resonating, and the clefts in the lionesses glowed – and he put one hand on the slab, caressing its smooth surface. It was Soloma's hand that his bumped into and, almost immediately, they were aware of the resonance echoing gently around the large cave. The clefts in the black lionesses glowed: silver – that was the one for the tin token that had become bronze and couldn't be used again; orange-red – that was the one he had tried the imitation copper in with disastrous results; translucent blue; and white.

There was a compulsion about the thing. The resonance was growing now. In fact it was beginning to be mildly dominant on the ears. In fact, more than that. They tried to step back from the table but were unable to do so. His hand and Soloma's were anchored to the slab by a strong force and despite all their tugging and pulling there was no release from it.

"Zadie," he said, trying to keep the rising panic out of his voice, "please put your copper token in the orange-red cleft."

She was undecided and delaying any movement. The noise was growing by the moment – a kind of growling resonance that was becoming painful and making it difficult to think. He wished that it would go away. He was desperate for it to cease. It was becoming more and more insistent, a series of roarings and growlings that were merging into an overwhelming sea of sound that excluded all else. If he could have freed his hands he would have crushed them against his ears to protect the drums that were threatening to burst. It wasn't just the sound; it was the great waves of pressure that were assaulting them.

"Zadie, put the token in!" he cried, "Please put the token in. We can't move! I'm losing my hearing!" and he saw rather than heard Soloma cry, "Please, Zadie."

Finally, that seemed to break through and Zadie shoved the token unceremoniously into the cleft. Nathan fell backwards, and Soloma on top of him, as the hands that they had been tugging at were suddenly released from the slab. As they got up the surface of the slate was bubbling and heaving and the deafening resonance had ceased. Instead, great bands of copper-red were extending across the ceiling of the cave and tracing down the walls, inter-linking with those spreading outwards from the base of the table; droplets of water fell and pools rippled in a mixture of molten setting suns and falling rubies. The veins grew richly and deeply, especially around the entrance next to the one that they had come in at and around the exit they sought. There they showed in overlapping archways, outlining the opening and beckoning into the passage beyond.

Meanwhile, the map table had formed – not the same as before – clearer inland and towards the moors, and down towards Camborne; less clear in other places; and, in many, still a flat, black slab. But there were definite valleys and hills, woods, and tiny settlements; and they stood considering it, breathing deeply in the stillness, recovering. Brea Hill was distinct with its settlement below it, where the church of St. Enodoc now stood, but the Camel was indistinct. Gulland stood out clearly but Trevennick was a blank. Tintagel was clear but only patches between it and Pentire.

"It's the copper country," said Nathan, breaking the silence and finding that he could hear clearly again. Before Zadie could respond, he turned to Soloma and asked, "Soloma, where is home?" and then, "Find home."

She looked up at him and then down at the map, walking slowly round it. Eventually, she stopped and waved her hand vaguely beyond Gulland.

"Well, that hasn't got us very far," said Zadie indignantly, "although, on the plus side, we're not deaf and we're not dead!"

The map table was stable. There was no sound other than the plink of water rubies, and the light showed no sign of fading. Nathan was appreciating the objections to his next intention. He could attempt it by stealth, and he contemplated that approach for some moments before deciding to be open about the matter.

"There's something I want to show you," he said to both of them, reaching into an inside pocket and fishing out a soft, cloth bag with a drawstring. It was small and he drew from it a beautiful object on a thin gold chain. They gasped at it and, although it wasn't the best light to see it by, its simplicity and elegance were magnetic.

"Where on earth did you get that?" exclaimed Zadie, whilst Soloma also cried out in her own language.

"You hold it a moment," he said, giving it to Zadie while he bent his head and withdrew a chain from around his neck. On its end was the bronze token that had once been tin. He laid it on his hand and invited Zadie to put the other by its side.

"They're identical in shape!" she exclaimed, "But that one is much more beautiful," pointing to the almost transparent one that was reflecting the copperish light but suggesting its own light within. "Is it another token? Where did you get it?"

He put the bronze token away again and told her the story of Mabel's tin box. "…four recesses in the box, for four different tokens," he ended.

"It seems authentic, from what you say," Zadie murmured as she handled it with something akin to awe.

"Yes. And I was able to make out something of an inscription on it under a strong magnifier." He paused.

"And …?" encouraged Zadie, still transfixed by it.

"Iglos," came the reply. "I couldn't make out the word under it … that was impossible as it has virtually no colour … only the slightest tinge of blue. I have the equipment to do it at the department but nothing at the bungalow," and he handed the object to Soloma, who stroked its surface with reverence.

"Why are you showing us now?" asked Zadie suddenly.

"Ah. Yes. Well. There were four recesses for four tokens in the box … and there are four black lionesses and four recesses in them."

Her eyes sharpened.

"You want to put that in one of those?" she said, pointing in disbelief.

"Yes. In the one that's tinged with blue, over there."

"No. I don't want an experience like the last one. We're returning Soloma home, not conducting an experiment, in case you've forgotten."

Zadie had a point and he looked across at Soloma, who was still in wet clothes. They ought to get her dried out soon.

"OK," Nathan responded and started lowering the token into the soft cloth bag.

"No. Wait. It's so beautiful. I mean, it might be harmed if you used it."

"It was made to be used," countered Nathan.

The discussion ran to and fro for some time. Eventually, Nathan was positioned on one side of the slab nearest to the black lioness with the blue recess, and Soloma and Zadie were on the other side. The map table was still showing the copper landscape and Zadie's hand was hovering over that lioness, ready to grab her token out of it.

"I'm putting it in now," came Nathan's voice.

For a moment it looked as if nothing was happening, and

then the map table slowly began to gain in definition. Blank area after blank area came into being. There was a valley at Trevennick but no bay, just woodland backed by a cliff; and there was the offshore area filling out in detail – open land with clumps of trees and little ridges and valleys; and a wide river streaming down from the Camel valley and wending its way round to the north of Gulland. Soloma gasped as the Little Lake where they had found her emerged. Onward the table unfolded until it rose in a higher white cliff with a large, irregular lake in front of it. Almost every detail of the map was formed. They became aware of the clarity with which they were seeing it, and they looked around.

Down the walls of the cave, every seeping flow of water was becoming a rivulet of flowing light. Liquid droplets of distilled light were dripping into pools that were themselves glowing like soft floodlights. The continued glow from the coppery veining gave it the impression of a setting sun in places, whereas in others the light was the light of the midday sun; and in others, still, the light was that of the stars on the clearest night. Then came the sunrise and, starting immediately above them in the centre of the cave ceiling, filaments of finest gold spread through the rock, dividing and rejoining, etching out each passage doorway and creating a crown of gold so infinitely beautiful that for a while they bowed their heads.

At last, they were drunk of the scene and Nathan spoke quietly to Soloma, "Where is home?"

She walked confidently to his side and pointed beyond the white cliff on the map.

"Well, I wasn't expecting that," he observed. "It looks like we've got to go onto the ice."

"That's impossible," objected Zadie.

"We can't go back. We only just managed to get in." They looked at each other. "However, I think there is a way of checking." He turned to Soloma again and said, "Find Nathan's home." The response was slower but she moved and pointed convincingly at the valley of Trevennick.

"Convinced?" he enquired of Zadie.

She nodded and he said, "I'm going to try two more questions on Soloma; then we must get out of here and get some warmth into her."

"Soloma, where is Iglos?"

She pointed to the tokens. No, that hadn't worked. Try the negative.

"Soloma, find NO Iglos."

She waved her arm over much of the map.

"I can see what you're driving at but I'm not sure that gets us very far," Zadie stated. "Don't you think we ought to go?"

"Yes," agreed Nathan, "We've been too long. I'll take this token out first, then you take yours out. The exit we want is over there, by the bottle, and the copper veining should direct us, anyway."

The golden crown receded as gently as it had begun and the white light ran back up the rivulets as they reached the exit. By the time they had stepped down its uneven passage only the copper was guiding, until a great streak ran from floor to ceiling in front of them. Soloma touched it first and a grey light filtered through the opening crack. A few more steps and it closed again behind them. They reached the mouth of the cave-like cleft in growing light. Nathan had his aerosol of fluorescent paint out again and marked the entry before they walked on out of the boulders and down onto the grassy slope where he had first looked up at the cliffs and thought he was dead.

Chapter 13   The Oddest Things

Clouds covered most of the sky but the wind was in the south and it was warmer as they settled near the stream where Nathan had washed the first time he and Zadie had come through the cave at Polgodoc.

"The weather is different this side of the cave," he observed casually as Soloma finished gathering dry wood for a fire and he lit it. He was busy unpacking his rucksack. "Unfortunately, what I want is right at the bottom … I hadn't intended using them until the return journey," he continued in a conversational way.

Zadie was watching both of them and chipped in, "You have some interesting things in there. What's that?"

"Packet of marine distress flares … thought they might be useful if we became separated … red, green, and white. The white one is fairly vicious."

"Cigars, again, I see – and plenty of matches this time." She was taking more interest now and he didn't mind as he knew she would have found an opportunity to investigate the contents at some point. "And what about that?" she pointed again.

"I don't think I'll need that now. It's a German sea-bed survey, dated 1938 … much better than the Admiralty charts and the best I could find for a map. However, the map table showed us much more," he answered, pulling out another aerosol can and laughing, "… and that must have fallen in by accident," as he lifted out a spray-on deodorant. Several items of clothing later he pulled out a most peculiar object. "Head torch," he explained, "…used to use it for climbing at night … very useful as it goes round the head on a strap, like this; the battery goes in a pocket, and both hands are free for climbing." He turned it on and they all laughed, Soloma looking up from the clear blaze of the fire she was tending.

"She's good with that fire," said Zadie softly.

"Yes. Very economical with the wood, too … gets a good

flame and makes it last much longer than I could ... no smoke, either. Nearly there now," he added. "I had intended buying fresh food from the shop but that all had to change with leaving in such a hurry." He lifted out several packages, followed by a set of tins and mugs that fitted neatly inside each other. "It's all dehydrated," he apologised. "What do you want – porridge with dried fruit, and call it breakfast, or sausage and mash, and make it lunch?"

"You've certainly prepared well," commented Zadie.

"I tried to," called back Nathan as he went to fetch water, "although I didn't intend starting these so early, and we have a lot further to go than I anticipated. Have a look for the spoons, will you? Oh, there should be a scouring pad, too."

It took little more than half an hour until he lifted the package out of the boiling water and divided the meal into the remaining tins. As he took his first mouthful, he spluttered through it and Zadie exclaimed, "It's not that bad!" not understanding his retort of, "You funny little thing!"

"It's not the food. Look!" he said, pointing at Soloma.

She had placed her tin to keep warm and was unpacking her leather pouch. As well as the sharp flints, a bar of soap from his bathroom and half a dozen tea bags had emerged. Soloma promptly popped a tea bag into one of the mugs and carefully poured the boiling water into it.

"I presume you have milk with you," ventured Zadie in a posh accent.

"Actually, yes," he replied in mimicry, producing a couple of small sachets, "and would Madam care for some coffee?"

It might have been dried milk and instant coffee but it tasted good, and they shared a bar of chocolate.

"What's the time?" asked Zadie, as Soloma covered up the traces of the fire.

"Just gone 2pm by my watch. About five hours of usable light, if that's what you're asking."

"Do you think it will rain?" she continued.

"Not while the wind stays in the south: the cloud is lifting, though," he answered, putting the binoculars in the top of his pack and tying it shut.

Zadie and Soloma had been ready to go for some minutes and he slung it over his shoulders, with a last look around to see that nothing had been left.

"What do you think happened in the cave?" said Zadie.

It was easier talking about it whilst they were walking, and Soloma was picking a good route towards the holly trees on the near skyline.

"You mean with the map table and the sound?" asked Nathan.

"Yes."

"I've no idea," he responded, and a few steps later, "Well, I do have an idea, but it has very little by way of facts to ground it … and it's not a very pleasant one."

"Go on, then; tell me. It's daylight," she encouraged.

"Well … the table responded to our touch – just like it did the first time – but I was concentrating on the copper lioness in my mind … and it was Soloma's hand touching with mine, not yours."

"So?" she prompted.

"I had nothing in my other hand … nothing to offer it. It was almost as if the lionesses were sensing a falsehood … someone who shouldn't have been there and was trying to cheat them."

"But you had the beautiful blue token, and I had the copper one," Zadie objected.

"Yes, but you weren't touching the table, and I was thinking copper. I told you it was a half-baked idea," he ended.

"Do you think the noise would have killed us?" she persisted.

"I don't know. Maybe we would have gone insane before we went deaf … or maybe deafness would have been a release."

"It's all a bit Pagan," she murmured.

"Much older, and much stranger," he responded.

"…but that crown was so beautiful, so delicate; it seemed to wrap around me: it was almost like imagining being inside a comfortable womb – protected and cared for," continued Zadie.

"Mmm … I hadn't thought of it like that. To me it was like something of unparalleled beauty being created by a master craftsman; eons of perfection compressed into a few moments; eternity touching time."

"I'd like to see the blue token again – in the daylight."

"Yes, so would I," he answered to the half-asked request. "I'll take it out when we next stop."

The holly bushes were upon them without them being aware of having walked so far. In the middle of the ring was the plinth of stone – solid black slate on the near side with its single recess of granite and solid granite on the far side with its recess of dark slate. A couple of black birds with red beaks flew overhead in a somewhat ungainly flapping flight. Soloma had already gathered up three of the ordinary, granite pass-keys lying near the plinth but was standing to one side of it.

"She wants something," said Zadie. "I think she wants you to join her."

Nathan stepped across and said, "What is it, Soloma?"

She tugged his hand gently and he walked a few paces beside her until the invisible barrier between the two geologies brought them to a halt and gently forced them back. Soloma repeated the process before turning to Zadie and saying, "Not Iglos," and pointed to the birds above, this time saying, "Iglos." She popped the granite token into the recess and stepped past the plinth, repeating "Iglos" again as the others joined her.

In the conversation that followed they felt that they were coming near to the meaning of a key word and Zadie was pursuing it with Soloma as they made for the next holly clump near the foot of Gulland. It was understandable, therefore, that she was not aware at first that Nathan was not following. Her immediate thought was fear that he had been distracted by the yew trees and the lure of the Serpentine beyond them. However, he was standing in clear view about two hundred yards away, looking down and prodding something with his boot. Zadie turned and cupped her hands, calling "Come on!" and waving him up the slope. Now, she had his attention and called again. Faintly, she heard the reply,

"'Fraid not. Come here!" and saw him beckoning to them. The subsequent exchange lasted several minutes. Eventually, it was clear that he was not going to budge and, with great reluctance, she set off back down the slope with Soloma; they were losing height and time, and would have to climb it all over again. Consequently, it was a terse voice that demanded, "What's wrong? Why won't you move?" when she and Soloma had trailed back to within ten yards of him.

"This," said Nathan quietly, lifting his boot to reveal an object beneath it.

"It's just a discarded flip-flop," began Zadie angrily, and then her voice petered away into a horrified silence. It was more a series of waves of horrified silence that rolled over her.

"That shouldn't be here..." she stammered, "... it's modern; it's our time."

He nodded.

"It means that someone else has been through the cave of Polgodoc recently ... and it's a child's size." She spoke her thoughts aloud and, as Soloma picked up the object, Nathan's mind was seared with an image of her playing with another flip-flop on top of the cliff.

"Same size, same coloured thong," he said, and then by way of explanation; "its pair was on the cliff top above the adit at Polgodoc. Soloma was playing with it before the helicopter came."

"...and the younger one of the missing girls was wearing flip-flops," added Zadie.

A fierce and urgent discussion followed. Nathan was convinced that both girls might have discovered the old mine on their own and somehow been accepted by the cave and through it. Zadie was determined that they had been abducted and brought through the cave, and kept pointing out that the news had reported a sighting of an adult male with a small girl near Lellizzick. The time, location, and description, had fitted one of the girls.

"Look! It doesn't matter!" she ended fiercely, "Whichever way it was, we must search for them."

"The noise that we've been making means they are not near this spot," countered Nathan, "...or that they can't hear."

"...or that they can't move!" came back the riposte.

Nevertheless, they did search, and thoroughly – and together, since Zadie did not trust Nathan anywhere near the clump of yew trees. Soloma seemed to understand what was wanted but not even she could find a trace of anything unusual. An hour and a half later they were back by the flip-flop.

"The days are shortening," said Nathan, "and I don't want to camp on this granite."

"Nor do I," Zadie agreed. "We could make our way to Gulland ... and we could see from there."

So they moved on, reclaiming the ground that Zadie and Soloma had trodden two hours before – a subdued threesome, glancing constantly to either side and around them.

The plinth in the centre of the next holly clump consisted of a darker rock veined with milky quartz on the farther side and Nathan picked up one of the tokens that Soloma seemed to be gathering together and put it in the recess, plucking it out and lobbing it back in the normal way as he reached the geology of Gulland. He waited a while for Zadie and Soloma to join him at the edge of the hollies and was looking at the hill, half a mile away, when Zadie's voice said, "She's a clever girl. We should have thought of that."

"Of what?"

"Soloma counted the tokens on each side of the plinth to see if there had been any movement in one direction recently," she continued.

"Anything?" he asked.

"No, nothing."

"Well, let's get up that hill then while there's enough light to see reasonably" and he led the way, but in his mind he thought there was little hope.

Chapter 14   **Two Small Sacrifices**

Half way up the southern slope of Gulland was a smoother patch with a part rim of higher rocks on its western edge, and they stopped to scan the landscape stretching below, taking turns with the binoculars until they were both convinced that there was nothing moving. It was Soloma who suddenly jumped down from between the rocks where she was perched and tugged them to the ground.

If it hadn't been for the look of alarm on Soloma's face and the determined way in which her young arms insisted upon them remaining lying down, they would probably have called out and waved as the group of six came into sight below them. Now they looked more closely, they could make out two white-bearded figures at its head. There was an air of disdain about the way they held their heads and their lack of speech to one another, looking straight ahead and walking – almost marching – at a steady pace across the uneven ground, as if it belonged to them. Long white furs, by the look of it, were gathered in around their waists with some form of belt and, instead of a leather pouch, a sheath hung from them. The two figures behind the bearded ones brought a cry from Zadie and the combined speed of Soloma and weight of Nathan flattened her to the ground as they hoped the sound had not carried against the wind. Both figures were smaller and unmistakably two young girls, suffering as they struggled to keep up the pace with heads bent down and continuous glances towards each other. Both had long hair and upon their head each wore a crude crown of flowers. As they watched, one of the girls stumbled and was dragged roughly to her feet by the man that followed, guttural words coming with the wind towards them as he threatened her. The other girl had stopped to help her and was jabbed sharply and shoved by another man. Both were forced to stumble forward more quickly to catch up with the old men, who had walked steadily on, unconcerned with what was happening behind. The unpleasant procession vanished from view into the holly clump.

"Was it them?" asked Nathan of Zadie, who had grabbed the binoculars at the first indication of being allowed to move a limb.

She shook her head. "Wrong colour hair, and too similar in stature," she added. "It looked thoroughly nasty though … almost like a prison party."

"…or worse," grimaced Nathan, and they both became aware of Soloma sobbing and shaking between them.

"What's wrong? What's going to happen to the girls?" he asked.

"Like Mabel," Soloma sobbed. She sobbed more heavily, her breath coming in rasping gasps as she picked up a sharp stone, miming an ugly charade, and drawing it repeatedly across her own torso, and her neck, before plunging it at her heart and licking and chewing like an animal.

Zadie cried, "It'll be just like those animals … those awful animals that wanted Soloma for a sacrifice! It'll be the Serpentine again … it's a ritual murder!" and she was no more able to stop herself bounding down the slope than when she had rushed to Soloma's assistance in the Little Lake.

"Wait! Wait!" yelled Nathan after her, "We're coming! Wait at the hollies!"

At least she had slowed a little and the last cry had produced a half-wave of acknowledgement, but Nathan was struggling under the additional weight of the rucksack and breathing heavily as he hurried up the last little slope to the knoll where Soloma had already caught and cornered Zadie. A few rays of sunlight finally penetrated below the cloud base in the distant west but it was already twilight within the group of holly trees as they stepped into them, talking rapidly and interrupting each other frequently.

"That's the best I can think of," Nathan was saying, "and we haven't time for a proper plan. It'll be dark in forty minutes. I'll leave the rucksack hanging on this branch. If it's gone, I'll assume you've come first and make my own way back to Gulland;

it'll slow me down too much to take it. Here, you have the head torch."

Zadie was about to speak but shook her head and mouthed something like good luck instead. Soloma was already on the other side of the plinth and pressed a token into the hand of each of them as they joined her.

"Bright girl," observed Zadie to Nathan, slipping it in a pocket. "We don't want to be scrabbling around in the dark for one of those if we're being chased."

They stepped out of the hollies into the fading light of the granite landscape and split up after a dozen paces.

"Remember, wait for the signal," called Nathan softly, "and try to get between them and the Serpentine."

He heard a soft "yes" come back from where Zadie had disappeared with Soloma as he strode over the crest in the landscape and made his way openly down the rock-strewn slope below. He found himself humming and singing the old hymn. Concealment didn't matter now for him. She was good in a crisis. There was a lot of love in her heart – an instinctive love that didn't question the danger to itself – and he wondered whether, if he had been on his own, he would now be huddled in the relative safety of Gulland justifying his lack of intervention. It would have been the logical course to take. After all, it wasn't his business … and he sang on.

They had heard him now and had stopped by the yew trees. He could just make out the men in conversation. They were moving to face him, the two younger men standing to either side of one of the white-bearded priests, and the other priest a short way behind with the two girls, close to the yew trees. He slowed his pace to give Zadie more time and ran his hands through his pockets. It looked like the two men had something sharp fastened to the end of their staves and the old man was fiddling with the sheath hanging from his belt. With a hundred yards to go, the dull, red tinge from the underside of the clouds reflecting the last distorted rays of the setted sun drew a reciprocal glint from the short, curved blade that the old priest held. Flint and copper then, he thought; sharp enough to make a mess of him and about as much of a welcome as he had expected.

The curved, copper knife was four yards from where Nathan stood, feet apart and hands in pockets, his apparent ease of stance belying the turmoil within. This wasn't his scene. Doubts were rising fast and the longer he stood, the more his plan seemed futile. He had no experience of dealing with this kind of situation and it was uncertain whether the knife or the face of the man holding it looked more wicked. The nose was hooked and had once been broken; the eyes above the tangled white beard that reached to the priest's belt were black and unyielding. The old man's gaze was compelling and Nathan found his own voice raw as he put together some of the words that Soloma had taught him in Trevennick.

"Give me the girls," he tried to command.

There wasn't the slightest flicker in any of the faces. No recognition of the words or reaction to them. He didn't doubt that his pronunciation was poor but they were simple words. Perhaps each group had its own language, or variant of it. If he couldn't make himself understood, the whole plan would fall. Perhaps he could turn and run. He had made an honourable attempt, his mind clamoured. It was nearly dark; he might get away. They might not chase him and leave the girls. But that would mean leaving Soloma and Zadie in dire danger. He would never be able to face them again. If he didn't do something, he wasn't going to have the option of facing them again and, somewhere, a glimmer of love cut through the screaming of his thoughts.

"Give me the girls!" he repeated more loudly.

He caught a look flicker between the men and the priest. At least he had been understood and they were seeking orders.

"No!" said the priest, followed by a command that Nathan did not understand.

The priest turned to the man on his right, repeating the command, and the man lowered his stave and slowly knelt, bowing his head and exposing his unprotected neck. Now the priest was repeating his command to Nathan.

If it had been intended to cow him into submission, it had the opposite effect. There was a cold clarity of purpose in Nathan's mind and his eyes flashed angrily. He would do no obeisance to this evil old man and his "No!" rang defiantly in response.

At a word from the priest, the second man started forward threateningly with his stave. Nathan moved quickly, jerking his hand from his pocket and the man stumbled to the ground screaming and scrabbling at his eyes, stave and command forgotten, as a jet of fluorescent paint hit him full in the face from the aerosol in Nathan's grip. The priest was kicking the first man to get up but he was staying on his knees, shielding his face.

Nathan advanced a pace and commanded, "Give me the girls!"

"No!" came the reply again.

He was barely two paces from the old man now and, as he looked beyond him, he could see the other priest holding a similar knife to the throat of one of the girls. Nathan reached in his pocket, bringing out a cigar. He lit it ostentatiously, flicking the match at the man cowering on the ground and saying slowly in English, "This is for the last time of asking. Give me the girls." He flung his arm up towards the darkened heavens above.

The priest lunged for Nathan with his knife and as he pressed the nozzle on the aerosol the bang caught everyone by surprise, even though Nathan had been counting for it. Nathan's hand jerked and the spray caught the tip of his cigar, bursting into a gush of flame that ignited the old man's beard. The distinctive smell of singed and burning human hair mingled with a hideous screaming as his attacker continued lunging on until he was blinded by the paint spray and had staggered past Nathan, still slashing with the knife in his darkness.

The other priest had stood and was looking up at the red fire descending from a thousand feet above and giving a garish illumination to the scene. Nathan started urgently towards him and the two prone figures of the girls, intent on felling him with a tackle before the knife could come into play on the young throats; but Zadie had other ideas. The bang was deafening as the incandescent white flare struck the clump of yew trees igniting them instantaneously and spewing its blinding brilliance into the darkness. In the few seconds before he lost his sight, Nathan saw the standing priest hit full square by a blob of molten magnesium, his robes and hair disintegrating as a torch. A bough of burning yew fell onto the bowl of serpentine eggs and great snarlings and growlings yowled and vibrated around them as a pulsating laser show of red and green lights radiated in every direction and showers of fine stones clattered down.

The trees were still burning: the noise of their incineration pressed upon his ears; he could feel the heat of it upon his face; and the smell of the sap vaporising assaulted his nostrils; but Nathan could not see. Only the brilliance of the flash was burnt upon his retina. He felt his eyes with his hands; closed or open, it was no different. He tried striking a match by feel but could not see it. This wasn't the time to lose his sight, and he cried out in the darkness.

There were voices – three of them – young voices, talking quickly and urgently, and he cried out again, "Soloma, I'm over here: I can't see."

Soon a pair of little arms hugged him and a voice said, "They help you. I help Zadie. She burnt," and he felt two different hands being placed in each of his and heard her feet scurrying away into the darkness.

It took an age to reach the holly clump. Despite the skill of the two girls, playing blind man's bluff up a rock-strewn slope wasn't the easiest of tasks and he fell twice. Several times he thought he heard snarlings behind and he wondered how badly Zadie was burnt, unable to shake the image of the second priest becoming a human torch from his mind and fearing for her. His body was needing a conscious effort of will to make each movement and he could feel the shock reaction beginning to grind and grip at his mind.

That was a definite snarl behind this time and it galvanised Nathan into moving forward as Zadie's voice floated down to him, "Keep going. Fifty yards to the hollies. It's fairly even," and he risked a stumbling run as the noises behind multiplied and grew louder. He sensed the trees upon him, tripping and falling forward into Zadie's arms.

"No time!" she cried. "Soloma has a token. Go with her!" and he felt a hand tug him past the plinth and off the granite geology. A moment later Zadie and the two girls were with them.

"Can you see anything?" asked Zadie anxiously.

"No ... although it seems fractionally less dark."

"That's because I'm shining the head torch straight into your eyes," Zadie continued. "Probably a good sign but it may take a while. I'm sorry but we can't stay here – those awful animals are on the loose again," and as if to emphasise the point there was a tearing and crackling at the holly behind.

"OK," Nathan replied, "if the girls guide me, I'll do the best I can. Are you alright? Soloma said you were burnt."

"I'm better than you. I'll manage."

"Are you using the torch?" asked Nathan, wondering at his blackness.

"No. If there is a pursuit it will give us away too easily. Soloma will guide. These girls see well by the starlight."

"Oh, have the clouds cleared then?" he questioned, searching for the company of a voice.

"Yes," she answered, "Where do you want to make for?"

"Gulland. The hazel thicket half way down the far slope. It will give us some cover. Soloma said you were burnt" – he was repeating himself now – "What happened? Tell me as we go."

"It took us a while to find a good position where we could see you and not be seen. We were about a hundred yards away behind some boulders when one of the men moved to attack you and then fell down."

"Yes. He was blinded by the paint spray."

"Then it got darker and I couldn't really see you, although Soloma seemed to. I nearly sent the flare up several times before I finally saw the light for the cigar. Then there was a burst of flame. Soloma kept pointing at something and I fired the next flare straight at it. I was a bit careless and burnt my hand and wrist, which was just as well really as I wasn't looking at the flare when it went off. It seemed to have quite an impact."

"Is it badly burnt?"

"No. It looks worse than it is. I've put something on it and bandaged it. I didn't bring much with me but I do have a few medical items."

"Is my rucksack still down at the hollies?"

"No. I'm carrying it."

"Shall I take it?"

"No. You worry about walking. And tell me what happened to you."

They were not far off the hazel thicket by the time Nathan had finished. Zadie was quiet.

After a long pause she said, "I don't like the thought of having killed a man."

"You didn't intend to," Nathan replied, "and there are two lives alive that wouldn't have been."

"That makes it sound like an equation. I still don't like it. One dead; two blinded; and one scared out of his mind," she added contemplatively.

"I don't think they will be fully blind," commented Nathan, "and someone set those animals loose … probably the old priest. If they catch us, don't expect any mercy."

"You think we'll be pursued, then?"

"Yes, but not tonight, unless the animals can pass the barrier."

"Perhaps that's why Soloma gathered up all the tokens."

"What?"

"She gathered up all the pass tokens for this geology at the plinth with the head torch and put them on this side of it," explained Zadie.

"Bright girl," they said together, as they found their feet reaching the mossy floor of the hazel thicket and lowered themselves onto the soft, welcoming ground. None seemed willing to prolong the hours of wakefulness with further conversation, and sleep rushed upon limbs and bodies, tired with exertion. Exhaustion watched over them, blotting the fears and images from their minds as they lay in jumbled proximity.

Far away, a creature howled.

Chapter 15   A Single Rose

The shadow of the rock extended over them as the sun rose. Zadie was peering through the edge of the thicket. Down below lay the Little Lake with its flat rock, from which she had rescued Soloma those few months ago. The lake was mirror still and catching the first few rays of light. It was altogether a remarkably still and clear dawning for the second week of September. Beyond the lake was the low rise down which they had watched Soloma and her sister come ... and beyond that was something that made Zadie gasp, riveting her attention so that she could not withdraw her gaze despite the arrival of three smaller figures alongside her.

It was a sheer piece of magic, a humbling awe, vastly greater in quality and quantity than the greatest imagination could create or the finest painter portray. It lived and changed as she stared unblinkingly, drinking the unparalleled splendour into her soul, intoxicated by it. Somehow, the slope up to the rise had assumed the shape and colour of a human face in the early flush of light, and rocks and rivulets appeared as lines of laughter and worry upon it. But it was what was beyond the face that held the mind and heart captive. The uppermost part of the great ice wall protruded as a narrow crown, adorned with gems of subtlest hue from faintest pink to lightest yellow and linked by a filigree of gold and silver, more delicate than human art could contrive and yet majestic in the size that her mind told her these slabs of distant, frozen artistry would be. And, as she watched, she saw the dark finger of Gulland's shadow moving from gem to gem until it shortened and faded and only the cold, ice crown was left radiating the whiteness of time immobilised.

Quietly she retreated, water from a pool in her tin, and she knelt beside Nathan's open rucksack, pouring dried porridge into the container.

He groaned.

"It has been the most superb dawn," she said, still in awe of it.

"Looks grey to me – and a bit foggy," he muttered, and she remembered his eyes.

"O good, so you can see something then?"

"Yes," he replied, "not particularly clearly if I look straight at it, but I can make out rocks and trees and figures."

Soloma gave him a hug and Nathan smiled at her, moving towards the group around the tin.

"What are you making?" he asked.

"Half the porridge. Do you think we can risk a fire?"

"Probably not … at least, not until we know if there are any signs of movement. Have you got the binoculars there?" he questioned.

"Yes. Do you want them?"

"No good to me. Give them to Soloma and ask her to go up the hill a bit. She knows how to use them."

Soloma disappeared with one of the girls, interpreting her task without any real need to be told, and Nathan prodded the rucksack with his foot.

"There should be some chocolate in the left hand bottom pocket. I can't see the buckle well enough. They are big bars. One for the girls and one for us should help."

By the time Soloma returned and gave the binoculars back to Zadie with a shake of the head, the cold porridge was mildly edible.

"You should have packed more spoons," Zadie chided playfully.

"I don't think sharing a spoon will be the greatest of our worries," he answered. "Besides, the girls will probably use their fingers," and he was quite right. The tin was emptied to the point where washing it out seemed an unnecessary task, even for porridge.

"How's the chocolate going?" he continued, savouring a slab in his mouth.

"They're following Soloma's lead," Zadie replied over her

shoulder as she packed away and watched the tentative nibbling turning to full acceptance of the strange food.

"Do we know any names?"

"Yes," Zadie answered, "The one with the longer hair is Tarma and the other one is Simona, or something similar. Soloma seems to know them."

Nathan tried the names and a greeting in their speech and was greeted respectfully in reply.

"Right, let's make a move then," he said, standing up and hoisting the rucksack onto his shoulders. "I can see well enough to carry this," he continued, forestalling Zadie's incipient objection, "and talking of seeing, let's keep an eye open behind. We'll be very visible in this light. Soloma, we will follow you," he ended, pointing to the distant west.

The girls moved remarkably quickly and quietly over the ground, whilst Nathan found the sound of his footsteps echoing heavily and was embarrassed at each crackle of twigs he failed to spot. Zadie was staying close enough to guide him over the difficult areas and their concentration on the simple task of walking brought them to the edge of the Little Lake without really having considered the implications of the spot.

Soloma was kneeling down and searching carefully through her leather pouch, while Zadie quietly amplified the scene to Nathan.

The little girl stood up slowly, holding something in her open palm. Silently she came to Nathan, taking his hand and leading him to the water's edge, before gently throwing the withered red rose from Lucinda's garden out onto the water. For a while it floated gracefully until it slipped slowly from view beneath the still surface.

"Like Mabel," Soloma said and, with the slightest of pauses, she turned and walked on up the slope.

It was more open country and as they followed a gulley notching through the crest of the low ridge they found themselves entering a stunted ring of holly. In the middle was a plinth, darker and veined with quartz on the near side, creamy pink on the far side; each half of the slab inset with a small amount of the opposite colour where the recess for a token lay.

"Very odd," Nathan was saying, fingering the token he had been given by Tarma. "It looks like limestone – maybe lightly metamorphosed limestone, but definitely limestone. That shouldn't be here. There is a little bit in Cornwall, of course, badly disfigured by tectonic upheavals but – "

"Nathan," interrupted Zadie, "would you mind sparing us the detailed analysis and put the chunk of rock in the hole – then we can all get to the far side."

"Sorry," he chuckled, doing as he was told, although a close observer would have seen the token disappear into a pocket as he made to lob it back to the other side of the plinth.

The landscape had certainly changed and sitting with their backs to a rock just beyond the stunted hollies they could see it falling away below them in gentle folds. There was much bare rock, and few bushes to break the barrenness. Only in the distance was a darker clump that could well be holly. Beyond that there was part of the marginal ice lake showing. The great ice wall stretched form north to south as far as the eye could see, although the sun was at its zenith and it had lost much of its reflected light. Nevertheless, it had grown in height with their greater proximity and, what it had lost in splendour, it had gained in impressiveness of size.

Soloma was sitting slightly apart and seemed to be asking Tarma and Simona a series of long and complicated questions to which they were replying with prompts from each other and pointings and gestures.

"She's plotting the way," observed Zadie.

"Yes," replied Nathan, "and not down to those hollies but up onto the ice."

"Your sight is improving."

"Yes," he continued. "I'm grateful for that, but the ice is worrying me. I would have brought other gear if I'd known we would have to go up onto it – ice axe, crampons, rope, cold weather stuff. What's more, at the present rate we'll reach it with the sun half way to the horizon and have to climb straight into the light."

"Let's take it a step at a time. If three little girls can manage it, then we can," Zadie responded.

"Sometimes being lighter is an advantage," Nathan countered. "Heavy people need more grip; they slip more easily."

"There were men with them…"

"True," said Nathan, finding the argument brought to a halt before it became divisive by Soloma coming across and gesturing to them to get going.

"She's beginning to take charge more," Zadie said without animosity.

"Good job too: we certainly can't," he said in acknowledgement as they walked on together.

"I suppose it's more like home territory – she's moving faster now – she's more sure and not looking to each side."

"Light," grunted Nathan, shifting the rucksack as he walked.

"What?"

"Light," he repeated. "Six hours maximum of usable light left; less if it becomes cloudy. She's got an overnight stopping point in mind."

"Don't you think they're hungry?"

"I'm sure they are … I am, and I'm trying not to think about it … but whatever's driving her is more urgent than hunger. We're going to struggle to keep up," he ended, and the conversation became intermittent in their endeavour to do so.

As it was, Soloma and Simona were waiting inside the hollies long before Nathan and Zadie were tackling the last gentle slope up to them. He had the distinct impression that Tarma had been detailed to lag behind and hurry them up the slope and he was glad of the chance to slip off the rucksack and lean against the plinth. The hollies were stunted and ordinary, barely much above his height, gnarled with age and slow growth in an inhospitable environment. But the plinth was extraordinary. The large block of creamy-pink limestone seemed to end abruptly and the other half appeared at first glance to be missing, until his mind took in the massive rectangular slab of crystal quartz seemingly growing from the ground, with a shallow recess of pink floating on its translucent surface. Even Zadie was impressed and they stood awhile looking alternately at the glass-clear tokens that Tarma had pressed into their hands and at the slab itself

"That really is quite something," said Nathan after they had passed through the invisible barrier and he stood running his fingers along the edges of the quartz slab and over its ultra-smooth surface. Zadie made no attempt to object as he pocketed the token, preferring to share in his appreciation.

"Let's go!" he said suddenly. "Where are the girls?"

"Just down the slope, there," Zadie answered. "Why?"

'Nothing."

"What do you mean, nothing?"

"Nothing," he repeated abruptly as she jogged to catch up with him.

"Well, it didn't seem like nothing. One moment you are caressing that rock, and the next we're plunging down this slope."

"It's probably nothing. I want to find Soloma. Where is she?" There was a terseness in his speech and it was not going down well with Zadie.

"Tell me what it is!" she demanded, reaching out an arm to stop him and finding it shrugged off. "Oh, very well, she's away to the right, there."

"Well spotted," Nathan acknowledged in a slightly more conciliatory tone. "Look, I don't want to alarm you but my peripheral vision is quite good now and the surface of that quartz was like a mirror. I thought I caught a flash of something just by the previous holly clump in the reflection."

"You mean we're being followed?"

"I didn't say that. If we are, it will be being pursued, not being followed. It would explain Soloma's haste … I want to find out what she knows," and the conversation continued in phrases as they both puffed for breath and tried to negotiate the uneven rubble of rock at speed. It shifted beneath them in places and they turned to watch a boulder half the size of a car topple noisily down the slope, gathering other fragments and rolling into the wide lake, its ripples dissipating over the surface long before they reached the opposite side half a mile away. Rounding another large boulder they almost bumped into the three girls, who had stopped at the noise.

"Soloma, are we being followed?" he burst out, pointing and forgetting to simplify the question.

"Yes, I think," came the reply.

"Hurry, then," he half-asked, half-commanded, seeking not to alarm the others.

Soloma nodded and they made the best speed they could through the jumble of rocks, heading northward with the ice-marginal lake slowly narrowing on their left. It was easier following the girls' footsteps and the shifting of a rock under their light touch gave some warning for the heavier feet. Even so there were several rock slides and Nathan begrudged the noise that they made.

"What is this stuff?" came Zadie's voice as they made a wider gravelly strip by the lake shore and were able to walk side by side.

"Moraine. Glacial moraine ... never seen it on this scale though ... only at the ends of valley glaciers in the high mountains ... this is vast. There will be rocks here from Wales and Ireland, probably Skye and Arran as well ... the ice sheet has come down the Irish Sea and its weight has gouged the sea-bed clean of everything that will detach. Some of the rocks will have been frozen into its base and used as giant chisels ... and it has simply bulldozed everything in front of it. Now it's retreating ... hence the lake ... and it's left all this as a giant geological rubbish tip."

"Stop here," said Soloma as they rounded a huge and very black boulder, and no sooner had they sat down than Soloma and Tarma shot off.

"That was fairly close to a command," mused Zadie.

"Yes, and Simona's been left behind to make sure we do stay put," replied Nathan as they watched the two girls scampering over the rocks and disappearing from sight.

The ice wall towered above them and the width of the lake was at a minimum – about a hundred yards – before it widened again to the north. Another huge black boulder lay on its side, sloping gently into the slightly milky water in front of them and they could see a narrower band of rock and boulders on the far side of the lake. The ice wall behind was not smooth but heavily indented, stained with rocks in places and laced with meltwater torrents, some of which emerged from its base. One spewed out some five hundred feet up and cascaded in a fan onto the rocks below, its sound a constant background to their thoughts.

"There's a tongue of ice to the left of that waterfall but it's dreadfully steep. She surely can't be meaning to go up that," said Nathan, voicing his thoughts, "and there's the lake to cross…"

"…and whatever might be in it," interjected Zadie, bringing several nasty memories to the fore.

"There's very little aerosol paint left," added Nathan, following another line of thought. "How many flares are there?"

"One red, one white, and two green," answered Zadie, "and, by the way, why did they have 'Admiralty Issue Only' stamped on the side?"

"Surplus stock, I suppose," he replied with some little disingenuity, and quickly changed the subject. "This black rock is basalt – volcanic lava – the nearest deposits are in Antrim, in The Giant's Causeway, and – "

"There they are!" broke in Zadie, sparing herself another geological lecture.

The two figures did not look like Soloma and Tarma. They were picking their way slowly and carefully over the uneven rocks and onto the shore, looking somewhat like upright turtles with feet and heads sticking out.

"Extraordinary!" exclaimed Zadie.

"What is it?"

"You'll see!"

"I thought I could see, but I can't, so to speak," Nathan said in frustration.

"Wait ten minutes and you will. This could be interesting. You'll just have to be patient," Zadie ended firmly.

Chapter 16   Coracles

They were assembled on the sloping black slab by the water. To one side of it in the deeper water four coracles bobbed. Soloma had tested all four and pronounced herself satisfied with a nod of the head and Zadie was eulogising over them to Nathan.

"So simple ... and so light ... double layer of skins sewn together with sinews and the seams sealed with some kind of animal fat – smells mildly fishy. The frame is bent to shape and lashed. The paddles are the heaviest part," she continued, lifting out one of the mis-shapen blades that was about the length of a man's arm.

"Where do I put my feet?" asked Nathan as he used the short strip of fibrous rope dangling from two of the craft to tie them together.

"You don't. You kneel on those cross-pieces that look like bamboo and rest your toes behind you on that one – at least, that's what Soloma did. Tarma seems to have done it before, as well. Look, she's showing Simona now."

"It sounds very easy," said Nathan suspiciously, lowering his rucksack into the second craft and clipping a couple of buckles in place.

"Not entirely," came the honest admission, "The one we made on an anthropology course was extremely unstable – and it leaked."

"Thanks a lot!"

"Anyway, the others are ready," she ended.

Despite her confidence, Zadie watched very carefully as Tarma clambered into a coracle and shuffled across on her knees for Simona to follow her in. They knelt side by side, filling the little craft and balancing it well as a pair. Simona pushed off gently under Tarma's instruction and they dug the paddles in lightly before Tarma said, "Stop," and used her blade to spin the coracle neatly round and bring it absolutely stationary facing the black slab and waiting for the others to follow. The girls knelt motionless and the craft had a good three inches of freeboard above the still surface of the lake.

"That looked a bit too easy," said Nathan to Zadie as he estimated the combined weight of the two girls and how much further his coracle was likely to sink in the water when he attempted the same feat.

Zadie and Soloma made an ill-matched pair and it was some time before Soloma was convinced that they had found the centre of gravity between them and was prepared to let go of the slab. Even so, she took Zadie for a short paddle in the shallow water before she was content to risk attempting the crossing. There was now no alternative for Nathan and his first attempt to lower himself into the coracle left him with one knee on the cross-pieces, the other stranded on the slab, and water pouring over the side of the coracle. It was with great difficulty that he regained the slab and emptied the coracle, which had turned from a light object that he could lift with a few fingers into a dead weight. On the third attempt he finally managed to get both knees and both feet in. He pushed off rather too vigorously, slopping water and wobbling dangerously. Concentrating on regaining stability was not helped by the suppressed giggle that reached him from a few yards away and he drove the paddle hard into the water, as one might with a canoe. This too was a mistake and, with neither keel nor rudder, the little craft spun on its axis, jerking the rope that was tied to the coracle with the rucksack in it, causing both craft to collide head on and rebound. A few fibres in the rope snapped ominously.

"You have to use both paddles at the same time – and gently," came a helpful comment from the audience. "You better go in the middle and we'll follow you."

Nathan bit off a retort and did as he was told, finding that the gentler his movements were, the greater his stability was, and the more progress he made. Keeping the coracle tied behind him moving at the same pace proved to be the key and he was surprised to find that the shallow draught and shape of the vessel meant that he could make way even where there was a current in the water.

His pleasure in having some mastery over direction and movement became dulled as they reached the mid-point of the lake and he found his mind engaged in an increasingly raucous argument: 'knees … must move knees … something's sticking into my left knee; can't move knees … will overturn the coracle; must move knee, this is agony; must move knee; only thirty yards to go now; don't look up again, that was a bad wobble; must be getting nearer; I must move; don't move …' and so it went on until he heard a voice say, "Come in slowly and straight: Tarma and Simona are standing in the water and will hold the coracle while you get out." Blessed relief flowed through his mind and having the icy water up to his knees as he disembarked awkwardly was small discomfort. Embarrassment followed as he saw the girls standing up to their thighs in the cold water and he realised the others had managed with little trouble.

"Sorry," he murmured, unclipping the rucksack and tipping the water out of his coracle.

"That's OK," responded Zadie consolingly, "you were on your own and it wasn't easy," and with a slight barb, "It's only your pride that's hurt."

Picking their way along the lake shore was more difficult on this side as there was a mass of jumbled boulders. The ice towered above, precipitous and over-bearing, its summit out of sight. After a while Nathan gave up trying to look up and concentrated on his footing.

"Was there any sign of anyone following?" he asked.

"No," replied Zadie. "We were obscured from view, unless they had passed the last holly ring, except on the lake and I couldn't look then. Soloma's still in a hurry, though. She shot off with Simona this time."

Tarma led them and he tried some questions in her language, eventually turning to Zadie and saying, "As far as I can make out we're looking for some kind of cave in the ice, but there are a lot of other words that I don't understand. It doesn't surprise me. She won't want to climb today."

"Why not?"

They had reached easier ground and could talk more readily now.

"Two reasons," he replied. "There's not enough light left to make the full height, even if there was an easy climb and, secondly, the wind."

"What wind? It's perfectly still here."

"At the moment, yes, but in a few hours there will be a cold gale howling down those slopes and cliffs above," Nathan stated confidently.

"How can you tell that?"

"The air is still, as you say, and as soon as the sun dips a little more it will be chilled from below by the surface of the ice. The cold air is denser and will flow down over the upper slopes and plunge down the edge of these cliffs. Ice sheets generate their own weather systems," he ended, just as they rounded two large black rocks, standing as sentinels, and found Soloma and Simona behind them peering into a low cave in the ice that had once been a meltwater channel but was now devoid of its stream.

Tarma stacked the coracle she was carrying neatly on top of the ones Soloma had already placed in the ice cave and then took the other one from Zadie, who was examining some broken fragments of paddle and had found another coracle hidden carefully in a recess. It was in need of patching and some pieces of skin lay nearby.

"Are we staying here tonight?" Nathan asked Soloma, trying a more complex question and surprised by the clear shake of the head he received in reply.

"She understands more than you think, Nathan," Zadie observed. "I don't know how they manage. They must be famished. They've had nothing since breakfast and done a day's work fit for a full grown man."

"Full grown man is feeling a bit faint, too," he agreed and broke out two of the remaining bars of chocolate. Soloma ate fast and lapped a little water from a pool in the wall of the ice cave before indicating that she wanted to move on.

Perversely, it seemed, she made them pick their way

slowly over the tumble of rocks rather than walking quickly along the sandy gravel by the lake shore. Nathan was beginning to raise objections until Zadie pointed out that they were leaving no footprints and that Soloma had already gone off to the left twice on her own to investigate two further caves in the ice.

"An hour of light left," muttered Nathan on the second occasion. "At least we won't be followed tonight."

"She's going more slowly now. Whatever she's looking for is nearby – and I don't think Tarma or Simona know about it as she's leaving them with us," commented Zadie.

Finally, a series of massive black rocks the size of houses blocked their way and extended right down into the water. They were forced to climb and squeeze through a narrow gap between two of them, emerging on the sloping surface of a third.

"Well that's torn it. We'll not get by that," stated Nathan as they looked down at the scene below.

A substantial meltwater stream was emerging from near the foot of the ice wall under pressure and spewing out like a sluice gate at the bottom of a large dam. Spray made the sloping rock slippery and the water was swirling and eddying in the plunge pool fifty feet beneath them. A slight slip invited crushed bones, if not death by drowning, and they recoiled back – except for Soloma who was making signs to Tarma, since she couldn't be heard above the roar of the water, and plucking at Nathan's sleeve. Cautiously he edged along the rock after her and was aware of Zadie following him. Near the end of the rock was an ice buttress, a sliver of the great wall above that had flowed almost completely across the rock. To go on would necessitate stepping out and round it with minimal finger grip on the ice and direct exposure to the drop below. Any slight slip, a shift in the rucksack, or a gust of wind, would result in only one conclusion. Soloma was gone and round before Nathan's mind could engage in further warnings, and he stepped after her.

"Zadie, don't look down!" he yelled back. "Grab my hand as soon as you can feel it!"

He virtually pulled her round the buttress as soon as the hands gripped and stayed to do the same with Simona and Tarma.

A retching sound was coming from behind him but since Zadie had eaten so little food there was nothing for her to bring up. He put his arm around her shoulders and guided her towards Soloma who was waiting at the end of the slab wearing a look that was torn between anxiety and satisfaction.

The ice cave behind her was high enough to enter without ducking and they could walk two abreast on its gravel-strewn floor. It was also fairly well level. Once it had been a meltwater channel, maybe as large as the one below, but now the water had found a lower level and abandoned it. It was blissfully quiet after the roaring outside.

Soloma sat in the middle of an expanse of gritty sand, smiling, and looking out through the entrance of the cave twenty yards away. Nathan released his arm from Zadie and slowly took off the rucksack, lowering himself beside them and saying, "You did wonderfully well, Soloma; you all did wonderfully well," as the others joined them. Soon, he started unpacking the rucksack.

"Looking for food?" said a recovering Zadie hopefully.

"Yes, amongst other things. Actually, I was searching for a pair of dry socks," he added, levering off his boots.

"You have dry socks in there!" she exclaimed in bemusement as the pile of items grew.

"Yes … and a pair of clean underwear … and a clean handkerchief."

She snorted.

"Anyway, here's one of the containers. If we can find a pool of water further back in the cave, it will save having to melt some ice. Come to think of it, Soloma seems to want you to go with her."

It was true. The little figure had barely rested five minutes before she was standing and beckoning Zadie.

"O, very well," Zadie said, "Mummy fetch the water – kitchen tap water, mind you, not bathroom tap!" and Nathan smiled, lifting an eyebrow in response.

He could hear them pottering further back in the cave and talking in an animated but contented tone. He picked up the binoculars. His sight was nearly back to normal now and the slightly arched mouth of the cave with its elevated position framed the distant landscape in the east. In fact, his compass suggested that he was looking almost due East. The landscape was bathed in the gentle golden-pink of the last half-hour of sunlight and, as he brought it into view, he reckoned he could make out the top half of Gulland gleaming as a broken dome ten miles distant, and beyond it the black line of the cliffs at Polgodoc. Somehow, it was a comforting scene and he was loathe to put the glasses down and tackle the mundane task of re-packing what wasn't needed and checking what was left of the food before the darkness fell. He looked across at Simona who was stretched out on her side, eyes closed, and then at Tarma, who was sitting, watching him and listening carefully to the voices from the back of the cave. On impulse, he passed the binoculars to her and could see her experimenting with them as he continued with his chore.

Zadie followed Soloma into the inner part of the cave. Although the light diminished rapidly, it had a quality about it that would have rendered the description 'gloomy' inappropriate. There was a tinge of gentle gold and pink reflecting from the distant landscape and bouncing round the walls of ice as the cave bent smoothly to her left and blocked the distant view. Suddenly, Soloma stopped and pointed, speaking excitedly. It was Zadie's turn to exclaim in surprise. Together – and with some difficulty – they lifted out the two coracles that were carefully tethered to a stake set across a recess in the ice wall of the cave, and put them on the floor. It was rather like a giant easter egg. The upper coracle was slightly larger than the lower one and fitted neatly over it, protecting the contents and keeping them dry. They spoke quickly in two competing languages and mostly at the same time as they unpacked and finally replaced the coracles, but not before Zadie had found a number of staves of wood wedged in the further depths of the recess.

"I think I'll leave them here for the morning," she said, as much to herself as to Soloma, savouring surprising Nathan with her find.

It was a strange pair that reappeared round the bend in the cave and, since they moved quietly and Nathan was busy with re-packing the rucksack, Simona had her eyes closed, and Tarma was using the binoculars, they were able to deposit the items on the sand before anyone had turned round. Afterwards, Zadie was able to say that she had never seen three faces respond in such perfect sequence of incredulity and pleasure as she did then, and it still brought a chuckle to her mind when she thought of it. Nathan's reaction was particularly pleasing as a jumble of "What? Where? How on earth?" escaped from his lips.

Chapter 17   Of Carnage and Caves

They were sitting in a circle in the last of the light chewing on dried fish and munching at what, to all intents and purposes, looked like health food bars made of some coarse grain with bits of hazel nut and baked with honey, and sipping water from a couple of shared enamel mugs to wash it down.

"I can't believe it," Nathan was saying, "loaves and fishes in an ice sheet!"

"It was very carefully packed and hidden," Zadie was replying in between chewing, as she described the recess and the coracles. "I don't think Soloma has been here before, but she knew of it and was definitely searching for it … rather like an emergency supply dump."

"Mmm, Scott of the Antarctic," murmured Nathan.

"I'd rather you had chosen Amunsden," came the riposte. "It was all so neatly wrapped inside skins, like a package, and buried in the centre of the furs. We left some of the food but brought all the furs for tonight … and," she added triumphantly, deciding to break her surprise, "there were staves!"

"Staves?" he echoed.

"Yes. Wooden staves, about shoulder height on me … with points on them."

"That's doubly good news," replied Nathan excitedly, forgetting to chew for a moment. "This is beginning to suggest that a route over the ice is possible, although I don't think this is the most obvious starting point. This sand was utterly undisturbed and there's no evidence of recent use … and the ice buttress that caused us trouble has taken a decade to creep and grow out over the rock slab."

There was not a crumb of food left when Tarma, whose eyesight was as good as her hearing, refilled the camping tin with water for Nathan and he emptied the remainder of the porridge into it so that it could soak overnight. The three girls curled up together on a blanket of furs, with more drawn over them, and Zadie and Nathan followed their example.

"I hope you don't snore or start talking in your sleep this time," said Zadie. "I'm exhausted."

"I think we all are," he replied, "but it is going to be a long and very dark night – no starlight in here – ten hours until we can see again. I don't want to use the head torch unless it's an emergency; any light from this cave would be like a lighthouse over the landscape all the way to Gulland."

"That was a nice spot. It felt kind of safe there," murmured Zadie.

"Yes," he agreed, "unlike the granite beyond it. Strange how some places have a feel about them. Polgodoc had a sense of awe; the granite was more an uneasy, dormant malice, something beneath the surface waiting to be disturbed; Gulland was at peace with itself; and this place feels neutral."

As they talked on, going over the landscape they had seen and their experiences, a single star rose in the distant east and comforted their thoughts as it progressed from floor to ceiling of the cave opening.

"What do you make of Soloma, Nathan?"

"She's an exceedingly brave and tough little girl. It's her will that has driven us on today, and she's accomplished something that would have been beyond me. She's done more than an adult could have. I haven't seen any fear in her face – just an utter determination to get us to safety – and it was only when we reached here that she smiled."

"Yes," mused Zadie, "It's almost like an adult in a child's frame … and Tarma, too; she hasn't flinched at anything. Simona's a bit different."

"I don't think Soloma trusts her entirely. She was only left with us to make sure we didn't do anything stupid when it was least dangerous," Nathan replied.

"They don't seem like children."

"What are you thinking, Zadie?"

"There's no play, and very little laughter," she observed.

"Soloma laughed with Mabel, and with Lucinda, and sometimes at the Bungalow," and then he added thoughtfully, "but you're right about the play: it was always constructive and for a purpose – like learning letters or words, or teaching me hers."

"It's strange."

"What's strange?" he asked.

"All my training, I've been digging up bits of societies like these and now I find myself in the middle of one. I dig up a bit of sharpened flint and put it on one side and label it 'cutting tool' or 'barb for fishing' and then I go on digging. I haven't the faintest idea of just how precious that ordinary item might have been to maintaining the daily struggle between life and death, or the sheer hard work of remaining alive – ordinary tasks consuming every moment of light. I'd never really appreciated what it meant to be without light at the flick of a switch and how it drives the whole rhythm of this society. And the children don't seem to have a childhood – maybe that's just an invention of our society – as soon as they can achieve a task it becomes theirs to do … and their society depends on them to do it."

"There are parts of our world that are still like that," said Nathan sadly, recalling some of the countries that he had visited and the worse pictures that he had seen: "child labour; slave labour; tasks and chores as soon as they can stand and hold a tool; nothing to hope for; no escape, only the release of an early death."

They fell silent as the Earth rolled onward through the night and, later, he asked, "Tell me about the dig you're going on in the Mediterranean."

"My first big break, really, if I get on it," she began. "Tomorrow will be Thursday and we are supposed to be assembling on Sunday evening – can't see me making that from here. Whatever else, time doesn't change in this place."

"Tell me anyway," repeated Nathan.

"It's an old site on a small island. New techniques – a kind of three-dimensional lateral radar, called Sidar3 – suggest that there is evidence of older civilisations, separated from the one that has been excavated by a layer of ash…" and she went on describing the possibilities to him until, somewhere in a complex analysis, Nathan fell asleep.

He woke around 2am. Something had disturbed him and he lay still, gathering his bearings. There must be a sliver of moon as there was the slightest light on the landscape beyond; at least, it was enough to dispel the disorienting effect of total blackness, and he practised focusing on Zadie's face to gauge how far he could see. He had just determined that he could make out her lips when they moved and whispered, "Nathan, are you awake?"

"Yes," was the reply that had always seemed rather stupid.

"I've been hearing things," Zadie mouthed very quietly.

"What sort of things?"

"A deep growling, and a kind of squeaking."

It was at the same moment that they both heard the noise. It was distant but penetrating and had a discordant element to it. Several times the noises came again and they found themselves straining to listen, holding their breath unnecessarily.

Finally Nathan said, "It's not an animal. It's the ice. Somewhere along this ice wall it's moving over the solid rock beneath – very, very slowly – that's the low grinding and growling. And somewhere up above it's deforming under the pressure and the movement – that's the squeaking, as ice moves on ice."

Zadie was relieved at first, until they both remembered the dawn on Gulland when they had watched a sky-scraper of ice tumble free from the ice wall and topple into the lake below. The picture that had been such a magnificent spectacle was a source of fear now, and they slept fitfully.

Pre-dawn light was flooding the cave with the faintest suggestion of pink when a quiet but persistent voice dragged Nathan out of one of his patches of sleep. He came to full awakefulness almost immediately and found himself looking into Soloma's dark eyes.

"What is it?" he whispered.

"Come," she replied.

Tarma was lying close to the mouth of the cave flat on her stomach and had moved the loose stones back from the edge. Soloma and Nathan joined her and he followed her line of vision until he could make out the file of figures working their way along the lake shore opposite.

"How many?" he asked.

"Six," replied Soloma, "and one."

Nathan worked his way carefully back from the edge and turned to fetch the binoculars. Zadie was sitting up looking at him.

"I'm afraid we might be having company," he told her, collecting the glasses. "Keep down low, if you're coming – the sun will be like a searchlight on the ice wall when it comes up and these people have good sight."

Four bodies were squeezed flat, peering out of the cave and watching intently.

"What are they doing?" asked Zadie.

Nathan spoke quickly, "Let's talk quietly. I know the clouds are showing a breeze from the south, but there are still some down-draughts from the night that could carry our voices over the roaring of the water below."

She nodded and accepted the mild rebuke.

"They could be scouting for more footprints. Soloma says Tarma saw them first, looking at the sand to either side of the black rock where we launched the coracles," he began in quiet commentary. "No. They've fanned out amongst the rocks. Now they're gathering together. They've found one coracle and are inspecting it … and there's the old priest talking to them and pointing."

"Get back, everybody! Now!" he commanded as the first dazzling ray of true sunlight burst onto the ice wall.

Tarma was the first to react and dived at Simona, who had quietly come and stood behind them and was rooted to the spot, illuminated like a flame in the light. Stones clattered over the lip of the cave and down over the rocks below as the two girls fell to the floor of the cave. Slowly, they all crawled back out of the line of sight.

The inside of the cave was brightly illumined a shade of orangey-red. Tarma was sitting talking with Simona on the furs; Soloma was sitting to one side, on her own; and Nathan and Zadie were arguing.

"We need to know what they are doing," Nathan was saying, "and we can't go near the mouth of the cave until we get some shadow."

"All night, I long for the light – and now we have light, you want darkness!"

"That's neither fair, nor accurate. I want to see as much as you. We just can't risk it again," he countered.

"So, what do we do – just sit and wait?" she demanded in frustration. "We're trapped!"

This was no good, thought Nathan. The last thing they needed was to start bickering amongst themselves. He reached into a pocket, feeling for a small, soft bag.

"I know it was a while ago, but I promised to show you this again when we next stopped in the light. Would you like to see it while we're waiting?"

It was a straight forward bribe, and they both knew it, as he drew the master token from the soft pouch. Its slender gold chain shimmered in the light and the translucent touch of blue in it appeared more beautiful than before. It was difficult to argue when confronted with such a thing of beauty and Zadie found herself drawn to it, touching it gently and letting the chain slip through her fingers. Soloma was there too, and caressed its surface when Zadie passed it to her, whilst Tarma and Simona gathered by her side as she let it spin gently and gave it back to Nathan. It was peculiarly attractive and each pair of eyes watched with regret as, eventually, he placed it back in its pouch.

Slowly, then more quickly, they were aware of the cave darkening unexpectedly, as if a curtain was being drawn across its entrance. Nathan edged towards the opening of the cave, lying with the binoculars out in front of him as the shadow of the rock encompassed them. Gulland stood as a broken mitre, proud and defiant in the distance; the sun, now directly behind it, cast rays of fiery red and gold as a corona around its crown, and the giant shadow moved slowly across the ice wall in response to the sun's rising arc. A hundred metres to either side was blinding orange, gold, and yellow, but where Zadie and Soloma lay with him was a single moving finger of deep shadow.

He was focused on the figures at almost the identical moment to Soloma's cry of, "There!" The coracle was in the pearly water, its milkiness in part from the debris of the melting ice and part from the down-draughts that were still roughening its surface. The paddler was making for a small island in the lake and having a tough time of it in the choppy water. Meanwhile, the old priest was standing in the shallows urging another man to wade across to the island, although the water was already above his waist. Or maybe he had been trying to help the man in the coracle.

"What do they want with the island?" asked Zadie. "Why is it important to them?"

It was a good question and he switched his gaze to it. There was nothing unusual, it seemed – and then a chill struck through him.

"Solid rock, not boulders," he said, "and there's something else … three of them."

"Three of what?" Zadie exclaimed.

"Three shaped features – not natural."

"What do they look like?"

"Pillars. Three dark pillars, about man height," Nathan answered with growing unease.

"What rock are they? … And what rock is the island?" asked Zadie urgently.

"The island's lighter. Could be granite. The pillars are dark but they're not basalt."

"Could they be serpentine?" she persisted.

He felt that the answer was being drawn unwillingly from his mind as he said, "Maybe. Here, you have a look."

Zadie was looking very carefully and voiced the thoughts of all three of them, "The last time we came across serpentine pillars, you touched the rock and we were surrounded by those evil animals that wanted Soloma as a sacrifice. They were horrid, horrifying: it chills me to even think of them. They were unreal."

"Their fangs and breath were real enough," said Nathan slowly, "and so was the evil."

It had been a stupefying evil that had reduced Soloma to a hunched down wreck of a being: evil beyond evil, un-mastered, unrelenting, overwhelming; rooted and grounded in evil; evil ancient beyond time; evil drawing strength from generations of practised evil; evil that even now was beginning to reach out and claw at their minds.

Nathan shuddered and saw that the old priest had drawn his curved knife. He was forcing the men into the water now.

"We had fire before. Fire destroyed them," intruded Zadie's voice. "Could we hit the pillars with a flare from here?"

"I don't think so," Nathan answered reluctantly. "It's too far, and the bang would be just as likely to bring a billion tonnes of ice down on top of us."

"They will be on the island soon. Maybe the animals can't cross the water..." but she tailed away unhopefully, recognising the old priest's determination.

"We'll be in the sun again in a couple of minutes," Nathan stated at the same moment as Soloma cried out and pointed.

Strong ripples were pulsing across the lake and there was a bulge of water on its surface – two bulges in fact – close together and moving fast. A distant yell came from the coracle and the men had turned. They were rushing, splashing, striving for the shore against the weight of the water. The priest had made it; so had one man; so had another. The coracle had no chance: it was butted into the air, its unbalanced human cargo thrown into the water and dismembered by a second set of razor teeth in one swift movement, the torso left to spread its stain and sink. Another man had gone, and then the last, attacked from both sides at once. For the only time, they saw the sleek body and powerful head of the aquatic murderer whose kin, or perhaps itself, had taken Soloma's sister in the Little Lake those short weeks ago. The water churned as human pieces were searched out and consumed, until the surface resembled a creamy yoghurt streaked with jam. One minute, the carnage had taken. One minute to end four lives. One minute to give five lives a chance. And the sun blazed above Gulland, blinding their view and forcing a retreat back into the cave.

The fragility of life had numbed them and there was little glee at their escape as they shared breakfast. Soloma told the others some, but not all, judging by their faces, and they concentrated on consuming the porridge that had swollen well overnight and the dried fruit that Nathan offered them from his much depleted stock.

Soon he said, "Two bars of chocolate left and three dehydrated meals, and that's it. Time to find out what Soloma intends." And he asked her, "Is there a way out of this cave?" pointing to the back.

"Yes," she said confidently.

"Do you know it? Have you been on it?"

This time he had to rephrase the question several times before Soloma shook her head. For once, disappointment and uncertainty showed on her young face.

He smiled at her, knowing now that she was working by what she had heard but not seen, and said, "Let's try together," and offered her his hand.

"How can we help her?" Zadie asked.

"I don't know," he answered. "She's attempting something that is beyond my experience. All I've done is child's play compared with what she is trying – up onto an ice sheet and across it with only a wooden stave, a few furs, and virtually no food. If it was me, it would have been planned for months; I'd have radio contact with a base, satellite images, GPS navigation, and a host of carefully chosen equipment. But one thing is sure: we're not going to let her down in the attempt!"

Chapter 18   Blue beyond a summer sky

The unwanted furs were carefully repacked into the coracles and a little more of the food removed. The remaining furs fitted the girls well and covered them to their ankles, whilst Zadie's reached to her knees. There was something comforting in their whiteness and the thought that they would be near invisible against the snow and ice – apart from Nathan, for whom no fur would fit. The staves felt a comfort in their hands, too, as they worked their way rapidly along the cave until a sharp bend cut off the last of the ricocheting, low-angle sunlight and the darkness began to deepen.

Just before it became totally dark the cave split. There was no difference in size in the two abandoned meltwater channels and even the head torch gave no clue as to which to take. A short exploration of each gave no help either and they were locked in debate, until Nathan said, "Do you mind if I have a cigar?" The improbability of the question brought Zadie to a halt in mid-sentence and the tone was more akin to reclining in a leather chair by a blazing fire after a good dinner party.

"Of course not," she replied automatically, watching in the torchlight as he took the tin from his rucksack and lit one with a match, breathing in just once before holding the glowing cigar steady in the passage. He repeated the process in the second passage, and suddenly she understood.

"Airflow!" she cried. "There's a tiny drift of air in this passage. Well done! I should have thought of that," and, if she could have seen it, Nathan blushed with pleasure. It seemed a shame to waste the cigar, small though it was, and he contemplated the unanticipated pleasure of the next few minutes.

"Zadie, you lead with Soloma. I'll bring up the rear. Caves and pot-holes are more your scene. What do you want to do with the head torch? Do you want it at the back or the front?"

"With me," she replied, gaining control of the situation,

"I'll tilt it up at the ceiling and it will give us good light from the ice. Oh, and I'll have the cigars and matches too. Now bunch up and stay within touching distance."

Soon they were making good progress, although Nathan occasionally hung back and then hurried to catch up. Zadie called back to him, "Nathan, are you doing anything? I keep hearing an odd sound."

"Just marking our way with the last of the fluorescent paint," he admitted and thought he heard a muttered, "Well, tell me next time."

Several times the passage split and narrowed and Nathan waited for the flare of a match and the aroma of cigar smoke to drift back to him. A couple of times the ceiling rose away in a great ice fissure and they had to squeeze through a narrow gap; and once another chasm cut across their route, bridged only by ice of unknown thickness, unbounded by walls and with the sound of fast-flowing water coming up from deep below. Whilst he didn't mind short caves, Nathan was rediscovering an antipathy to the extended dark passages. That had been a nasty crossing and they had taken it one at a time. Darkness made the time stretch longer but eventually there was a lessening in its intensity and, coming through a narrow squeeze, the passage widened out and Zadie was able to turn off the head torch. Nathan checked his watch. An hour's walking with it on: that would leave two hours of battery. Their spirits lifted with the light and they half-ran round a bend, looking forward to seeing a glimpse of sky, only to come to a grinding halt.

It was a relatively small obstacle but an exceedingly awkward one. It stretched from wall to wall and overhung about twenty feet above them. At its base was something of a hollow and beyond it was bright light. Several pieces of language that he wouldn't be teaching Soloma escaped from Nathan's lips as they stood contemplating the perfectly formed waterfall of ice that the meltwater had once carved at this spot.

Several minutes later Zadie said, "This is your area. Can you climb it?"

"With the right equipment, yes, but not with what we have.

And, even then, that overhang will be nearly impossible. Besides, even if I did succeed, it would take me several hours of careful work – and how would you all get up?"

"So, what do we do?"

"Look for alternatives … and, if we can't find any we go back to the last split in the passage. Here, share half a bar of chocolate with the girls, and we'll have the other half when we are out," he answered to cover his concern and encourage them. "I'm going to have a scout around the walls."

Surprisingly soon he wandered back over to them and said, "I think whatever Soloma heard was right. There's evidence of indents – cut indents – in the wall, but they are old and there has been enough moist air drifting in for the ice to regrow and smooth them over. Ten minutes work with an ice axe would do it. However, it'll be more like an hour with the penknife, when I find where I have put it."

"You can climb it, then?" asked Zadie.

"Yes," he replied.

"What about us?"

"Let me get up there first and then we'll sort that out," he said confidently. "I'll leave the rucksack with you. I can't climb with that – it's all a question of balance."

The little group of four sat and watched Nathan climb. Each smoothed recess took three or four minutes of work with the penknife to scratch and prise some of the ice loose until there was enough irregularity for a finger or toe grip. At any one point he had two feet and one hand anchored and was working at it with the free hand, occasionally moving it to his mouth and breathing on it to restore the feeling that was being numbed by the ice. The left handholds were taking longer as he was less dextrous with it and, at one point, he remained stationary for nearly ten minutes. He worked in silence, his concentration focused entirely upon the few inches in front of him. Suddenly, with three quick movements, he was up and over the lip and out of sight.

"Well done!" called out Zadie.

"Thanks ... give me five minutes to get my limbs working

again," floated back to her in reply before a variety of other sounds culminated in a prolonged silence.

Eventually, Nathan's head reappeared and said, "Zadie, can you get one of the girls to stand on your shoulders and hold a wooden stave out to me please. I think I will just be able to reach it."

Simona was the lightest and, at the third attempt, she had managed to scramble up Zadie's back and perch on her shoulders with them both leaning against the wall. She was flailing around with one hand trying to find the end of the stave that Tarma was holding up to her, without looking down and unbalancing the precarious pyramid. Soloma was guiding operations in her language with instructions that Zadie guessed to be variants on 'left a bit', 'right a bit', 'up a bit', 'down a bit', and she was suddenly seized with the humour of the occasion – it was rather like a party game – and had to resist the temptation to laugh and bring them all down. Nathan had to lean over rather further than he liked to gain the end of the stave being waved by Simona and when she released her grip of it he nearly slid forward with the additional weight. Finally, though, he had worked his way back out of sight and a muffled hammering, as of stone on wood, echoed back down.

He reappeared, looking pleased with himself, and called out, "OK, I'm going to throw something down to you. I want you to tie it to the rucksack and hold the rucksack above your head as high as you can." He disappeared again.

The rope landed near Zadie's feet and brought an immediate cry of delight. It might have been old, fibrous, and thin, but it was definitely rope. What was more, if Nathan had found it, it had been put close by for this very place and was another sign that a way forward might be possible. Soloma was examining it, too, and told Zadie that it was old. She tested it with the weight of the rucksack and several strands of fibre snapped. Nevertheless, they followed Nathan's request and he reeled it in delicately, keeping the speed as constant as he could and sliding it up the smooth ice wall to prevent it swinging, before grabbing its strap at the first opportunity. The rope came down again and the staves went up one by one. It came down once more and Nathan's head reappeared.

"Right," he said, "Your turn now. The rope won't hold your weight but you can use it to help balance if you wobble. One of you hold it taut that end and I'll keep the tension here. I want Soloma up last and Tarma first. No offence, but the way Soloma tackled those cliffs at Polgodoc I think she may not need the rope."

Tarma came carefully and Simona followed her with an easy climbing motion. Zadie didn't want to leave Soloma to last and turned to look back at her after three holds, which resulted in her sliding back down unceremoniously and having to start again. Nathan could feel the tension in the rope varying as it was being touched frequently and he bit back the urge to call out. Any suggestions were likely to be unhelpful in mid climb. An arm came into reach and he steadied it, pulling her gently over the last lip of ice. He was about to peer over again when Soloma's head and shoulders appeared and she stepped lightly beside him.

"Well done, all of you," he said warmly. "Pick up a stave and go and have a look at the view. I'll be with you in a moment."

Having coiled the rope and tucked it away, he strode out of the cave to join them where they were sitting on a boulder, drinking in the sunshine and the surroundings. It was certainly spectacular. To their left was an ice wall, towering steeply but not as vertiginously as the ice wall fronting the lake that they had come from. To the right was a modestly steep slope of ice, rising up to the summit of the ice sheet, maybe eight hundred metres higher. In places it was riven with crevasses as the surface had flowed forward faster than the base, and at one point it had spread laterally producing a small forest of seracs – pinnacles of ice created by an intersecting set of fissures as it split and spread. Nearer, it was black, not white, where a litter of moraine covered half the surface of the slope up to the summit. Across from them was a broken wall of ice, blue in tinge at its base, and making a clean cliff a hundred metres high before it rose irregularly to the ice plateau beyond. It was a kind of amphitheatre of ice encompassing a jewel of unparalleled beauty – a lake as blue as the summer sky and with the appearance of solidity – a great splash of azure paste from an artist's palette, radiating its colour in the weak sunlight.

"That lake," said Zadie, "I've never seen anything like it: water can't be that colour; it's unreal. It's kind of majestic and delicate at the same time. I keep staring at it, thinking it will suddenly change. It almost looks good enough to eat."

"Talking of which," said a voice behind her, "here's the other half of the chocolate to share." He went on, "Yes. I never thought I'd see this. I had to tear myself away from it to come back into the cave. I've seen pictures – there's just one place where it's like this – but the pictures don't do it justice, not in any way. I can tell you the theory but experiencing the reality is altogether different. If there was no other reason for our journey, I would have come for this."

"So, what is it? Why is it so wonderfully blue?"

Nathan told her about the pictures he had seen of the Patagonian ice sheet – the third largest in the world – and how it was in rapid retreat. At its edge, wedged between the melting ice and abandoned moraine, was a larger lake than this. There was a local name for its colour 'dulce de glaciar', glacier cream, which came from the old, old ice, squeezed by a hundred thousand years of pressure beneath a thousand metres of overlying ice until even the air trapped in it had been forced out. Blue ice, he called it, and pointed at the lower ice wall opposite.

"Never thought I'd see it," he ended. "Mind you, it explains a lot. This is the true edge of the ice sheet, and it's melting rapidly." (Zadie translated this as 'might retreat a few metres in a century'.) "What we came through is a huge block of abandoned ice detached from it and about half a mile wide and eight hundred metres high. The lake would have been higher in the past, too; hence the abandoned meltwater channels and the old waterfall we had to climb."

Surprisingly, he was quite willing to leave the spot now, almost as if to linger would be greedy, a surfeit of the sublime, and he called over to the others, "Zadie, you lead with Tarma. Keep on the black stuff and stop if there are any crevasses in sight. I'll come with Soloma – I want to find out what she knows about direction – and if there are any clear, surface meltwater streams, have a drink: water will be a problem once we're up on top. It should take an hour and a half if it's as good going as it looks."

In truth, bringing up the rear meant he was not risking taking the party at a speed too great for them and he could pause and look at the lake when he wanted. Soloma was good company and a conversation in bits of two languages, aided by gestures and pointing, began to give him a picture of what lay ahead. 'Home' apparently could be reached well before sunset and lay almost due west of a black rock cairn. Soloma had given directions and time from pointing at the sun, once she understood what Nathan wanted. The black rock cairn had taken rather longer to decipher. It was the worrying factor. Finding a small cairn in an ice wilderness was not going to be the easiest of tasks. Even with a map and GPS it would be difficult. At least the weather was holding and the party was moving at a good pace. Nathan sent Soloma on to keep Simona company whilst he worried at the problem of the cairn in his mind.

It had been his intention to call a halt just below the summit, partly as an excuse to sit and look back at the increasingly small sliver of lake that was visible, but he was lost in his thoughts and there was no distinct change of slope so it was much to his surprise when he found himself looking across a vast, unbroken sea of ice. The plateau stretched to the horizon, merging indistinctly with the high white cloud, occasional patches of rippled blue giving the only indication that the one was earth and the other sky. Zadie had halted and they took their break, grouped together in the light southerly breeze, and at least two of them feeling like intruders in an alien environment.

"That's fifteen," he said, looking at his watch. "Time we moved on. I think we'll let the girls lead this time. They've as good a chance as I have and there was something that Soloma was saying that I didn't understand. She was quite definite about it though."

Soloma certainly seemed confident and it was more noticeable that Tarma and Simona were both contributing thoughts to her as they walked, making good progress at first. Then the ice surface became ridged – not dramatically so but in a series of long, low ridges about three metres high and forty metres apart. The intervening troughs had loose, powdery snow, shin-deep in them and it made the going harder, particularly as they were taking each ridge at an angle. Zadie finally expressed her exasperation to Nathan.

"I hate these ridges! Can't we take them at right angles? That would be easier."

"Mmm," Nathan began unhelpfully, "you haven't noticed then?"

"Noticed what?"

"She's using them as a map – them, and the angle of the sun. On my compass, we've been following an almost constant bearing of 280° – West by North. This is the sixteenth ridge, and prior to the ridges we had twenty minutes walking on flattish ice on the same bearing," he replied.

"You are counting all that! I suppose you're bored with my conversation."

"No," he laughed. "Just thought it might be useful if ever we try a return journey…"

"Fair enough. I'll start considering the ridges as friends now. What are they, anyway?"

"Sastrugi," he answered.

"Show off! What does that mean?"

"Ice pressure ridges – the opposite of crevasses. The ice behind is moving faster than the ice in front and it is buckling the surface upwards like a corrugated roof. I haven't come across them before," he added, "and I agree they're not very pleasant. Caused Scott a lot of trouble with dogs and sleds. Fortunately, we are not carrying much. They may end soon if Soloma's timings are right."

The words had hardly been spoken when they saw the girls ahead stopping at the crest of ridge number twenty. The ice before them was flat again and all three girls were scanning it carefully in the milky sunlight. Zadie had the binoculars from Nathan's pack and was quartering the landscape. Finding the marker cairn was vital. This was not the place to start using guesswork and estimates. Soloma had said that 'home' was directly west from the cairn and about two hours travel. A fruitless quarter of an hour was beginning to prey on them all. Zadie reckoned Tarma had the best sight and had given her the glasses in frustration. Gently the sun edged clear of the high dappled cloud and Tarma cried out, pointing to their left. They had it now. There, in an ocean of unmitigated white was a single black speck, perhaps half a mile distant, although there was nothing to judge distances by, and slightly to the west of their line of travel.

In fact, the distance must have been less as it took only a few minutes to reach the cairn. Zadie was thinking how such a small thing could mean so much and of the labour involved in bringing stones an unknown distance to build something barely a metre high and two across. She could feel the excitement rising – both intellectual and emotional – at their journey being close to an end and the chance to see an ancient community in action. The girls were talking freely and pointing to the west where a strange cloud hung. Nathan was looking at it too, through the binoculars. It was not at all like the mixture of dappled cirro-cumulus or the thin blankets of cirro-stratus stretched high above. Rather, it was a vertical tower, a rising veil catching the light slightly with the sun past its zenith. It was too thin to be smoke and there was no discolouration of the light or opacity that smoke would yield. Zadie had suggested smoke from a volcano, only to be told that the nearest volcanically active areas were in Iceland and the Canaries, and that volcanoes didn't smoke – they either gave off steam or ash in columns, if they weren't throwing out cinders or lava. Most of the time they did nothing. Nevertheless, it was fascinating, and the fascination grew as they walked directly towards it.

Another marker cairn came and went. The ethereal cloud was billowy with shades of subtle light illumining the motions within it and it had grown to bar the horizon beyond. Soloma was heading directly for it and its mysterious quality held their attention.

As a consequence, danger was upon them almost before they realised it and Nathan's cry of "Stop!" only just reached the girls a hundred yards ahead. Zadie and he ran clumsily on the ice to catch up as the thick fog bank rolled in from the south and enveloped them, distorting sound, disorienting, darkening the light; and bringing a chill, damp cold that seeped rapidly into the exposed flesh and spread through the lungs and body. They stopped, knowing that the others were within fifty yards but out of sight.

"Alright, we'll do this on a bearing," Nathan said urgently to Zadie. "See if you can get Soloma to keep calling out – but she must stay where she is."

The luminous point on the compass steadied on due west in Nathan's open palm and the strange dialogue between Zadie and Soloma echoed and rolled with the fog bank, sometimes seeming loud enough to touch its owner, at other moments so faint it was hardly heard – and always shifting, shifting its direction. Without a solid reference point it was difficult to tell any slopes on the ground and Nathan dared not look below the open compass to his footing.

"That's sixty paces on 270°. They should be within twenty metres of us, if they didn't veer off line before they stopped. Try calling again," he said.

The reply sounded faint but the varying denseness of the fog and the slow, swirling currents of chilled air within it acted like echoing boards and heavy curtains to redirect and muffle voice and sound. They took another ten paces on the same bearing and tried again. It wasn't easy to find anything in the world of dampened white – white ground, white fog; white below, white above; white enveloping everything – and the three figures they sought were dressed in white furs. Again, they found themselves longing for one point of blackness in the world of white.

This time the reply was stronger. They were straining their sight into the fog on their left, following the sound. Zadie looked at Nathan, pleading in her eyes to be allowed to run at the sound and find the little girl she loved. Abruptly, she pointed behind him in the opposite direction. It seemed to them both that on the wavering edge of indistinct visibility was a slight darkening, a formless beginning of a shadow.

Nathan nodded and said, "Five steps only. Keep within sight of me. I don't want to lose you as well."

Already the dense fog was enveloping her and it was only the dark boots beneath the fur that gave any surety of her position to Nathan. Suddenly, she shrieked and was gone.

Nathan stared at the point where she had been. Already his mind was playing on uncertainties and seeking to drag his eyes to either side or down to the compass. There was nothing else to do now.

He called out and plunged after her.

Chapter 19   The World in the White

It was a bare twelve steps and Nathan virtually fell over them. Zadie was hugging and shaking the slender form, wrapping her inside her own fur and holding her against her own body.

"She's so cold," she said, sobbing simultaneously from relief and pity. "Poor little thing, she's nearly frozen."

In a last, desperate attempt to provide a marker for the nearby voices that she had heard but had not seen, Soloma had stripped off her white fur and stood, then sat, in the cold fog. Ten minutes more and she would have lost her sense of feeling altogether and the numbed mind would have started acting irrationally as hypothermia set in. It had been both a brave and foolish act, thought Nathan, as he thrust her own fur back around her and forced her to stamp her feet and move her limbs. A slow smile spread through Soloma's eyes.

"Here. Make them eat this – and you have some too," he ordered, breaking the last bar of chocolate into uneven pieces with hands that were clumsy with the cold. "It's the best I can do; I haven't got the right stuff or the right equipment – hot, sweet tea would be better – but at least it has some sugar in it." Quickly, he went on, "We can't stay here. This fog is drawing cold from the ice: it's virtually freezing and it's draining us by the minute. We can't wait for it to lift: we must move, or we'll be a human cairn for some hunter to stumble on in a decade's time. Now listen. I'll explain the principles of navigating in white-out conditions. It sounds simple but it's horrid for the person in front and it's not as accurate as it sounds. Zadie, you'll understand. Soloma knows enough words to grasp some of it, especially left and right. Tarma, I'm sorry, but you'll have to have these round you," he said, tying the wet (and smelly) pair of thick red walking socks round her like a scarf.

The strange party moved off slowly. Zadie was in front

wearing the head torch so that it pointed directly back behind her. Soloma was alongside her, with a brief to make sure that she didn't lose sight of Tarma five paces behind them. Five more paces behind was Nathan, the compass held at face level in his open palm and its luminous dial pointing due west. Simona was beside him to guide his feet. Nathan's parting briefing had been to go slowly and to repeat every instruction he gave back along the line. The theory was simple: line up Tarma, whose red sock scarf he could see, with Zadie, whose figure he couldn't see but whose light he could; set them off on the bearing, keep them in a straight line, and keep walking. In practice, there was a huge amount that could go wrong even without the additional problems of language.

After a few minutes, Nathan yelled, "Left one pace," and some seconds later Tarma called over her shoulder, "Left." Intermittently, he yelled again as they moved on without any sense of accomplishing distance. It didn't matter that Tarma didn't understand the words, although he suspected she did. All she had to do was repeat them and keep following Zadie. If Soloma's timings were anywhere near right they were about forty minutes normal walking from her 'home'. This would take them three times as long in these conditions and he dreaded the thought that they might encounter more pressure ridges on the ice.

Zadie was not liking it. It was a weird sensation and her mind was beginning to scream at her. It was like stepping into nothingness. There were no markers or rocks to break the whiteness. There was nothing that she could fasten her view on ahead and she was reduced to watching her feet move over the equally white surface below, forcing her mind to admit that they were moving forward and resisting the urge to turn and look behind or dash madly to one side. Time seemed to have stopped as well, and the occasional faint call of, "Left" or "Right," was becoming a treasured moment of sanity to hold onto. She longed for light – real light – and clarity – something tangible outside of her being that she could lock onto … anything … anything at all that would give a point of reference in this interminable whiteness of insubstantiality. It wouldn't be so bad if Nathan was beside her; she harboured a thought that she might be growing fond of him and entertained a debate in her mind for a while as to whether it was fear driving her to yearn for reassurance or just wanting to pass the job of stepping out into this wretched nothingness to someone else.

A long while later, Zadie heard a faint cry of, "Stop," and Tarma, Nathan and Simona joined her.

"Not nice," said Nathan. "That's a really unpleasant job, leading like that: thank you."

The professional comment warmed her and Zadie replied, "This fog doesn't seem quite the same. It's moving differently … and it's not quite as cold."

"Yes," he answered, "and I've had the impression that we've been moving very gently downhill for a while, judging by your head torch."

They reformed the line and went on again. There was definitely a change and in a matter of minutes Nathan was gaining glimpses of Tarma's figure and then of Zadie's ahead. They stopped again and turned off the torch. It seemed perceptibly lighter ahead and the slightest bit less white, like a touch of frosted jasmine on a winter's morning.

"We'll try a line abreast for two hundred paces," said Nathan, "but let me keep two steps ahead."

Zadie felt a huge well of relief that she could follow something she could see, as Nathan led. The light was growing and stretching across their course, the faintest shade of primrose now. Whatever it was, it was becoming taller and wider. A second colour emerged and Nathan's foot struck a rock – its simple blackness both instantly comforting and immediately concerning. The ground was sloping and more rocks appeared. His mind played on the thought of nearing the edge of an ice cliff or stepping into a crevasse as he picked his way slowly downslope, abandoning the compass and using the gradient as a guide. It was a warmer wetness, and rocks were becoming more common than ice; soon there was solid rock in patches, pink and slippery, and steep; and, finally, a glimpse of some half-living plant. The fog was thinning – golden and spiralling upwards, prisms of water scattering light in a shimmering of rainbow hues – until, as suddenly as it had come, a breath of air drew the veil away and they staggered, stunned by what they saw.

Below them was a landscape, circled by sloping ice, but green and brown, and pink and black. It filled a great bowl in the ice and around its perimeter rose a cylindrical curtain of shifting mist or spray. A gentle hill lay in the middle with narrow fields contoured around it to the south and wooded strips to its north. A scattering of huts straggled near its crown; there were streams and pools and, above all, there were figures moving. Three tracks led through the mist from the ice to three large, dark black rocks and snaked on down to meet up before ascending the hill.

"Home!" said Soloma simply.

The nearest track was a few hundred yards to their right and the girls were tugging at Nathan and Zadie to move across the steep slope towards it, their enthusiasm making light of weary limbs. Soon, they were on it and moving easily down the slope towards the rock. Not for the first time Nathan gasped as they approached. The rock was carved out of basalt and its familiar shape sent his mind back to the mouth of the bay he loved at Trevennick. No wonder Soloma had been so content to sit on the cliff top and look at it, for here was its verisimilitude in triplicate welcoming the ways to her home. The head was well-shaped, standing alert above the resting paws, and behind it was a cleft, before the lithe back and tail of the crouching lioness stretched away.

The girls climbed up, placing a palm in the cleft before skipping round the hind-quarters of the black lioness and waiting. Zadie and Nathan repeated their actions more slowly and were adjacent to the rear paws when they were brought firmly but irresistibly to a halt.

"Barrier," they said together. But the girls had passed through and there were no tokens to be seen. Soloma was speaking and telling them to wait. "Soon," she had said and disappeared down the track with Tarma and Simona, leaving Zadie and Nathan to perch beside the path watching them until their view was blocked by vegetation.

"Why can they get in and not us?" asked Nathan in frustration.

"I think," said Zadie, "that they belong here and the rock has welcomed them as its own. Anyway, Soloma didn't seem surprised that we couldn't follow – and she told us to wait."

"Wait for what?"

"For whom, I suspect," she answered. "A welcoming party probably. A pity: I wanted to see her meet her mother. Still, it gives us a chance to think – and I'd like to get a better look, so pass me the binoculars, will you."

As she examined the scene below, Nathan strolled to a nearby stream and drank awhile. He was stroking the smooth head of the lioness and looking at Zadie's gold-blond hair as she studied the village and fields below. The hair was ruffled and unkempt but it had a lustre in the late afternoon light and soon he found himself running his hand gently over it and through it.

"We've come a long way," he murmured.

"Yes," she replied, lifting her face to his and kissing him, the glasses forgotten in her lap.

They sat together, hand in hand, at peace with each other's company and content to exchange thoughts without speaking. There was movement on the path below but they sat on, untroubled.

At last, Zadie stirred and said, "They're close now. I'd rather be standing to meet them," and they rose to wait the few minutes more.

It was a small party that was coming, unarmed and slowly. Tarma was there, along with a boy and several other girls, and a woman who might have been her mother. The group stopped a few feet away, separated from them only by the invisible barrier, and the woman called a greeting, to which Nathan replied. She stepped through the barrier and placed the palm of her hand in the cleft of the lioness and, a moment later, Tarma was there too, leading them on down the track.

At the bottom of the slope there were stepping stones across a stream, a warm mist playing on its surface. It became apparent that they were not to ascend the hill directly but to follow round it. They passed a strip of hazel and saw two children hurry away with the nuts they had been gathering. Tarma and the boy were talking and pointing and Nathan gathered the gist of some of the conversation, translating it for Zadie, who was busy with her own pointing and commentary. Hazel and holly gave way to something strikingly akin to bamboo and then to narrow fields curving with the slope and waving gently with waist high grasses. They were more like terraces than strip lynchets and in some places the vegetation had been cut. There were no animals but several fields had been dug and Zadie cried out with delight, pointing out to Nathan the digging tools lying nearby.

The path wended its way gently downwards until voices could be heard, and round the corner a series of pools came into sight. A coracle lay bobbing in the water on the farther side, its occupants having made a hasty exit; and three large, golden fish lay on a stone still flapping on their threaded line. Two slender barbed shafts were alongside and, as they looked across the three large pools, they saw the tell-tale ripples of other fish moving in the depths.

"Neat," said Zadie. "Fish ponds – meat and protein all year round. The medieval monasteries did the same. Mind you, they had rabbit warrens and dovecots, too."

As they walked and watched, they were increasingly conscious of being watched but seeing no-one as voices evaporated before their arrival.

"I don't understand. It seems like they accept us, but are afraid of us," Zadie mused, "and Soloma's nowhere to be seen."

"I think we are being stalled," Nathan replied; "given a tour whilst Soloma tells the elders, or however this village is organised, about us. When they are ready, we'll be brought before the head-man."

"You might be right about the stalling but I think you might have a surprise about the head-man. Now, these look interesting," she continued, pointing to a series of pools fed by two separate streams.

The pools were fairly large, about six in number and varying in depth, separated by areas of flattish rock. Investigating further, they were struck by the warmth of the water and Zadie plunged her arms into the nearest pool, sluicing her face with water. Nathan turned to ask Tarma about them but found that no-one was there.

"Strange," he said, "they've gone," and, tasting the water, "This is spring water – hot spring water – and the other stream is cold and drinkable. I'm beginning to understand why this place is free of ice: the warmth is coming from the rocks themselves – geothermal heat – the hot springs keep it ice-free, and that also explains the mist rising around the edge…"

"Well, you carry on looking at the geology. Meanwhile, I'm going to have a wash while there's no-one around. I stink," announced Zadie, discarding garments and immersing herself in the deepest warm pool.

The sound of her splashing and the concept of a wash became unbearable, and soon Nathan was dangling his legs in the water. Suddenly, there was a noisy disturbance and several girls joined Zadie in the pool, laughing and pointing at her. The noise re-doubled as she responded by rolling on her back and kicking water at them whilst the girls half stood and scooped wavefuls of water back at her. She was outnumbered and getting the worst of the water fight, much to Nathan's amusement, when Soloma approached unheard behind him and said, "Time to come."

He busied himself with his pack whilst Soloma quelled the fight and Zadie retrieved various items of clothing. She was in a good mood when she joined him, the thick white fur draped over an arm, and the girls following a short distance behind as they made their way up the hill with Soloma. The path zigzagged between the fields and, when they reached the area of huts, small groups of people were standing outside looking at them.

"Notice anything?" asked Zadie, interrupting Nathan's conversation with Soloma. He had been trying to gain information about where they were going and who they would be meeting but he was finding Soloma somewhat evasive – deliberately so, he thought.

"They seem to be friendly," he proffered in reply.

"Anything more detailed? It's fairly obvious," persisted Zadie.

"There's some smoke from fires … probably starting to cook … it's near the end of the light," he tried.

"Sometimes you are so unobservant. What about the people?"

He looked and thought. The figures were quite short and slim in build. Perhaps food wasn't plentiful. Since he had no idea what to expect, he was struggling to follow Zadie's reasoning and contented himself by muttering, "You're the expert. Tell me."

"In that case, the expert says 'gender'. There are no men, and very few boys."

At that moment, they came to a flatter area with an almost circular pool. Around its edges were deposits in pastel shades of lemon and pink and, in the middle, a fragile growth of white protruded above the surface of the water and extended in an irregular, widening shape beneath it. A few red petals floated on the water, and a few more had become becalmed in a tiny embayment near the centre, in what was unmistakably living white coral. It was so extraordinary that Nathan stopped and Zadie bumped straight into him.

"Come," called Soloma.

A short way further up was a slightly more substantial hut, built into the hillslope and facing south. Skins to cover the doorway were hooked up carelessly on the flimsy wooden wall made from horizontal lengths cut from the same bamboo-like vegetation they had seen earlier. Soloma ducked inside, beckoning them to follow.

Chapter 20   Elana

It was a single room built against the rock of the hillside, dim compared to the outside, although some light filtered through the gaps in the walls and more spilt in through the doorway behind them. Towards one side was the makings of a hearth, and a residual smell of smoke and cooking pervaded the atmosphere. Various implements were neatly grouped along with a few utensils and, at other points, furs were spread over the dried leaves of the bamboo-like plant. A small slab of pink rock made a flat table. On it rested a miniature carving of a lioness – black as the basalt it was carved from and perfect in its imitation of the three guardians of the paths into this strange land. The other objects were less recognisable, obscured by their familiarity, until it became clear that they were a bar of soap and a handful of tea-bags.

Alongside the table a figure sat. The hair was white and shoulder length. A short chain of copper links hung round the neck. The face was creased by the battering of elements and time but the eyes were bright, sparking through the aura of dignity and sadness that it gave. With surprising agility the figure rose, greeting Nathan and Zadie, and gesturing to them to sit. Nathan returned the greeting and, for whatever reason, felt moved to give the slightest inclination of his head in deference to the elderly figure.

"Welcome," she said, and Zadie and Nathan looked at each other in astonishment.

"I see from your reaction that I have not lost the art of words, long though it is since I have spoken your language," the old lady continued in a slightly halting, stilted way as she sought for words, long familiar, long unused. "Soloma has told me much, and she will tell me more when you are gone. I thank you for bringing her back to me. I had thought she was dead and grieved her passing. You have travelled far, and not with ease. Tonight you shall stay here with me in safety; and tomorrow you must go. I will give you such food and help as we can spare."

Zadie felt as if a cold hand had gripped her inside and blurted out, "Why must we go?"

There was no anger in the reply, only a certain measured sadness. "You must go because the weather is changing: soon we will be locked in for winter and travel will not be possible. You must go because there have been deaths: evil will seek vengeance. It would have been better had there been no witnesses left in your encounter at the stones of sacrifice. It will take them a while to gather the men they need; there are barely five hundred in total in what you know as Cornwall and they are well dispersed. If you go now, you have the better chance. And it will be better for my people if you were not known to have stayed here.

"I'm sorry," said Zadie. "It's just that I had been looking forward to seeing Soloma meeting her mother and being with her family."

"You were the last to see her mother alive," the old lady said slowly. "It was she who was fishing at the little lake when the creature took her. Strange – it was always a safe place to fish … they would not have anticipated danger … not there. I am her family now, and she is my child – my great-grandchild." After a pause, she went on, "The furs that you have brought back were made by her grandmother, Varda, my daughter. They were well made – others have not had her skill – and that route has not been used for a generation. Even then it was a secret route, used only in time of great urgency. I thought it had been closed by the ice. Soloma's mother must have learnt of it at her mother's knee and told Soloma of it. So," she sighed, "you have seen the Secret Lake. Is it still beautiful beyond a summer sky?"

"It is very beautiful … the most beautiful lake I have ever seen," replied Nathan courteously and truly.

"I would have liked to have seen it once more," came the wistful response, "but few winters are left to me now and I must remain with my people."

"Soloma will prepare food for us," she said, nodding towards the girl. "The fish have been caught. Indeed, you saw them yourselves. And while she cooks, you may ask me questions. My name is Elana, although once it was Eleanor."

"Thank you," Nathan said and asked, "Elana, how long have you been here and how did you come to be here?"

"The answer to your first question is fifty years. That to your second question is a longer tale, but I will tell it briefly. Soloma can listen too, for there are parts she does not know.

"It was late summer," began Elana, "soon after the war. I was walking the cliffs with my beloved. He was on leave and hoped to come home and settle down. We were talking about those hopes and watching the waves crashing against the cliffs when a squall came in from the horizon. We sheltered in a cave and it was while the rain came down that he proposed to me and produced a ring. I was in love with him and wished with all my heart that we should be together. The last thing I remember was kissing him, and then I fell into a darkness. I did not know whether I was in a dream or waking; whether I was dead or alive. I crawled around, seeking a way out of my darkness, hoping to find his arms again. Hours later, I tumbled into a strange place where there were stars and the smell of wet grass, but no-one heard my cries. He did not come to me.

"When morning came, I saw a landscape that I knew but it was not as I knew it. There were no fields or walls; no people; no animals; and there was a great plain stretching out where there should have been sea. I wandered that day and the next, searching for company and something to eat. That night I sheltered in holly bushes where there was a strange stone, and in the morning two women found me. In truth, they were little more than girls, only a few years older than Soloma, and bearing the extra burden of pregnancy. They shared the little food they had with me and taught me where to look for berries as we came towards the west. I will never forget my first sight of the ice: it was both terrible and beautiful in the rising sun. Two days we were on it. They were dreadful days. The food ran out. There was no water to drink, and no way of knowing where we were going. We stumbled into this place at darkness on the second day.

"I do not remember much about the next weeks. I think I was ill. But they treated me with kindness and I recovered, learning their language and their ways, until I could be of use and not be a burden upon them. It was different then – less food and less people. They could have let me starve but they were generous with what they had."

Elana sighed at some old memory and Nathan asked, "Did you ever try to go back to your own home?"

"Yes," she answered. "Twice I tried. They told me of a legend that somewhere there was an opening to the east through which a person might pass but not return. The second time, I reached the cliffs I knew but there were men there, strange men. I did not stay. Each day this seemed more like my home and, although I wandered far when I was young, always I returned. Soon it was my home. I brought things back with me and taught some things in exchange for what they taught me. The hazel coppice that you saw comes from nuts I found on a distant hillslope. We separated the streams and created the wash-pools, and made the implements with which to dig. Gradually the land became more productive and fed more mouths, until it is as you see it now. Usually, we have enough for the winter."

"Where are the men?" asked Zadie. "There must be men as you have children."

"They come," answered Elana; "once, sometimes twice, a year ... always from the south ... only a few. They wait by the guardian for us to let them in. They choose and go again."

Zadie and Nathan asked several questions at once, and Elana held up her hand. The light was nearly gone and Soloma turned the fish on the hot stones, carefully feeding the fire to keep a small blaze lit.

"I will tell you more," Elana began again, "for I see that you are curious and I cannot think that it will harm. It is in the spring that the men come. They bring gifts with them: copper or tin that they have smelted; furs from the winter hunting; sometimes strips of dried meat if they have had a good winter. They cannot pass the guardian unless we let them in. A child may pass freely but no adult may enter unless they are let in by one who has given birth. That is why you could not pass until Tarma's mother let you in.

"They stay a day and choose a wife, as you would say, from amongst the girls who are of age. Then they leave. The girl goes with them and tends and cooks for them, and others, over the summer while they are busy mining. That is why Soloma was away: her mother was teaching her the land beyond the ice. The men looked long at her this year: she is taller and fairer of face, like most of mine, and soon she will be chosen. Sometimes they stay with the men one summer, sometimes a year or more, but when they are pregnant they return, often at this time of year. The winter does not support un-needed mouths on that land either, and we can care the better for them. When I came here they laughed at me and told me I was too old to be chosen. They thought when I was wandering that I was seeking a man. A few are never chosen, and a few are chosen twice. Tarma's mother they ask for much as she gave birth to twins – our only twins, Tarma and her brother, Ruan. They bring her many gifts, but she is strong-willed and will not go again. Sometimes we send gifts back with them – ornaments of copper that we have made – to the men that we knew."

"What happens to the boys?" Zadie asked.

"When they are strong enough to be of use the men may take them. We do not see them again until they return for a girl. Some we never see again: the mining is dangerous. Most long to go and plead to be taken with the men. Ruan is the oldest here. It is unusual for a boy to stay so long but he has his mother's will and a love for his sister: they are rarely parted," explained Elana.

"They were parted," observed Nathan carefully, sensing that he was entering unwelcome ground.

"Yes," said Elana.

"And I think not willingly," he continued.

"You are right. It is not something of which I am proud. Some things I have changed but the old lore is hard to alter … and some evil is beyond me," replied Elana.

The pause lengthened into awkwardness and indecision

before she finally continued, "Only a few times in my lifetime, the men have come again – older men with one of the Mortan – the priests. They come when they have lost many in the mining, or in fighting, and they need more hands. They demand the boys to replace their losses. Late this summer they came. We had too few for them and Ruan refused to go on his own. If we cannot meet their needs they will take two girls. We refused to let them in, and none would yield a girl to them. Tarma and Simona were returning from gathering berries high up on the slopes beyond the guardian. They took them before we realised, and were gone. We have no weapons; it was nearing night; and there are no tracks left on the ice. Ruan and his mother went after them at dawn. It was four days before they returned, empty-handed. The others feared the Mortan and were whispering in their huts."

"Did they know what would happen to the girls?" asked Nathan.

"Yes," Elana answered sadly. "It is part of the old lore passed down the generations, from grandmother to child, that if insufficient males are born a female child will be sacrificed to appease the wrath of the evil ones and prevent disaster." She went on, "You look at me as if I do not realise but I, and I alone of those now living, have seen it. I know what happens. Long ago, I followed them with Varda. We were near a hill far from the ice when we saw it happen. I will not repeat what they did, nor talk of the malice of that place whilst it is dark. There was nothing we could do. We were seen and pursued, at first by half-creatures filled with evil cunning, and then by men, until we crossed the Great Lake and sheltered in a cave. That is how we discovered the route through the ice and past the Secret Lake.

"Perhaps you think that we were cowards; that we should have tried to stop them and died in some vain attempt. Perhaps you think I have had the power to stop it since. I tell you, it was worse in the past. You saw a pool with white coral below this hut. It was the custom to make sacrifice there each year. A baby girl was placed on the white coral in the centre and left overnight. The coral is sharp and the flesh is soft; the child could not crawl through the water. The white was stained red in the morning, and the cries were more than an ear could bear. When I became leader I put a stop to it. Now we cast petals on the water instead. They know I love flowers and bring me a few whenever they find them."

Horrors of imagination and memories suppressed lasted until Soloma moved forward to the old lady with a piece of fish. She nodded, satisfied, and each was served. At a word from Elana, Soloma joined her and ate too, before fetching honey-cakes of grain and nuts. There was a quietness about the meal as each digested their own thoughts, and when it was ended Nathan thanked Elana in her own tongue.

"Soloma has taught you well," she observed. "I think I will teach her your language more fully this winter, and Tarma too. The winters are long and it will give me something to do now that my hands are too feeble to mend or make."

They spoke late of many things, watching the dying embers of the fire and finding a strange bond in doing so. Elana told of a northern route across the ice that was marked by cairns and took two days to reach a point where ice-fall and rock had shallowed the Great Lake so that it was fordable with care. From Nathan's description, she recognised the hill of Gulland and the Little Lake – but of Polgodoc they said nothing. Zadie was quiet for a long while and was troubling over something in her mind.

Eventually, she asked, "Are your people afraid of us? When we were walking around the fields, and at the fish-ponds, we could hear voices but they vanished before we saw them."

Elana's expression was no longer visible as she replied, "The answer is both no and yes. It was not you they were afraid of, but Tarma." Nathan looked up in surprise as she continued, "Yes, they had grieved her loss. They had assumed she was sacrificed and gone from them, along with Simona. When you brought them back, they thought they were spirits returned to haunt them because they had denied the Mortan. Tarma's mother, Meroa, was having none of it. I told you that she was strong-willed. She could feel her daughter's flesh and saw her eat. She was not going to hide her away, but others feared that if Tarma looked them in the eye they would suffer her fate. Simona has not been so lucky. Her mother has hidden her and refused her food, declaring that as she is a ghost she has no need to eat. She is fearful that a sacrifice has been rejected and doom will follow.

"The unexpected brings uncertainty, and uncertainty breeds speculation; whispers arise, and half-memories surface from the past. There is evil without, but the greater evil is within. However, it is true that they fear you to some extent. I told you the legend of the opening in the East. It has another part I have not told – that strangers may come from the East bearing knowledge that is wonderful, but always in time of great trouble. Soon after I arrived there was an awful winter. Normally it is dry here, as we are in the middle of the ice and the streams melt any snow, but that year it rained for many days. The stored grain became wet and there was illness and death. I went away, and when I came back I was heavy with Varda. The guardian recognised me as its own and death had taken those who had spoken most against my life. It was only then that I was fully accepted.

"Now, we have spoken much – and much of it I would have preferred to speak in the light. Rest now, and consider which way you will take in the morning. I will wake you before the light comes."

"I have one last question," stated Nathan.

"Ask then, and this shall be the last."

"There is a word that we have come across. It seems important. Soloma tried to explain it but I could not understand her meaning."

"What is it?"

"IGLOS," he spelt to her.

"It means, 'open', 'without barrier', 'free to all'. It is a good word to take to your dreaming. Sleep now in peace. The furs are by you."

Chapter 21   **Departure**

Nathan woke to Zadie's light touch and found Soloma standing by him, silhouetted against the slightest fire, holding a package.

"Food," she said, placing it by his rucksack and fetching furs and staves.

"There are honey-cakes and dried fish," came Elana's voice; "enough for two days. Have breakfast while you walk. Go before the village is awake."

He finished tying his boots and thanked the old lady, who stood outside the doorway in the lessening darkness of pre-dawn.

"And there is this," she added. "I do not know which way you will choose, but it is the best I can do," and she drew from behind her a coil of some material.

"Rope!" he exclaimed.

"Yes. It is good and new, although not as long as you might wish. It will bear Zadie's weight but not yours," she added.

He stooped on instinct, lifting the old hand in his, and kissing it gently. "Thank you, Elana," he said, and it seemed to him that there was a wateriness in the eyes that looked back at him.

"Not for fifty years have I been treated thus," she said. "Fare well. The girls will go with you to the cairn. Remember me to Cornwall."

There was an urgency in Soloma's wait and they were off and down the hill before their thoughts had begun to gel. Tarma joined them at the stream and, as they toiled up towards the black lioness, the light was growing stronger. At its paws they paused, but there was no barrier to exit for adult or for child and, turning, they caught one last glimpse of an elderly figure resting beside a doorway, before the warm mist enveloped them.

Once they had reached the flat ice, the girls were going at a cracking pace and there was little time to talk. Medium cloud was spilling in from the west, obscuring the sun but leaving its position clear enough for only the occasional check on the compass as they headed into its rising arc. Barely an hour elapsed before a black speck emerged directly ahead and Nathan was left wondering at the girls' skill in navigation over a surface that yielded nothing with which to have distinguished direction in its white monotony of shape and form. All too soon the speck had grown distinct and the awfulness of parting loomed larger with each slowing step. The cairn was taking on a meaning of its own. Part of Nathan's mind was detached, working on distances and bearings and times, and part was trying to push down the emotions that kept intruding, clamouring for attention.

Eventually, he gave up. "I will miss her," he said to Zadie.

She turned her face, the tear marks on her cheeks, and asked, "Which one?"

"Well, all of them – Simona and Tarma, Elana, but most of all Soloma."

"So will I," she answered, and with a few more unwilling steps they found themselves at the cairn.

Food delayed the final parting for a few stolen minutes, but it was a futility. Neither Tarma nor Soloma would take from their supplies and in the end a moment came when all four seemed to realise the inevitability of it all and they stood facing each other. He would like to have made some fine speech but all he managed was, "Goodbye." He didn't hear what Zadie said as she hugged each girl in turn, and he bent to kiss Tarma and then Soloma. They stepped back, the cairn between them. Soloma was rummaging in her leather pouch and stepped forward again pressing two objects into Nathan's palm. Looking down, he saw that one was light and battered – the last red petal of a crumpled flower that had journeyed with Soloma from Trevennick to the land of the lioness. The other was solid, gleaming a little even in the overcast light, and he smiled at the gift of pure hewn copper. His heart welled up for the little girl and he bent his head, reaching out a chain over it. The once-tin token that was now bronze dangled on its end and, gently, he placed it over her head and tucked it beneath her fur. He kissed her again on her forehead and said, "Look after your people, Soloma." In a matter of moments, each pair had turned and gone their own ways.

Side by side they walked, each engrossed in their turmoil of thoughts until, at length, Zadie's broke the surface into speech.

"There was so much I wanted to ask ... so much I wanted to see. We find a whole world and yet we have so little time in it..."

"I'm not sure it didn't find us," he answered thoughtfully. "We didn't seek to find it; we haven't sought any of this ... and we still have to return to our world, if we can. And if we do, there will be something of this place and these people that stays with us; but I know what you mean."

"What were you thinking about?" she asked.

"Socks," replied Nathan.

"Did you say 'socks'?" exclaimed Zadie.

"Yes, I said socks – my red socks – the pair I tied around Tarma's neck. I was wondering what will become of them."

"You can think of socks at a time like this? That's the most utterly unimportant thing I can imagine!"

"I always think of the little things when I'm trying to crowd out the big ones."

"So what were the big ones?" Zadie persisted.

"I was trying not to think about the coral pool and what used to happen there ... and wondering what I would have done. I know you wouldn't have let it happen."

"You care more than you know, Nathan. You can only take each event as it comes. You didn't hesitate to rescue Tarma and Simona – and you were prepared to bring Soloma back here by yourself, if necessary."

"But I did hesitate!" he burst out. "I had to think whilst you plunged straight off down the hill at Gulland."

"And if you hadn't stopped to think, we wouldn't have succeeded in rescuing them. What would I have done? Run up and shouted, 'Stop!' 'Stop!' and had my throat cut? What good would that have done?" she comforted him.

"I suppose you're right," he ventured insecurely.

"I am right," Zadie affirmed. "You are too hard on yourself. It needed both of us. And now I'm trusting you to get us back across this ice."

"Thanks," he muttered gratefully. "You are generous in your words."

"It's not generosity," she answered, halting him. "It's truth. I haven't been with you so long not to see something of what's under that thick skin of yours!" and they laughed a wholesome laugh together.

"Well, this is the moment of decision," Nathan stated. "That's five hundred paces from the cairn. If we turn for the cave, this is where we turn; otherwise, we go straight on and trust to Elana's northern route."

Somehow it didn't surprise Zadie that Nathan had carried on counting to himself despite their conversation and she thought, 'little things', but said, "I'll back your judgement."

It would have been easier if she had wanted to debate the choice, to share responsibility for it. He had been marshalling the arguments in his mind: an unknown route relying on finding the marker cairns that would mean spending a night on the ice, but which had been travelled relatively frequently by Elana's people; versus a known route that could certainly prove dangerous – ice, cave, lake, creatures – but was shorter.

"Very well," he answered, surprising himself with the brevity of his decision-making, "I'll go for the known dangers rather than the unknown. We turn here – but the cave is yours to get us through."

"Good," said Zadie. "Get me there and I will."

The first pressure ridge in the ice came up quickly and they halted as Nathan explained the problem of keeping to the reciprocal bearing of the journey with the girls. Since there were only two of them, he couldn't use a line of three for accuracy, and the troughs and ridges were sufficiently awkward for him to have to watch his feet rather than a compass needle. Furthermore, when in a trough he wouldn't be able to see Zadie in the next trough. In the end, she went ahead from one ridge to the next, moving to left or right as directed by Nathan and waiting for him to catch up with her before moving on. It was unpleasant work, and slow, with little chance for conversation.

Zadie was counting ridges and it was in trough eighteen that she suddenly shrieked and stopped, pointing at the ground in front of her. It was certainly large and unwelcome. At least, whatever had made the crisp print in the snow beside her was certainly large, and potentially unwelcome. Woolly mammoths and sabre-toothed tigers – hungry sabre-toothed tigers – assailed her mind.

"It's a fresh print, and it's very large! And there's another one over there, and there!" she exclaimed to an out of breath Nathan.

Nathan smiled before saying, "Well that's a stroke of luck. I think we'll follow them for a bit."

"Are you mad?"

"No. Very sane. Don't be afraid. There will be some smaller prints nearby – a whole family of them, in fact," and he laughed. "Look," and he put his boot beside the print and then carefully enlarged it; "good match, isn't it? The snow has sublimed in the sun and ablated on the edge of the prints, enlarging them. You are looking at the legend of the yeti. These are our own tracks. Come on. I don't have to be so careful with the compass now and I can walk with you."

Zadie's embarrassment at her scare melted in the company of walking together again. Soon ridge twenty gave way to flat ice, and an increasing bevel down, until a sliver of sky blue edged out of the white ahead like a painted crescent moon. More of the blue moon emerged and they were on the dark moraine, working their way carefully down towards the Secret Lake.

"Did you mark the exit from the cave?" Zadie asked, looking at the ice wall rearing up in front and thinking that there were rather more openings into it than she had remembered.

"Yes. Old rope and empty aerosol of fluorescent paint in a crevice just inside it," Nathan answered. "We're at about the right elevation from the lake now and just need to get a line on the blue ice. There should be two large, flat rocks where we ate before."

However, there were rather a larger number of flat rocks, most of which looked identical. If it hadn't been for the superlatives of the view, Zadie would have grown anxious as Nathan searched, but there was something inherently peaceful, almost restorative, about the surface of the Secret Lake. Eventually, her gaze was broken by a shout from further up the slope and she clambered up to him with some regret.

"It seems like it is inviting you to walk on it, to eat it," she said to him.

Explanation was unnecessary and he replied, "It is a precious spot. We'll not see the like of this place again. I'm glad we came this way. Even in the darkest night, I will remember this."

Food was needful and they sat awhile. The lake made dried fish and honey-cakes seem like a feast and Nathan lit a cigar as Zadie laid back against him. Neither was inclined to stir, and it was Zadie who broke the unspoken soliloquy of nature.

"How much light have we got?"

Nathan found his watch and answered, "Four hours or so. You're right. We must move."

"No," Zadie said, "I meant how much light in your head torch?"

"Probably thirty minutes, maybe more. I didn't time how long we used it for in the fog," he answered again.

Zadie measured the probabilities in her mind before responding, "Enough for one attempt, then. We have to get it right in the cave, first time. There won't be enough battery to take a wrong turning and back-track. What's more, we can't use your cigar trick: the air could flow out through any exit on the far side. Whatever happens, I'll remember this view. I'm going to take it with me – inside of me."

Staring over the edge of the ice waterfall, the light was already dim below. Zadie was tied under the armpits with the rope that Elana had provided and Nathan was scrabbling for a firm footing from which to make a belay. Soon she was working her way carefully down the tiny holds in the ice wall of the passage, the rope bearing most of her weight, Nathan unsighted and tensing for the sudden jerk that would indicate a slip. Minutes stretched by until suddenly the rope went slack.

"OK. I'm down," came the muffled cry. "Rope's free!"

Nathan lowered the rucksack to Zadie's waiting grasp and cast the end down to her. He would have to free-climb down the ice. He had known all along that there was no alternative, and the task was no less daunting for the prior knowledge. It was one thing going up when he could see and reach ahead but quite another going down, feeling for barely existent grips, whilst knowing that if he looked down his precarious balance would be gone. He lowered himself gingerly over the edge and felt blindly for the first toe-hold. The moment followed when he had to release the last secure finger grip and start down the smooth, vertical wall of ice. It was difficult work and it was taking him a very long time. He was barely a third of the way down and already his fingers were numb and his mind was beginning to suggest letting go and risking a slide to the bottom.

"Left foot three inches down and six inches right," intruded a voice from below. "Right foot straight down three inches," and so it went on. "Nearly there now; two more steps."

He let go and slid the rest. The undignified ending would have failed a climbing test but he didn't care. He was down and safe; the rest didn't matter, except to thank Zadie for her intervention, and he stood toying with the rucksack, looking back at the climb down. She had watched him carefully as he had climbed down, and it had seemed to her that he had become stuck a third of the way down and had been beginning to lose confidence before she had started calling out directions. It was a horrid thing to see a competent performer becoming hesitant and insecure. She had seen it once in a fellow caver who was utterly competent but had lost his nerve. He had fallen and smashed his leg. It had taken a day for a fully equipped rescue party to get him out of the cave system.

Zadie suspected that Nathan's memory for any landscape or rockface was near photographic but that in a cave system he would be almost useless. If Nathan had known what she was thinking he would probably have agreed; anything above ground and he was fine – anything where he could get a relative bearing. Complex dark holes were not his scene, and all that he could remember of the internal plumbing of this large chunk of ice was that there was a rather nasty ice-bridge, over a chasm that he had seen neither the top nor bottom of, part way through it.

"Rope up," Zadie heard her own voice saying, whilst she chucked him an end of Elana's rope.

It wasn't strictly necessary – at least not until the ice-bridge – but it might help Nathan's confidence to feel the link around him and the mechanical task of making the fastenings would help. She needed to get him moving again. He responded automatically, and set off like a hesitant dog on an unfamiliar, dark walk. All too soon, the passage started bending and contracting until they reached the first of several narrow squeezes. Zadie had begrudged turning on the head torch, leaving it to the last glimmering of light before putting it on its lower setting to conserve the battery. Nathan had used the fluorescent spray paint wisely on the journey through with the girls, although it took Zadie a while to pick the angle and height that he had been marking at and she preferred to use the marks as confirmation of her own mental map of the ice-cave system, rather than rely on looking for them in advance.

Progress was good until she came to a bifurcation in the cave that she didn't remember. There was no marker visible. It wasn't a time to open a debate on which route to take and she placed Nathan at the split and paid out the rope as far as it would take her in the left hand passage. It was sloping downwards, which was correct, but seemed to change angle more rapidly than anything she had remembered coming. Two steps further and her foot hovered above a chasm as the light disappeared from the ceiling into its impenetrable height. Nathan had felt the slight tug on the rope as Zadie had used it to steady herself and turn carefully back. It had not been a pleasant wait in the dark and he was glad to follow her along the right hand passage, keeping slightly more tension in the rope. Shortly, she stopped and he edged slowly to a halt behind her. The light was disappearing into the unscalable heights and from the unplumbed depths the gushing and roar of water arose.

"This is the ice-bridge," Zadie said calmly. "We are half way. The other side of it the passage will soon open out and there will be some gravel on the floor for a section. I am going to have to use the full light from the head torch in front of me now. You'll be in the dark for a few moments. I'll give three slow tugs on the rope when I'm across. I won't hear you from the far side, so give me two tugs to say you are coming. I'll give you as much light as I can."

Without further ado, and to shorten the time he was left in the dark, Zadie stepped onto the narrow bridge and walked steadily across as Nathan paid out the rope. Nathan started sweating as the darkness began to enfold him and all he could see was a light that seemed to be floating away from him, diminishing to the unjudgeable intensity and location of a glow-worm. He was nearly at the end of paying out the rope and was seized with fear that it wouldn't be long enough for Zadie to cross the bridge. He knelt and leant forward to give it an extra yard and, at that moment, it stopped running through fingers that were clammy from within and numbed from without. One tug came; there was another; that was three. The light was turned directly towards him and part of his mind screamed that this wasn't going to help as it bounced off the surface of the bridge, emphasising its narrowness and the deep darkness on either side. It had been better coming when he had seen less and had been driven by the desire to follow the girls across. He half shut his eyes and began crawling forward, the loose rope beginning to dangle dangerously over the edge beside him. Zadie sensed him moving without giving any signal. Suddenly, he could feel the rope being taken in ... now there was a steady tension on it. Zadie was reeling him in. He shut his eyes, blocking out the constant reminder of the narrowness and drop, and shuffled forward on hands and knees, following the tension of the rope. His fingers felt the edge from time to time and his ears were burdened by the roaring from below. Time hung still and he forced himself on, until at last he could hear her voice and breathing and, opening his eyes, he saw her a few feet away.

"Well done," Zadie's greeting came, and they were off again. Just as she had said, soon there was gravel underfoot, and he was able to walk with her. He could feel his composure returning as he walked alongside, and finally there was a glimmering of light again. Zadie needed no prompting to turn off the head torch and, as they rounded the final bend, the opening to the cave gave sight of a fragment of distant landscape. The broken crown of Gulland had never seemed so beautiful to Nathan.

"That was fifty-five minutes – thirty with the light on," observed Zadie, holding Nathan's wrist to look at his watch and surreptitiously checking his pulse at the same time. "What do you want to do – have a meal and stay the night here, or push on?"

Nathan's mind was working again now and he answered, "First of all, I want to use the binoculars to see if anything is moving out there." They both lay, taking turns to scan the landscape stretching from the lake below to Gulland in the distance, as he continued, "We've got cloud, and the light behind us, at the moment. If it's clear in the morning, we're very visible from here to the lake. What's more, there are those creatures in the lake." Zadie shuddered involuntarily. "Each time we've seen them attack, it has been early in the morning. I think I'd like to reach the first hollies, if we can. There are three hours of light left," he ended.

Zadie had been quietly anticipating the security of the cave for the night and it took her a while to consider the arguments. She was still undecided when Nathan stood beside her and said, "Look, you were wonderful in the cave – I know I went to pieces – but I'm back together again now … I just came a bit unstuck on the inside. I can manage the climb down from here fine."

Zadie smiled and made to move towards the mouth of the cave when Nathan stopped her.

"You can't go like that."

"Why not?"

"The fur," he answered.

"I rather like it … and it's very warm," Zadie retorted.

"Yes. It's also blindingly white. You'll be like a mobile lighthouse in that landscape … and, if you fall into the lake, it'll drag you straight down. No," he continued in response to her look, "even if I took everything out of the rucksack, it wouldn't fit."

Zadie turned the fur inside out but it was still too white. She stroked it longingly for a last time as she put it back in the coracles in their recess. Bit by bit they were leaving people and things behind: Elana and her land; Tarma and Soloma at the cairn; the staves at the entrance to the cave by the Secret Lake; the fur here – soon it would be time for the rope. And each time she felt that it was a piece of herself that she was parting with. The thoughts preoccupied her and enabled Nathan to negotiate the ice buttress and pull her round on the rope onto the sloping ledge beside him before the fears of falling into the plunge pool below had taken hold.

Working down the rockfall took time and, as they skirted along the western shore of the large lake, Nathan wished he had taken more notice of which of the many indentures in the foot of the great ice wall, towering above, Soloma had used to hide the coracles. Each abortive trip from shore to ice wall consumed further time and the shadow of the ice was already deep, and deepening fast. It was not until the fifth attempt that they were successful in finding the coracles and, even then, they nearly missed them. Soloma had hidden them well from any casual eye.

"The current runs from left to right," stated Nathan, looking across towards the black slab of basalt sloping into the water on the far side of the lake. "So if we start here, it should carry us towards the landing point."

Getting into the coracles was easier said than done. It had been difficult enough from a relatively flat rock the first time. From smoothed, wet boulders it was nigh on impossible. In the end, Nathan stood up to his thighs in the cold water and Zadie boarded the craft he was holding. He tied the rucksack alongside her and she gave just enough control to his coracle for him to clamber in and drip water into its base.

"You'll be cold tonight. A nice fur would have warmed you up," called Zadie as she began paddling.

Nathan grunted and followed her. The anxiety of attack from below by unknown creatures ate into them as they crossed; and the minutes dragged, whilst the light diminished. For a period it appeared that they were making very little progress, until the current came to their aid. The little craft slid neatly alongside the black slab and only Nathan got wet as they disembarked. They hid the coracles in a boulder field away from their intended direction of travel, packing the paddles and rope inside them. With one coracle turned upside down on top of the other one, they formed a passable boulder that would not attract attention easily.

The trek back to the slab and on to the hollies was unpleasant. It was increasingly difficult to see beyond the immediate area and the footing was insecure. Nathan was following the lakeshore, but slightly away from the easier going where they would leave footprints, and was looking for a small stream entering the lake from the east. The ice wall was lost in darkness by the time they found it and headed half-left up an irregular slope of more solid rock that would have been quite good going in the light. However, in the dark it was tiring and difficult. Abruptly, they were brought to a gentle but firm halt.

"Barrier," said Nathan. "At least we know that we're close to the hollies."

"Close left, or close right?" questioned Zadie.

"Right, I think," Nathan replied.

As it turned out, he was right, and it was only a further hundred yards of stumbling and fumbling before the prickles of the ancient group of hollies welcomed them into their embrace. Normally, dried holly leaves would not be most people's choice for bedding but in this case Zadie and Nathan found them more than acceptable as they settled down inside the ring. The rucksack wasn't really big enough for a pillow for two, but they each took comfort from the other's regular breathing and Nathan was asleep before Zadie's wondering mind closed into a darkness that was complete.

Chapter 22   The Mortan's Revenge

There was a tap dripping in the kitchen. That was the trouble with an old bungalow … there was always something to do. He would ignore it. It wasn't time to get up yet. No, it wasn't the kitchen tap – that went 'plink' and was much more regular. This was a softer 'plunk'. It was annoyingly irregular … and now his nose was tickling … the dog must have slept on the bed again while he was out, and left some hairs there. He resisted the urge to swat them away. He was surprisingly weary for a good night's sleep. With great reluctance he opened an eye to look out of the bedroom window. The window wouldn't come into focus. It was all distorted and had a blue patch with green and white flecks in the middle of the white cloud … and there was a dark spot in the blue. That must be a bird wheeling high above. His nose tickled again, and from behind the tickling a soft voice said, "Welcome to the world."

Zadie's face snapped into view and he rolled off the rucksack, prickling his own face on the fallen holly leaves. He was fully awake now, and wet. It had rained in the night and, although the hollies had provided some shelter, he was damp and stiff.

"How long have you been awake?" asked Nathan.

"About an hour, on and off. It's been light a while. I didn't want to move in case I disturbed you. You were talking in your sleep," Zadie added.

"Anything incriminating?"

Zadie blushed. "Not much. Some odd bits about a girl…. It was mostly about fixing the plumbing."

"Well, how about some breakfast?" suggested Nathan, changing tack. "I don't suppose we can risk a fire?"

"Yes to food, and no to fire," Zadie answered firmly.

Nathan unpacked most of the rucksack, looking for the dehydrated food and putting it to soak in a tin, whilst Zadie wandered off with the binoculars. She shook her head in response to the unspoken enquiry upon her return and expressed mild surprise at the mess Nathan was stirring.

"Sorry," he said, "cold, rehydrated curry isn't everybody's choice of breakfast but deliveries have been a bit difficult of late."

In the end it appeared more edible than she had thought.

"Is it Saturday?" she asked between chewing a less rehydrated piece of meat.

"Probably," Nathan answered. "Why?"

"Because I'm due to assemble with the rest of the group on Sunday."

"What group?" replied Nathan, discarding the piece of meat that his teeth had given up on after several minutes chewing. "The group going on an archaeological dig in the Mediterranean for six months. Remember? I told you about it."

"Yes. I mean, yes, I remember now," he corrected himself, separating the rest of the meat from the rice before continuing, "All being well, it's a day from here to Polgodoc. You could still make it."

Talking of days and times spurred movement and eventually they departed at 10.00. At 10.02 they ground to a standstill. By 10.10, a thorough search on hands and knees around the plinth in the centre of the hollies had convinced them that there were no pass keys to let them through to the creamy-pink geology beyond.

"Somebody's playing us at our own game," observed Nathan, recalling how they had delayed their pursuers after rescuing Simona and Tarma.

"Yes," agreed Zadie. "Trap us here where there's no food to be gathered and no place to hide. If we try going back across the lake, there's a good chance that the creatures will get us. If we light a fire to cook, someone will see the smoke – or maybe they'll just come back in a week to check out what's happened."

Something jogged in Nathan's mind. He had been interested in the limestone and a few minutes later Zadie had retrieved two items from a side pocket of the rucksack. He looked at the two tokens – the one clear and glassy quartz, the other creamy-pink and dull in comparison.

"I didn't see you pocket that one on the way," Zadie commented.

"No," he replied, "I didn't think you would agree with me doing so. Anyway, it will be useful now – and I'll keep the quartz one, if you don't mind."

He placed the token in its recess and Zadie held his hand as he plucked it out again and they walked through the invisible barrier to the far side of the plinth. Then he lobbed the token gently towards the hollies where they had slept.

"Why did you throw it away?" demanded Zadie.

He paused, and answered with some sadness, "I don't think we'll be needing it again … and if anyone else is trapped on that side of the barrier they're likely to be friend rather than foe."

Zadie accepted the explanation and they began picking a course towards the next geology – the one that would give access to Gulland. The holly clump was not visible until they had descended into a shallow valley and climbed out of it again. A few scrubby bushes began to appear on the slopes in favoured crannies. They were being watered by a moderate shower of rain and surface water began to flow between the rocks. In a sense, they were grateful for the curtain that it drew on their progress and the noise of it lessened their fear of voices carrying to some malintentioned ear. There were several debates in their conversation that kept overlapping each other before separating again and then rejoining: one was the weather and visibility – the showers were becoming less continuous and the cloud showed signs of breaking; another concerned the route round Gulland and across the granite beyond; whilst the third related to the tokens and the plinths. It was to the lattermost of these that the conversation returned as the clump of hollies drew nearer.

"I don't accept that," Zadie was saying, "I know my copper master key let us off the granite once but that doesn't mean it will work with every geology … and it was life or death then … and it was Soloma who grabbed it and thrust it in the recess, not us. Besides, the Mortan who followed us knew a way of getting past the plinth without a token, or by-passing the barrier, and maybe they have the power to block the use of special keys."

"That's too much speculation," objected Nathan. "He might just have had a spare ordinary token, or known where one was kept."

"Now you're speculating," she countered.

"OK," he ended. "If there are tokens, we'll use them – we're nearly there now – and if there aren't, we may have no choice. Either way, I don't want to go via the Little Lake or round the south side of Gulland – it's too visible from too far away," and as if to emphasise his point, a patch of sunlight burst onto the shiny, wet leaves of the hollies ahead.

As it turned out, ordinary tokens were scattered near the base of the plinth, its creamy-pink half washed clean by the rain and the dark-veined recess glistening expectantly. They passed the barrier singly and struck off to the north as soon as a cleft in the landscape allowed. It was strange how they both felt drawn to Gulland. Zadie's objection was only superficial when Nathan suggested climbing as far as the hazel coppice, and she didn't comment as their feet led them on and upwards until they were lying back against the rocks near its crown, warmed by the early afternoon sun.

"We spent our second night here," said Nathan between mouthfuls of honey-cake, as if recalling some long-past honeymoon.

"Do you remember the ice wall in the dawn?" continued Zadie, verbalising his thoughts. "It was amazing. Strange to think we've been up on the ice sheet. We ought to be able to see the cave from here."

He passed the binoculars to her and delved more deeply into the rucksack while she scanned the distant lake. The ice wall was shadowed in the light but darker specks and glints of water gushing from its base guided her view until, with the aid of the compass, Zadie was convinced that she could see it.

"Gulland was kind to us with its shadow that morning," she murmured and, more strongly, "What on earth are you doing?"

Nathan had a map open on his knees. It was written in German and he was drawing lines on it with a blunt pencil, and annotating distances and bearings.

"Just making a record," he replied. "See if you can find any evidence of Elana's northern route or any other clumps of holly, will you?"

"Why? You're not thinking of coming back here, are you?" questioned Zadie in surprise.

In all honesty Nathan had not entertained any such thoughts, at least not consciously. It was more a professional curiosity. It also helped him to feel that he could locate Soloma in some small way, and the seeming objectivity of the map reduced uncertainties and fears to the comfort of words and lines. Something of this subconscious thought conveyed itself to Zadie and she found herself drawn into helping him, at first unwillingly and then with enthusiasm. The Little Lake was plotted, and the cave. Away to the north were two darker points on the landscape that might be clumps of holly and, in the ice wall itself, two areas of darker colour that could be falls of rock.

"Will you give me a copy when we get back?" she asked him, thinking that she might frame it and put it on her bedroom wall in the small flat she called home. He nodded and folded the map neatly before they climbed the few steps to the actual summit and lay scrutinising the landscape to the south and east. Nothing moved. There was no alternative route across the granite – just the two clumps of holly, innocuous in the sunshine, and a badly burnt patch of yew midway between them.

"It's gone three o'clock," he said quietly to her. "If you don't mind, I'd rather stick to the shadow and go down that side of Gulland and round its base."

Although Zadie agreed, she had a feeling that Nathan was delaying the moment at which they would have to face the granite. It was understandable, given their experiences on it, but picking a less direct route made it nearly an hour to reach the first clump of hollies. Not that it mattered: the overnight train from Penzance to Paddington stopped late at Bodmin Road. She might even have some decent sleep on it. Nevertheless, she was curious and asked him directly.

"Sort of," came the answer, "I was aiming to climb the cliff at dusk."

"Why?"

"The two girls who went missing. I don't know who might be watching what, or where, and I would prefer not to be too obvious."

Zadie had buried the memory of the young girls' abduction and now it was exhumed in her mind, the horror of it grew – particularly if that flip-flop meant they had been brought out of their world and into this. She walked in silence beside Nathan as they toiled up the hill to the hollies and was pleased to see the tokens scattered by the base of the plinth.

"They must be choughs," commented Nathan of the pair of birds that seemed to make this place their home. He had watched their ungainly flight for a few minutes when Zadie bent to pick up a token. Suddenly, without warning, he threw himself at Zadie, knocking her off her feet and crushing her against a tree stump with the full weight of his body and the rucksack combined.

Her eyes were pained and watering, and the shallow, gasping breath from her winded body was barely able to enunciate the startled, "What...?"

"Did you touch it?" he demanded, brushing back her hair.

"Touch what?"

"Touch the token?"

"No, why?"

"They're serpentine," he answered slowly, kneeling at a respectful distance and eyeing the nearest of them.

"A trap," mouthed Zadie.

"Yes. And I bet they would let us in but there are no tokens to get out again on the other side ... probably wake those dreadful animals, as well."

They sat and looked at each other for some time until Zadie was breathing normally again. She felt her ribs but there was no searing pain from a break, only a dull, bruising ache where the copper token had transferred the force to her body. With some difficulty she lifted the chain over her head, allowing it to dangle in front of her as she inspected the token for damage.

Slowly Zadie stood and said, "Alright. We'll have to use it now."

"And take this section as fast as we can," added Nathan. "Are you OK to walk? Sorry I hit you so hard."

She tested her limbs and nodded before approaching the plinth and reaching for his hand. There was nothing unusual to observe of the recess and she plunged the token in, lifting it out again and stepping to the far side with him. As they had suspected, no tokens were visible on the ground. Beyond the exit from the hollies the landscape was clearly lit, and they stood like swimmers on the edge of a deep pool before launching down the slope. Thirty minutes later they were at its foot and hurrying.

"You certainly made a mess of those yews with that flare," said Nathan, fingering his pocket, "and took out two of the pillars."

"A pity I didn't take them all out," Zadie answered as they moved more slowly uphill. "Where are the rest of the flares?"

Nathan produced one carefully from his pocket and she nodded approvingly. The holly clump was moving nearer with a stubborn slowness, its dark leaves reflecting the low angle sunlight. The pair of choughs alighted on its higher branches and watched them struggle up the slope. Nathan had loosened his beautiful blue token from its pouch in case they had to run but he let it slip back through his fingers and breathed in relief as they entered beneath the birds' steady stare. A cursory glance showed none of the dark slate tokens that should have been there and they were through with Zadie's copper key without a time to pause.

"We'll have a drink by the stream," promised Nathan. "Then it's the cave."

The cliffs of Polgodoc were already looming in studied neutrality. There was the chimney rock away to the left; and further on the right, the head of the lioness that guarded the bay below Trevennick peered watchfully out to the West. Zadie drank as Nathan surveyed the familiar scene, reddened by the low sun.

"It didn't feel right," Zadie commented.

"What didn't feel right?"

"When I put the key in the recess, it didn't feel right. There was the very slightest vibration," she answered as she tucked it out of sight on its chain.

"Well, let's not worry now," he said, worrying. "It's a mile from here to the cave – less maybe. Let's go."

They were half way there when they were spotted, at almost the same moment as Nathan spotted the figures moving swiftly along the cliff. There were a dozen, at least, and several dressed like Mortan.

"Run!" he cried, pointing to the figures, but Zadie matched his slower pace. "Go on!" he cried again. "It's the third cleft from the left!" and, reluctantly, she drew ahead. It would be a close race. They had the longer distance but the men would have to descend the cliff. He pictured its line in his mind as he ran as best he could with the rucksack. There were two small valleys where the cliff bent inland – that would give them a few minutes more; it all depended on how well the men knew the way down. He looked again and saw with fear that the men had no intention of following the path he visualised. They were gathered by a headland no more than two hundred metres from the cave and had started working their way down its crumbling face. It was blindingly obvious as a route now – dangerous but short. A curved knife glinted. They would cut off Zadie with ease and prevent him reaching her, as well.

Nathan slowed and stopped, steadying his breathing, watching the descent. He lay against a rock, his arm still and as far away from him as possible. He turned his face and shut his eyes, pulling at the cord with his other hand. The whoosh brought Zadie to a standstill and the bang reverberated back to Nathan as the white, incandescent flare exploded against the headland. Crumbling rock mingled with yells and a slow avalanche of limbs and boulders, whilst thrift and scrubby bushes became a pyre of flame, the smoke obliterating the scene.

He didn't wait to see the outcome and brushed aside Zadie's, "Good shot!" as he struggled up to her, angry that she had stopped to wait for him.

"Keep going!" he cried, dragging her forward. "It won't have got all of them."

The slope seemed longer and more uneven, and each pace dreadfully slow, despite the urgency that drove them towards the cliffs of Polgodoc. There was movement on the cliff-top and shouting; and as they dived into the third cleft in the cliff, a rock, followed by a boulder, narrowly missed their heads. Angry voices and scattering stones could be heard behind them.

"If this isn't the right cleft…" Nathan left the trailing sentence unfinished.

"I'm up against the wall. I can't see! I need a hand!" Zadie exclaimed.

"What do you need?"

"A hand – your hand! We came in together; we've got to go out together!" she exclaimed again, feeling for it in the dark.

They grasped hands and, for an awful moment, nothing happened. Then a faint red glow cut the wall in front, the vein stretching from floor to ceiling and widening, deepening in its coppery colour until it throbbed, waiting for an offering of its own. Zadie was jammed against Nathan and was scrabbling to lift her chain, without success. He reached into his pocket with his free hand, thrusting the object into the recess. Nothing happened, except the throbbing became more urgent and the angry voices closer.

"What's wrong? What are you doing?" she cried.

"Wrong rock! It was the blue token! I've got it now!" he answered, plunging the chunk of copper that Soloma had given him into the throbbing heart ahead.

Voices were behind them as the rock split and they tumbled through its entrance, willing it to close again, and speeding up the uneven floor. A solid clunk echoed behind.

"Keep going," said Nathan, stepping past the flat, black map table with its lionesses before it became a temptation. "Can you use your copper key to give us a bit more light, please."

Zadie avoided leaning against the dark black slab as she got her breath back. She could move now, and settled the copper token in her palm. The veining in the walls and ceiling responded to the master key and great lines of coppery red spilt across the floor, some beckoning into an exit beyond. Nathan put his chunk of copper away and fiddled in the rucksack.

"Do you think the Mortan know how to get into this place?" questioned Zadie.

"Exactly the same nasty thought that was going through my mind," replied Nathan without looking up. "I think the answer is probably yes … and I don't want to stay to find out. Ah! Got it now," he said, lifting out the head torch and flicking it across the far wall. "We definitely don't want the exit the copper is inviting us to take, but I can't see any fluorescent paint."

"I told you the rocks wouldn't let you get away with that one," Zadie commented with mild satisfaction.

A dull bang echoed through the cave, rolling back off the walls, followed by further thuds and echoes.

"I don't think they'll break in that way," said Nathan confidently, continuing to search the pockets of his rucksack for the piece of tin that Wilf had given him and eventually locating it. A gentle silvery light spread through the nearby rock as the chunk of tin lay in his hand, and he looked for confirmation of the exit.

Zadie was becoming agitated.

"I think the Mortan know something we don't. Hurry up, Nathan. That noise is growing in intensity. None of the echoes are fading. Remember what happened before!"

She was quite right. He was struggling to hear her now and she grabbed at him, tugging and yelling, "We said 'Middle in, Middle out'. There's no time to confirm it. Come on!"

The coppery lights faded as Zadie clenched her fist. The tin veining was only weakly illumined from the lump in Nathan's palm and they stumbled towards the exit that it suggested, and up the uneven steps of the curving passage. It was only a few short shuffles before the blank, rock wall at its end met their touch but the rolling thunderous echoes were pummelling their senses as they leant against it.

They fell forward together.

Chapter 23   Home?

The wet floor of the adit rose to greet Zadie and Nathan. The salty Cornish air rushed into their lungs, and the rock shut firmly behind them, closing out the thunder of the Mortan.

Waves swashed in the gulley that split the adit in two and sucked gently out again, rolling the smaller pebbles in their retreat. The simple sound brought the realisation of how much Nathan had missed it.

"High tide," he murmured in appreciation.

"I can't see a thing," Zadie objected.

"Nor can I, but I can hear it and smell it," Nathan answered.

"Can we have some light, please? It's nearly pitch black in here."

Reluctantly he broke the soothing spell of quiet sound that was washing over him, cleansing his mind from fear and uncertainty. The beam from the head torch was feeble now as the battery was finally failing but in its dim illumination they cried out together.

"Fog!" said he, unable to make out even the entrance to the narrow adit with any clarity.

"Plank!" said she, looking at the gap in the floor a few feet ahead.

"That explains why it's so dark," he continued. "It must be pretty dense to block out the last of the light."

"We were followed down here, then," said Zadie, pursuing her own thoughts. "They must have been looking for the missing girls."

"Or wanting to ask us a few questions, if they spotted us," he finished for her.

The discoveries spurred them from immobility. Their new world, which was really old, had shut with the rock behind and now, back in their old world, there were immediate problems to face. The plank was worn and had the letters WD stencilled on it, but it was solid and bore their weight as they stooped and shuffled out of the adit onto the ledge beyond. The sound of the waves below was muffled by the fog but neither needed a reminder of the drop below as they edged along the ledge to its extremity.

"You take the head torch. There's a little battery left, and I can do this climb by feel," Nathan stated in a matter of fact kind of way. "The first foothold is on the right."

He watched Zadie launch herself and steady on the rockface. Soon only a slight luminescence in the fog told him that she was climbing and, with a last glance back at the unseen mouth of the adit, he jumped to follow her. The clammy fog had made the holds slippery and cold, and for a fleeting moment his mind thought of ice. Then he was climbing, left and right, like a ladder, and up over the top of the cliff to the waiting figure.

"The battery is dead," said Zadie. "I'll follow you. You know the path."

As they moved up the hidden valley of Polgodoc, there was a gradual lightening in the fog, as if a series of dark shutters were being withdrawn. In a matter of ten paces up, they burst through its damp embrace. The moon and stars were shining on a white sea of cloud that rolled into the distance before them, its surface almost perfectly flat and still. By the time they gained the lane the skeletal hills were emerging like the half-clothed bones of some complex creature at rest in a mattress of soft, white wool, its sleep watched over by the firmament above.

"I never thought fog could be so beautiful," Zadie observed, as they gained more height and veered onto the high path across the fields.

"It's odd," replied Nathan.

"Well, I think it's beautiful," she said again.

"No. That's not what's odd," he answered. "I can't see the lights of St. Columb or St. Issey, and there's no glow from the village lights beneath the fog. They should be visible from here."

"Maybe it's a power cut," she suggested, and pointed

towards the south-east. "There's a big glow on the horizon over there."

"Yes," he agreed, "you may be right. It could be Bodmin, although it's a bit big for that … perhaps Plymouth … you can see a long way from here on a clear day."

"Where are we going?"

"Little Vennick. I left the landrover there. I'll run you over to Bodmin Road and see you onto the train," he added.

They walked in silence for a while until Nathan said, half in question, "Zadie?"

She walked on, anticipating no need to answer yet.

"Zadie," he began again, "we've been together all this time, and I know virtually nothing about you."

"You know lots about me. In some ways you know me better than I know myself," she said gently.

"I didn't mean that," he tried again, "I meant I know nothing about your life, your background. We've never had time just to sit and talk."

"Does my background matter to you?" she answered.

Nathan looked away at the landscape that he loved.

"No," he said slowly. "No. It doesn't matter at all."

Zadie smiled.

"When the dig is over I'll come down and stay – then we can talk – and I'll write sometime," she promised.

"I'd like that," Nathan replied. Mixed emotions churned within him.

"As for the moment, I'll tell you a bit," she continued. And she did, speaking of parents who had separated; of being sent to boarding school; and of working her way through university.

"It wasn't that they didn't care," she said in response to a question, "more that they had their independent lives – busy lives – and boarding school was convenient. They came to all the events – I was a kind of fixture in their diaries – 'Zadie in concert'; 'Zadie, lacrosse match'; 'Zadie, exeat'; 'Zadie, parents' meeting'; etc – and it was fun when they came, or when they took my friends out. I made some good friends. There were others like me but there were 'normal people' too. Sometimes they would invite me out, or we'd meet up in the holidays. Of course, there was the other side of things. Sometimes we got in trouble but it was the kind of place where there was space to make mistakes, to get things wrong; and there were people there to pick you up – teachers and tutors, as well as friends – and it didn't matter if I was seen to work. Mind you, there are good schools and bad schools; I guess I was lucky mine was a good school. Anyway, it was better than wasting my life going out in the city every night and failing my exams. It made it easier when I went to university, too; I was sort of independent by the time I went there and had my own goals … and made my own mistakes.

"You're not everyone," Nathan observed.

"Glad you've noticed!" Zadie replied. "No. It wouldn't have suited everyone, and I've met a lot of great people who came through the comprehensives, but I don't begrudge them sending me there. It suited me and I had some of the best years of my life there. And they still care. It's a kind of adult love: they're there when I need them and when I get back to London there'll be two messages on the ansaphone wishing me well on the dig and to say that they will miss me."

Mention of the dig stirred the green creature within Nathan as he thought of her in close company with a small group of people for six months and he slammed the door shut on it with another question.

"So what's your connection with Cornwall?"

"It goes back a long way. My grandmother on my mother's side was Cornish, and generations before her … lived over Tintagel way … hence my middle name," Zadie responded. "But basically, I just like the place … especially the north coast … and especially out of season."

"Are you going to tell me it?" asked Nathan.

"Tell you what?"

"Your middle name?" he pursued.

"Not sure. It's private … and you might laugh." But she continued, "Oh, very well: it's Barwith."

"That's a nice name," Nathan said, rolling it on his tongue, "unusual too."

Soon Nathan found himself under examination. She was probing carefully and knew rather more about him than he had expected.

Eventually, she laughed at his surprise and observed, "You'll have to learn to talk less in your sleep. At least I have a surname to write to now ... Mr. Petrox!"

Broken slate crunched under their feet as they turned up the track to Little Vennick. Mabel's old farmhouse was in darkness, outlined against the glow from the horizon. For a moment he worried about the geese and disturbing her. Then he remembered the geese were dead. Mabel was dead. Grief touched him and his hand strayed to a single, crumpled, red petal, lying in the soft pouch containing the blue token. The landrover looked shiny in the moonlight and the key was in the ignition. He pressed the button to warm the ignition coil and was pleased to see there was plenty of fuel for a run to Bodmin and back.

"I'm going to free-wheel down to the main road before I turn the lights on," he said as Zadie looked across at him. "It's very late, or early if you prefer; unlikely that anyone will see, but there's no point in taking a chance on the last lap."

"If your watch is right, I've missed the overnight already. There's an early morning train though; I can catch that," Zadie stated.

There was absolutely no traffic on the main road and the moon was illuminating the landscape clearly as they drove. Nathan was feeling very hungry and beginning to be light-headed.

"What's wrong with your dashboard lights?" Zadie asked.

"Haven't worked for years," answered Nathan cheerily.

"Well, what about the headlights?" she demanded.

Now that she brought it to his attention he became aware that he was obtaining very little light indeed whenever they were in shadow – barely a dim outline from each sidelight. He flicked the switch again and tried the full beam, to no avail.

"Sorry. There was a fault on them but I thought I had it

fixed … must have got some water in the electrics while we were away … last time I used them was going to see Wilf."

"You can't drive to Bodmin like this, and there's fog ahead," Zadie added for good measure. "Can you make Wadebridge? There's an overnight taxi firm there, and I'll risk a hire."

Nathan nodded sadly as he rounded the first bend on the hill down into the valley ahead and they plunged into the soft, wet blanket of dense fog. Darkness closed around them. He braked hard, slowing to walking pace. There was a narrow stone bridge at the bottom of the hill and he was straining for sight of it, knowing that the road turned sharply at that point and not wishing to test the strength of its fragile parapet. Zadie screamed. He uttered an oath and skidded to a standstill, stalling the engine. Two vehicles scraped past him in the opposite direction, travelling far too fast for the conditions and looming out of the darkness without any warning lights.

"Idiots! Absolute idiots!" Nathan was muttering as the landrover chugged up the hill beyond the bridge and out into the moonlight.

"And I wonder what they were saying about you," observed Zadie, having recovered her composure.

Soon there was fog again and it was very slow going with the road descending in a series of bends. The fronts of three cottages, built close against the road, passed by at touching distance to Zadie, and Nathan swore. Zadie didn't need the words to sense his pent up frustration as he wrenched the wheel on another turn.

"I've missed the Wadebridge turn," Nathan growled. "This road goes down to the quayside at Padstow. There'll be some green railings coming up soon, and a car park. I'll stop and see if I can fix the lights."

For the first time, there was a stirring in the air and dim shadows of stone-built houses emerged from the thinning fog. Zadie caught a glimpse of the monolithic Metropole Hotel, its mock castellations showing against the lighter fog. Nathan had intended going straight on at the old hairpin bend at the bottom of Station Road. Instead, he brought the vehicle to a screeching halt in front of a battered pair of wooden gates. He stared at the untidy pile of coal beyond them. Foreign voices floated out of the growing light and he swivelled at the unmistakable wheezing sound, disbelief flooding through him as the moonlight struck the plume of steam dissipating from the edge of his visibility. Doors slammed and a command rang out. Coughing chuffs of smoke punctured the air, drifting incoherently and raining flecks of rusty soot as the engine slowly gathered way, its firebox flickering against the brass controls.

A uniformed figure leant over him from behind, startling him, and breathing its aroma of unfiltered cigarettes and stale fish and chips. A rifle was slung carelessly over a shoulder, and the Cockney accent said, "Look, mate, move this scrap 'eap before them soldiers gets 'ere. That captain's got 'is eye on you halready", and then more confidentially, "Bad night. Plymouth got 'it again."

As in a dream, Nathan turned the vehicle. They drove in silence past the blacked out windows of the town and onto the top road. Wind was scattering the fog and by the old, stone bridge they saw the screech marks of their tyres. There were no road markings nor signposts at the junctions. Near Trewosa, two horses were pulling an empty farm wagon into a field. The moon was setting a dull orange in the far west as the sun rose in the east and they pulled to a halt outside the farmhouse at Little Vennick.

Side by side they stood as Nathan lifted the heavy lion-head on the door, waiting as the echo from the bronze knocker faded, and pushing at the unlocked door. The house was dark and quiet. Drawing the thick velvet curtain in the kitchen, the dawn light showed up the table. A fresh newspaper lay folded beside a plate of hard-boiled eggs and bread, and a note that read, 'Help yourself, Love, M'.

"What's the date?" asked Nathan, pointing to the paper.
Zadie picked it up and put it down again.

For a long while she stood, staring unseeingly into his eyes. Then she heard her own distant voice.

"It says, September the tenth ... nineteen forty-one."

END OF BOOK ONE

Acknowledgements

'Abide with me', Henry Francis Lyte, 1847.
'The day Thou gavest', John Ellerton, 1870.
'And did those feet', William Blake, 1804.
The paraphrase on page 91 is from The Song of Solomon, ch. 8,
v.7, King James version of the bible.

Further copies of **The Three Camels** may be ordered through booksellers. They are also available by post from:

The Bookroom, Bryanston Conference Centre, Blandford, Dorset   DT11 0PX   (01258 452411)

Author's Note

My very grateful thanks are extended to the poet David Caddy, to Richard D'Silva, and to Elisabeth Jenkins, without whose enthusiasm, interest, and technical advice this book would not have been published.

No novel is entirely new. It is the product of life's experience and society's impact. To a greater or lesser extent this is modified by the physical environment in which one exists. If I have borrowed unwittingly from the ideas of those authors whose works I have read, I apologise: no man is an island, isolated from the mainstream that flows around him. If I have given pleasure to the reader of this novel or raised questions in his or her mind, I am glad. And if any should wonder what happens next in this world of partial reality, the second book is written and due to be published in October 2009 under the title *The Camel of Soloma*.

By the Same Author

'The Camel of Soloma'
(ISBN 978-0-9559577-1-0)